WALKING DAVIS

WALKING DAVIS

A Novel by
David Ely

CHARTERHOUSE
New York

LIBRARY OF CONGRESS CATALOG CARD NUMBER: 72-84217

MANUFACTURED IN THE UNITED STATES OF AMERICA

Lovingly dedicated to my children
Michael, Pamela, David, Margaret

Part
ONE

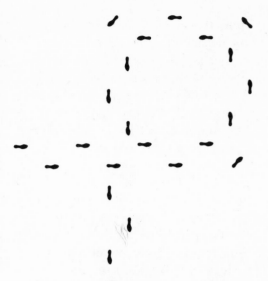

ON March 17, 197—, at half-past ten o'clock in the morning, Pierce Davis set out from his home town of Spark, Iowa, to walk around the world.

He'd hoped to get an earlier start, but was delayed for several reasons. The night before, his wife, Natalie, had insisted on washing the five pairs of new socks he'd bought for his trip, and they were still damp in the morning. He had to use her hair-dryer on them. Then, his father, the town physician, was called away in the early morning to treat an ailing farmer, and Pierce didn't think it would be right to leave on such an important journey without saying one last goodbye. Dr. Davis did not return until noon, however, and Pierce, feeling unable to wait past ten-thirty, had already gone. (As it happened, they passed each other several miles east of Spark on the Des Moines highway. Unfortunately, the doctor, in his car, did not seem to notice his son trudging along

3

the roadside. Pierce waved, but the car sped past him and was soon lost to sight around the curve at Johnson's Wayside Diner.)

Pierce had been told that a television crew might come to take films of his departure. The TV crew never arrived, but a photographer and a reporter from one of the Des Moines newspapers did appear at the last minute. The photographer took a picture of Pierce grinning up at a mileage sign (Des Moines 37, Davenport 196), and the reporter asked a few ironical questions, clearly indicating his opinion that Pierce would quit the first week. Then they offered him a lift to Des Moines—which, of course, Pierce was bound to decline—and drove off at high speed.

The older residents of Spark took little notice of Pierce's leaving. The younger ones were much diverted by his venture, but (it being a weekday) they were either in school or at their jobs, and so Pierce began his long walk attended by four dogs and the postman, John R. Bushby, who accompanied him along Main Street as far as Grove Avenue, where his delivery route started.

At the last house before the sidewalks ended and the fields began, Pierce was greeted by Mrs. Muncie, a retired schoolteacher, who had come out to the road to leave her garbage.

"Where are you going, Pierce?" the old lady asked, and when Pierce replied (loudly, for she was rather deaf): "Around the world, Mrs. Muncie," she gave her white head a shake.

"Better not," she said.

But she winked at him and smiled, and Pierce smiled back at her courteously as he passed by.

At the town limits the dogs turned back, as though required to do so by local ordinance, and Pierce went on alone.

4

Pierce Davis was no eccentric, nor was he a simpleton. The idea of walking around the world wasn't his; in fact, when it first had been broached to him, he thought it preposterous. He had been willing to admit that it might make sense to the sponsor—a huge farm seed and equipment business with headquarters in Duluth—but he hadn't felt that he was the man for the job.

Even so, the idea had appealed to him. There was something splendid about it. He'd wake some nights excited, having dreamed of world-walking through strange lands and among exotic peoples, and the catarrhal breathing of his wife nearby seemed to echo the rhythm of his slow and giant strides. Those dreams had finally persuaded him, for he'd hoped since childhood that some special destiny awaited him, and he guessed this might be it.

He hoped—but he wasn't sure. He knew he had no claim on fate. He wasn't gifted, he had no particular talent, nor was he markedly different from the other boys in the town of Spark with whom he'd grown to manhood. He'd seen what they'd seen, and done as they'd done. He had fidgeted in the same schoolrooms and church pews, kissed the same girls, chased the same cats, and raided the same orchards in autumn. His only distinctive characteristic was one which at times served him badly: he was an easy laugher. When something amused him, he wouldn't just smile or snicker, he'd burst out laughing—and there was nothing wrong with that, except that Pierce sometimes laughed too loudly, or in inappropriate circumstances, and it occasionally occurred to him that this laughter of his had a life of its own, for it often caught him by surprise by erupting when he didn't really feel like laughing. He laughed in the way certain women blush or men perspire, in response to a sudden change in emotional temperature. Once in court, testifying as a witness to a traffic accident, he laughed so under cross-examination that the judge rebuked him.

Because of this habit, Pierce drew a little more attention in Spark than he would have otherwise. By some, he was considered an unusually cheerful young fellow; by others, a fool. No one, however, really thought he was anything out of the ordinary, and this general opinion Pierce himself shared.

Still, there must have been some hint that he wasn't really like the others, or at least that he was like them but with a slight difference, almost imperceptible perhaps, some little quirk of character, a minor chromosome displacement, some latent oddity or aptitude—something, anyway, that would impel him to undertake the lonely and unusual role of world-walker.

Whatever it was, it was undoubtedly something simple. Pierce was an uncomplicated fellow, and his subsequent career—if world-walking can be called a career—was itself, strictly speaking, nothing more than a prolonged succession of the humblest of human actions, that of putting one foot ahead of the other.

Pierce Davis and his sponsor assumed that his real difficulties would lie far ahead, in remote continents where he might be waylaid and robbed, or stoned, or set upon by wild beasts, or mistaken for a foreign mercenary in some little war and hung up by the thumbs to wither in the sun. As far as his native land was concerned, no special problems were foreseen.

But when he tried to enter the federal superhighway system at an access point in Dallas County, after a brisk three-hour walk from Spark, he was stopped at the toll-booth and turned back.

"No hitchhiking," said the attendant.

"I'm not hitchhiking, I'm walking," said Pierce.

The attendant shook his head. He knew better. "Not allowed," he said.

Pierce tried to convince him, in vain. The more Pierce talked, the more the man became irritated, as though he were being asked to approve of some indecent act. "Nope," he kept saying between his teeth, "not permitted." And he glared at Pierce with unconcealed dislike.

Pierce backed off. Then, seeing a state police trooper lounging in a patrol car parked nearby, he went over to explain the situation and to seek the trooper's support.

The trooper didn't seem to understand, though. "What do you mean, you're walking?" he asked suspiciously.

"Walking, just walking," said Pierce, and as the trooper continued to stare at him, he added: "You know, like this." And he took a few steps.

The trooper eased himself out of the patrol car. He had sized Pierce up and he wanted to be ready for anything. What the trooper saw was a husky young man in his late twenties with protruding ears and an open, friendly face, but he knew from experience that such honest-looking fellows were often the worst.

"Where you headed, buddy?" the trooper asked.

Pierce hesitated. He didn't think the trooper would react favorably to an announcement about world-walking. "Des Moines," was all he said.

"You got business in Des Moines?"

"Well, I'm not actually stopping there."

The trooper hitched his belt to bring his pistol holster around a bit. "You got some identification on you, buddy?"

Pierce didn't like the trooper's attitude, but he was even-tempered and considerate of other people's problems, so he swung his knapsack from his shoulders and unbuckled the straps. He took out his passport, which was thickened with visas, and he took out his folder of letters of introduction and identification, which were in virtually every major language in the world. After the trooper had pawed through this material, he was even more convinced that he was dealing with a troublesome character, maybe a foreigner. Still, there was no evidence of criminality or espionage, so he contented himself with repeating the tollbooth attendant's injunction: "No hitchhiking."

"I'm just walking," Pierce said again.

"Not on this highway, you don't," said the trooper. "The government built this highway for cars. People don't walk on it. You want to go somewhere, you get a car, you take a bus or something. That's what it's built for. They didn't put no sidewalks on it."

"I'd walk in the center strip where the grass is," Pierce said.

"That grass got planted for looks, not to walk on," the trooper said, becoming annoyed. "You start letting one man walk and pretty soon they's a parade out there and people getting run down crossing and all." His voice had hoarsened. A vein bulged on his forehead, above his dark glasses. "And suppose when you got to take a leak, you go in front of little children and women in the cars passing by?"

"Well, I sure wouldn't do that," Pierce began to

protest, but then, feeling laughter surge within him, he had to close his mouth tight and bite his lips, which made him look idiotic. The trooper stared at him aggressively for a moment and then continued his explanation in a disgusted tone:

"And then maybe there's some woman alone with a flat tire or out of gas and hoping a decent man will stop to help but instead here comes along a bum walking where there ain't nobody supposed to walk and this woman she realizes how helpless she is."

"What's wrong with walking?" Pierce found the trooper's increasingly angry reaction unsettling. "Just because a man walks doesn't mean he's a bum. Walking, it's good for you."

"Not here it ain't."

"It's a healthy exercise. It—"

"Listen, buddy." The trooper was menacing now, offended by the grimaces Pierce had been forced to make to suppress his laughter. "People think they can do whatever they want to regardless. Well, I'm telling you you can't. They built it for cars, how many times I got to tell you? You got no business walking. Nobody walks."

"I walk," said Pierce. One bark of laughter escaped. "Sorry," he said, again biting his lips and grinning helplessly at the infuriated officer.

"No, you don't, you don't walk. Don't tell me you walk, I don't want to hear it." The trooper actually seemed to be trembling, he was so enraged. "You drive a car, you take a bus, you ride in something maybe a train I don't care, but I'm telling you no walking. Walking is hitchhiking, we don't allow it. Walking, you don't do it, understand? Walking nobody does." He clenched his fists and fairly shouted at Pierce: *I don't want to hear no more about this walking, you hear me? Nobody walks.*

9

Pierce glanced over at the attendant, blurred behind the glass of the booth, beyond which, on the superhighway, the automobiles raced by so rapidly that he couldn't be sure that anyone was inside them, and he glanced at the trooper, a glowering figure all leather and whipcord and metal, masked by the dark glasses, and glistening in the sharp March sunlight as though, like his patrol car, he were freshly polished.

Pierce gave up. "Okay," he said, shouldering his knapsack. As he turned and walked off, he tried to persuade himself that the trooper undoubtedly had valid reasons for refusing to let him use the superhighway. He was troubled, though. The trooper's attitude had implied that walking itself was virtually a criminal activity, and it occurred to Pierce that this aversion probably would be shared to a large degree by motorists, too. Very well, he told himself, henceforth he'd use the back roads, which would be quieter and more pleasant, anyway, and where he'd be accepted without question merely as a fellow strolling along with a pack on his back.

Thus he tried to comfort himself. But he couldn't help wondering whether he wouldn't find himself in a certain amount of difficulty wherever he went and by whatever route, from the sheer fact of being a walker. A man who walked when everyone else didn't—well, wouldn't such a man be regarded as a bit abnormal?

Surely not, thought Pierce. Still, he was a little discouraged, and he decided that he would go no farther that day than the next town on his map, and find lodging there well before darkness fell.

Dr. Davis, driving back to Spark, had in fact seen from afar the familiar figure of his son, walking. He'd thought of stopping for a few farewell words, but at the same time the sight of Pierce so strongly renewed certain vexatious sensations within him that, being well read in psychology, the doctor judged that there was a slight but definite possibility that instead of bringing the car to a halt beside Pierce, he might be nipped by a psychotic trauma at the very last second and run him down. Besides, Dr. Davis had a little cold and knew it would only get worse if he had to roll down his window or open the door just to exchange a remark or two with Pierce, whom he believed he'd be seeing again soon enough, as he shared with the Des Moines reporter the conviction that Pierce wouldn't get far. In any case, Dr. Davis ignored Pierce's wave, kept his eyes fixed on the road ahead, and drove grimly by, both hands on the wheel. *Good luck, Pierce,* he thought, but he didn't really mean it, for luck and Pierce had no connection in his mind.

His son was one of those fine, clean, strong young fellows of whom much (but not too much) is expected, yet who accomplish next to nothing, and for no apparent reason. As Dr. Davis well knew, Pierce had had many advantages, but they seemed to be of little use to him. Pierce was high-spirited, cheerful, and sincere. He could sing, he could dance, he knew how to repair machinery, he had the gift of meeting people easily, and he could drink if he needed to and hold it well, but these and a dozen other little knacks and capacities benefited him hardly at all. At the age of twenty-eight, Pierce Davis was already a man whose future was dim.

The doctor was of the third generation of Davises in Spark since the arrival there in 1868 of a bearded, bandy-legged little Union Army veteran from Wisconsin named Wiley Davis, who bought farmland and married a strapping Polish girl to do his work for him. As the town grew and prospered, subsequent Davises pursued careers as shopkeepers and artisans, and, later, as professional men. Dr. Davis's elder brother, Phil, was judge of the probate court, and various cousins and nephews in Des Moines and elsewhere had set themselves up comfortably as engineers, dentists, teachers, and businessmen.

The achievements of the other Davises made Pierce's lack of success appear to be downright failure. This wasn't fair to him. He had had just one real setback—he'd flunked out of medical school at the end of the first year—and in more favorable surroundings might justly have felt that he was making some progress in life, for he worked diligently as a mechanic in a big garage and was studying accounting at night by a correspondence course. Would he some day be able to found his own garage business or car dealership? Did he have a future as an accountant, or, through accounting, in business management or public service? He doubted it. So did his father. No one else really thought he could, either. That was the curse of Pierce Davis. Wherever he turned he saw disappointment—on the faces of his wife, his father, his Uncle Phil, the various cousins Davis, himself in the mirror, and even (he imagined) his little daughter, Stephanie, age two. "I'm licked," Pierce would sometimes whisper to himself, but he didn't know why that should be, and often he'd set off at a trot along the farm roads that led away from Spark, but which led nowhere for him, and he'd run for hours under the heavy summer sun or in the dusty autumn air when the fields were stripped and he could hear the hogs grunting miles away. He'd run until he could run no more; then he'd listen to the crickets or the crows for a while before turning to walk back home.

When Pierce first mentioned the world-walk to his father, Dr. Davis had said politely that it sounded very interesting, but he'd given Pierce the familiar disappointed glance, as though Pierce had already failed in the attempt, and Pierce, feeling discouraged, hadn't raised the subject again until a few days before his actual departure. Dr. Davis hadn't reacted much. Was it, Pierce wondered, because of a feeling that nothing his son did could be of any real importance? And was the old doctor right? This troubled Pierce no little, and he was glad when the day came for him to leave Spark. All he had to do was walk. That didn't seem so hard.

On the second morning of the world-walk, as Pierce Davis was proceeding through the south Des Moines suburbs shielded by his waterproof poncho from intermittent rainshowers, the story of his enterprise appeared in the Des Moines newspaper as a little front-page feature in which his first name was spelled "Pearce" and his age, by a typographical error, was given as eighty-two. The reporter, treating the project with a supercilious touch, wrote of Pierce as "the Magellan of the highways," although he grudgingly included the fact that Pierce had some claim to athletic distinction, having won three intercollegiate cross-country events during his undergraduate years at the University of Iowa.

The story was picked up as a light paragraph by a press service, and so was printed here and there in various newspapers scattered across the country. Within a few days a dim response passed through the national consciousness, for the idea of world-walking stimulated certain types of adventurers and cranks and publicity-seekers, and although this phenomenon expired well before reaching the proportions of a fad, it did produce a few more little news stories.

In Salem, Oregon, three high-school boys who'd read about Pierce set off in the direction of Alaska, spent the night in a barn, which they burned to the ground the next morning through carelessness with their cigarettes, and, having escaped the flames, were arrested and returned home to appear before the juvenile court.

A sixteen-year-old runaway girl from East Lansing, Michigan, had also read about Pierce, for she said she'd simply gone world-walking, too. (This seemed doubtful, however, as the police found her in a motel outside Flint with a sailor.)

In Chicago a legless Army veteran announced he'd circle the globe in his powered wheelchair. In Boise, Idaho, a retired circus acrobat proposed to do his world-walking on his hands—and actually traversed eight blocks of the business district in that manner before he quit. Then there were others elsewhere who, in various ways, declared how they'd outdo Pierce's effort—by hopping one-legged around the world, or by crawling around it on all fours, or by using a pogo stick to do it in jumps, or by stalking on stilts, or by walking backward, and, inevitably, there appeared several citizens who claimed that they'd walked around the world already—an Arkansas hog farmer swore he'd done it not once but twice, back in the 1950s—but no one bothered to investigate such declarations, and at the end of the week these first and feeble evidences of public interest in world-walking had died out completely, by which time the world-walker himself was crossing the Mississippi River at Davenport, nursing a head cold and limping from blisters, feeling tired and lonely, and wondering if he wouldn't have been better off to have remained at home with his wife and child, where at least he would have been comfortable.

*   *   *

Natalie Leonard had married Pierce Davis when he was
in medical school. She was a doctor's daughter, and she
had assumed, naturally, that she would become, like her
mother, a doctor's wife, a calling she had trained for virtually from infancy and which appealed to her fondness
for secrecy and power: through her husband she would
be privy to the most intimate details of town life.

When Pierce told her he had flunked out, Natalie
had seen her life in ruins. From that day she had thought
frequently of divorce or separation—Pierce had, in a
sense, grossly deceived her—yet she never could bring herself to the point of leaving him; his failure had clouded
her opinion of herself, and she was afraid that she would
be unable to do better the next time, if indeed there
would be a next time.

"I'm still young," she'd tell herself, staring into the
mirror, but she was a year older than Pierce and looked
more than that, for tiny lines were working through her
skin, and the veins on her hands seemed thicker every
time she inspected them. Pierce, by contrast, appeared
boyish. He missed being handsome by reason of his jug
ears and prominent teeth, but he was husky and well
proportioned, his eyes were as blue as a baby's, his skin
fresh, and his movements as vigorous as the laughter
which would seize him for no apparent reason. Sometimes in the evenings, when Natalie watched him frowning over his accounting textbooks, his burnt-blond hair
tumbled over his forehead, with his body as relaxed as a
child's, she felt hatred rise hysterically within her, and
she had to bite her lips and clench her fists to keep from
shouting at him: "You flunked out—why? Why did you
flunk out? Tell me why, why, why!"

Pierce had tried to say why at the time. He'd gotten the impression that the practice of medicine was itself a form of illness. His fellow students hung about the dissecting tables too avidly for his taste, and the professors seemed too brutal and knowing. After each lecture or laboratory period Pierce had felt slightly unwell, as though his own organs had been handled by the instructor for demonstration purposes. Nor had his father's example inspired him. Pierce saw that Dr. Davis was irritated by the trivial ailments of his patients, which were mostly neurotic in origin. The only times he seemed professionally stimulated were in gory emergencies, as when farmers got caught in their reapers. Such observations so troubled Pierce that he lost the vision he'd had of himself as a doctor, and having lost that, he lost heart, lost class standing, and finally lost everything.

His attempts to explain this were meaningless to Natalie. She was outraged that such qualms had denied her what she felt was hers by right. "I should have been a doctor's wife," she kept thinking, as the months and years passed by. She tried to do her best for Pierce, she tried to overcome her resentment, she even tried to revive her old feelings of affection and passion for him, but she couldn't, she really couldn't. Every day, in various ways, she was reminded of what should have been. In the mornings, when she saw Pierce leave for the garage, she was galled because he was carrying a lunchbox instead of a little black medical satchel, and in the evenings, when the telephone rang and Pierce had to go out for a while, she suffered at the thought that he was merely towing a wrecked car or replacing a battery. She hated his hands, which no amount of scrubbing would free of grease stains, and when she carried the family laundry to the South Street coin wash, she was so ashamed of his grimy overalls that she stuffed them into the machine swiftly, when no one was looking, and thought to herself for the twentieth time in the day: "I should have been a doctor's wife!" She might have been soothed by Pierce's mother, a large and placid lady, but unfortunately the elder Mrs. Davis had been killed in a traffic accident several years before while visiting a sister in St. Louis. Natalie had no close friends in Spark. Her attitude toward Pierce's relatives was guarded and defensive. Her only satisfaction was in little Stephanie, who, being dark and small-boned, resembled her and not Pierce, and as often as she could she took Stephanie up to her parents' home in Clarion, in north Iowa, so that the child would know what it meant to live in a doctor's house.

Natalie decided that if anything happened to Pierce, she would take Stephanie to Clarion for good. She couldn't be a doctor's wife, but she could be the doctor's daughter again—if anything happened to Pierce. Such thoughts made her feel guilty, but she couldn't help speculating. It made her almost happy at times. For his part, Pierce knew he didn't have a successful marriage and that it was probably his fault, and what had occurred to Natalie also began occurring to him—namely, that he might make some amends to his disappointed wife by vanishing.

Obviously Natalie hadn't opposed the world-walk, although she'd maintained her customary reserve. "It's your decision," she had told him. Inwardly she had exulted. Pierce's sponsor, the agricultural company in Duluth, was contractually committed to send her each month the equivalent of Pierce's wages at the garage, and on top of that had provided her with a handsome insurance policy as protection in case Pierce got killed or maimed.

For reasons of her own, she was the only one who believed in the world-walk—even Pierce had doubts—and at the same time she was convinced that she'd never see him again.

The world-walking idea had originated in the imagination of a fifty-eight-year-old businessman named Charles L. Mordenstahl, the executive vice-president of the Duluth agricultural company. Mr. Mordenstahl was a fleshy, handsome man, supercharged and overburdened, who knew from experience when to surrender to his enthusiasms. Thus he allowed the world-walking concept to possess him (just as, the previous year, he had permitted himself to be seized by the idea of creating lightly perfumed fertilizers for more gracious farm living).

Like most American businesses of size, Mr. Mordenstahl's company had for some years been establishing itself in foreign markets, in a variety of ways. In some countries it owned plants outright; in others it operated in partnership with local entrepreneurs, or sold licenses for the use of its patents. In addition, the company participated in research-and-development programs conducted for the benefit of world agriculture both by the U.S. government and by the United Nations. There was a constant flow of technicians to and from these public agencies, and when project opportunities materialized, Mr. Mordenstahl's company was often the successful bidder. He himself frequently was required to fly to such places as Ceylon and Argentina, either to pose ceremonially with indigenous ministers of agriculture for photographs at the official openings of new fertilizer plants, or to deal personally with some organizational crisis. Competition worried him, though—competition not only from rival U.S. companies, but also from the Germans, the Russians, and the Chinese—and within his own company he had enemies who lusted for his blood and his job, so that altogether Mr. Mordenstahl lived the frantic, overwrought life of an American businessman with increasing international interests, hounded by the dynamism of his personality and his position into a relentless hunt for new ideas.

The world-walk, he decided finally, would symbolize the spirit of American agriculture—youthful, vigorous, resourceful—moving inexorably across the rural face of the earth. The world-walker himself Mr. Mordenstahl envisioned as a hardy young giant who would stroll from farm to farm and village to village, distributing free packets of seeds and counseling the peasants on their soil problems. Such activity, well publicized and suitably backed up by technical experts, would help create that climate of respect and friendship which the Chinese in particular were so damnably good at, and which, according to the latest information, was beginning to pay off for them in the tangible form of contracts. Mr. Mordenstahl determined to launch a single walker as a pilot project, and then, if all went well, more walkers would follow— not to circle the earth (for he shrewdly judged that a true spectacular could be done just once), but rather to walk continents and countries, even regions and districts.

His staff had proceeded to make the customary preliminary analysis. This confirmed most satisfactorily Mr. Mordenstahl's judgment that the venture wouldn't cost much, that it would yield desirable benefits if it succeeded (and that it would be simple to drop if it didn't), and, in short, that it would be well worth trying.

Except that it couldn't be done.

The staff study pointed out that a man could fly

around the world in an airplane, balloon, or rocket, that he could circumnavigate it by ship or submarine (or, in theory, under his own power as a swimmer), but that because of the various intervening oceans, it was a physical and literal impossibility to do the job by foot (except at the Poles, which wouldn't count).

Mr. Mordenstahl had considered this objection briefly. Then he dismissed it. The world-walk concept had fastened too strongly on his imagination to be shaken loose by such a quibble. He thanked his assistants, informed them that the project would go forward without delay, and instructed them to start compiling a list of prospective world-walkers from which one finally would be selected.

Pierce hadn't been discouraged when the Iowa trooper kept him off the superhighway, for he had supposed that it would be more agreeable to walk the back roads where he could exchange a few friendly words with farmers in their fields as he proceeded from one little town to the next.

But he'd found it wasn't quite like that, neither in Iowa nor in Illinois. The roads were quiet enough; much quieter, indeed, than he'd expected. Only infrequently did a car or truck pass by; there were no other walkers or hikers, nor were there bicycle-riders or motorcyclists, and the surrounding fields were empty. Sometimes in the distance giant farm machines could be seen toiling along in their dust, and there were farmhouses here and there, set well back from the road under fine old trees planted a century ago, but Pierce, in the countryside of mid-America, found himself very much alone.

This hadn't troubled him at first, but as he passed day after day in rural solitude, he became more reflective, particularly in the late afternoons when the shadows lengthened, and he kept glancing ahead and behind and to the sides, not so much hoping to spy out his fellow citizens as simply wondering exactly where they'd gone.

To be sure, Pierce was aware that the land didn't need much labor any more, so that most farm people had left to work in the cities, and he knew, too, that many of the villages had been deserted and lay dying, but even so he wasn't prepared for the hushed and empty land through which he walked.

"Hey," said Pierce aloud, to hear the sound of a human voice. "Hi there, Illinois." Suppose he stumbled and broke an ankle—who'd come by to help him? He noticed that the road was pitted. Its edges were crumbling. Evidently it wasn't used enough to warrant resurfacing. From time to time he glimpsed city towers on the horizon or heard faint urban rumblings, but such distant signs of human activity served only to emphasize the loneliness of the countryside.

The little towns were sad and withered. Some houses were vacant and boarded up, others slumped in discouragement in weedy yards, and the faces Pierce saw at the windows were old. More than once he passed through a whole town without seeing a single child.

It was only with some difficulty that he found lodgings at night, for the old-fashioned bed-and-breakfast establishments once common in country towns no longer existed, and he'd been forced to stop at sleazy motels, which survived as trysting places for adulterers, where his arrival alone and on foot was regarded by the proprietors as sinister. Eating likewise was a problem. There were just a few dim diners on the route he was following, and he had to provision himself at grocery stores to be sure he wouldn't miss his midday meal.

Thus for hours at a time Pierce trudged in solitude through an abandoned land. He began to feel like a trespasser, as though the people who'd formerly dwelt in the towns and on the farms had been rejected by some natural force which, after a few decades of submission to mankind, had reasserted itself, expelling the intruders. Which of course he realized was nonsense, as the land was producing more food every year, under scientific management. Still, it was strange to find all that fertile springtime earth stretching mile after mile, capable of feeding thousands upon thousands of humans, but without another soul anywhere in sight.

"I'm thinking too much," he said aloud, and his words seemed to evoke a momentary shocked stillness all around him—among the roadside trees, the weeds that matted the shoulders of the road, the rivulets that ran at the edges of the loamy fields—and he added, both as a joke and as a self-conscious gesture to whatever it was that disturbed him: "Don't worry about me. I won't bother you."

He spoke in a low voice, almost a whisper, as though he didn't want to call any particular attention to himself. The land seemed hostile, and so did the old people in the dying towns. In fact, he felt that he was walking the battlefield of a war not yet decided.

"This is *Illinois*," he reminded himself. "I'm fifty miles north of *Peoria*." Nothing at all extraordinary could possibly exist so close to Peoria, could it? And yet, walking along that crumbling highway between those rich, forsaken fields, he found himself reflecting that Illinois and Peoria were just names, that the land itself had endured many long centuries, that the rocks were far older than any human memorial, that mankind was of little importance in the ageless musings of soil and stone, sun and storm—and that he, Pierce Davis, counted for no more here than a robin in a tree.

"I've been by myself too much lately," he said. "Walking, it's lonely." That was it, he thought. The countryside wasn't any different from that around Spark, he was just seeing it in terms of his own loneliness, and the reaction of the people he'd passed by, maybe that, too, was largely imaginary.

Or maybe not.

He was baffled. Was his walking changing him and the way he saw the world, or was it forcing him to see the world as it really was? He couldn't tell. All he was sure of was that he was alone. That was a fact, all right. He'd never been so alone before. He was thinking about himself, as he'd often done in the past, but it was in a new way now, because he didn't have anybody else to think about at the same time. He had to think of himself not as Natalie's husband or Stephanie's father or Dr. Davis's son, but as the walker—Pierce Davis, the walker.

And then he had a premonition that his awareness of his own personality might undergo some sort of change. His sense of his own identity was bound up with other people's lives and other people's view of him—and if this were taken away with nothing put in its place but the solitude of a world-walk, his very name might be threatened.

"Didn't figure on this," Pierce complained. "It's a hell of a way to start out." He kept glancing up and around, as though he expected some response from the sky, from the fenceposts, from the pebbles. "It won't be so easy," he said. "I didn't think it would be easy, but I was thinking about things like mountains and deserts."

The sun stared down from its tremendous height. The empty road ran miles ahead, miles behind, and on each side the abundant earth lay silent.

Pierce was more than a little worried now. Was he to be snubbed by his fellow man and by nature, too, and beyond this, to be deprived of that complete sense of himself which he'd had for as long as he could remember? Maybe he ought to quit. Then he thought of what his father would say and how his wife would look and what he would think of himself, and he swore he'd come to terms with whatever the world-walk might require of him.

"Listen," he exclaimed. "I'm Pierce Davis from Spark, Iowa, and I've been hired to walk around the world, that's all."

He kept on going.

Pierce Davis hadn't been the sponsor's first choice as the world-walker. Nor had he been second choice, or third, or even fourth. He was, in fact, forty-third.

The other forty-two had declined the offer, one after another, when approached by Mr. Mordenstahl's assistants. They couldn't leave their jobs or their families, or they demanded a stipend far higher than Mr. Mordenstahl felt it proper to pay, or they thought the idea so ridiculous that they refused to consider it seriously (which had been Pierce's initial reaction, too).

The list of potential world-walkers had been compiled from the athletic records of several Midwestern universities, including the University of Iowa, and as Mr. Mordenstahl's assistants paid special heed to sporting events requiring stamina, Pierce's brief eminence as a cross-country runner was enough to mark him for further investigation.

Despite his lowly position on the list, Pierce did possess all the necessary qualifications. That is, his skin was white, his appearance was personable, and (by American standards) he was well-spoken. He had no criminal or delinquent record, nor was there any indication that he was queer. He was a college graduate from a Protestant middle-class background, which, with his maturity in years and his small-town upbringing, was some guarantee that he wouldn't suddenly turn radical or religious or in any predictable way embarrass his sponsor or his nation. He wasn't a farmer, it was true, but real farmers who qualified in other respects were scarce, and these few proved to be surly and intractable types, so that finally it was judged sufficient that Pierce had a general familiarity with outdoor life and had worked one summer painting barns.

Mr. Mordenstahl himself approved the final selection, after Pierce had been flown to Duluth and interviewed for hours by the executive staff. Mr. Mordenstahl hadn't been enthusiastic, though. He found Pierce suspiciously naïve and even-tempered. "Are you sure this guy isn't mentally defective?" Mr. Mordenstahl kept asking his assistants. Still, no better candidate than Pierce was available, and so the job was offered to him and then pressed upon him in subsequent weeks until he at length consented.

Now, while Pierce was experiencing certain insights on the secondary-road system in north-central Illinois, Mr. Mordenstahl was becoming restless. It had been agreed that the American and European legs of the journey would be largely exploratory and experimental, to test the walker's capacity to carry out such a fatiguing

25

undertaking. The real targets were the Middle East and particularly Asia, where millions of peasants and land-lords constituted the greatest undeveloped market in the world. Even so, Mr. Mordenstahl was disappointed that Pierce had gotten such a meager press sendoff. His public-relations aide had counseled a low-key publicity approach as being more dignified and cheaper, too, but Mr. Mordenstahl still wanted lots of clippings instead of the few he had. "This story will build," the public-relations man had predicted. But it hadn't.

And where was the world-walker? Mr. Mordenstahl had received a single postcard, mailed from Iowa City, in which Pierce had reported rain and blisters. After that, nothing. "Is he hiding or what?" Mr. Mordenstahl grumbled. He was starting to have doubts—doubts about Pierce, about the world-walk, about the security of his own position, which was menaced not only by all his foes and rivals and ill-wishers, but also by the charts and graphs that showed small progress in sales. "Expand or die," thought Mr. Mordenstahl. He took to biting his nails and doodling during conferences. And he wondered: Had the world-walk idea been a mistake? Had he been betrayed by his enthusiasm into an error of judgment?

In the early afternoon of March 29 Pierce Davis was trudging along a state highway some fifteen miles south-east of Kankakee, Illinois, not far from the Indiana border. He was tired and discouraged. The wind had whipped him all day, he'd been rained on three separate times, and in the dingy motel shack where he'd spent the night bedbugs had feasted at his waist and shoulders, where his belt and packstraps now chafed the welts.

The loneliness of his walk weighed on him more and more. He was oppressed by the silence, by the emptiness, and by the slow unfolding of a road that seemed always the same. Sometimes he suspected he was being followed by someone. He imagined it was another walker, a shadow always just out of sight around a bend in the road or hidden by a hillside. Once or twice, feeling foolish as he did so, he crouched behind a tree, lying in wait for this phantom walker, who never appeared. At other times he was touched by quick fantasies of death: a speeding car would come singing up behind him and hurtle him, broken, into the ditch; a ragged sword of lightning would cleave him head to toe, or a pack of wild dogs would swarm out of one of those far abandoned farmyards, racing toward the unprotected man, the exposed and lonely walker.

He crested a modest hill. The clouds parted; the sun gave a summery glare to the land beyond. The landscape was the same, but the sudden spell of sunlight seemed to fix it as still as a desert. For a few moments he paused, listening, but heard not a single sound, and went on, trying to step more lightly, for he had the sensation that something was awaiting him, which made his scalp tingle even before he saw an automobile stopped on the highway with a man standing motionless beside it.

The car was black; the man was, too. He was a tall and narrow man, who looked dangerously hard, and he was sheathed in a dark suit from which a white shirt gleamed. Beneath his black hat, bony features set off a severe gaze from yellow-tinged eyes.

"Car broke down?" asked Pierce, as soon as he was within reasonable speaking distance.

The black man nodded.

"Mind if I take a look?" said Pierce. "I'm a mechanic by trade."

"Be much obliged," said the man.

Pierce removed his knapsack and set it down, then opened the hood and began examining the parts and connections. "What, it just quit on you?" he asked.

"Stalled five times," the motorist said. "The last time, it gave up."

"Well, you've got a battery problem."

"I figured that. I've been here an hour, and in that time four cars and a pickup truck have gone by, counting both ways, and not a one would so much as slow down, let alone give me a push." The man spoke with an accent which Pierce guessed might be West Indian. He seemed withdrawn and slightly suspicious.

"Maybe we can get it going," said Pierce, closing the hood.

The two of them, pushing together, managed to roll the car ahead to a point where the road began to slope down. Then the man got in behind the wheel, and Pierce pushed alone. When the car was rolling as fast as he could run, he stopped and watched as it trundled off. Farther down the road it bucked and shuddered as the clutch was let in. The points began firing, a plume of blue exhaust appeared from the tailpipe, and the car went off at a considerable speed, as though the driver were anxious to get as far as he could before it stalled again.

Pierce returned to where his knapsack lay, swung it up on his shoulders, and resumed his walk.

Half an hour later he saw the car again. It was stopped just over another small rise, and the driver was leaning against it, smoking a cigarette.

"Same trouble?" asked Pierce as he came up.

"I waited for you," the man said. "I'll give you a lift. I couldn't stop back there, but here I can roll it again and

I can take you as far as the next town or wherever they've got a garage."

"Well, thanks, but I can't. I'm walking."

"I see you're walking, but you did me a favor so I want to do you one."

"I sure thank you, but you go on ahead and don't wait for me."

"I've already waited," said the driver, taking a last quick drag on his cigarette and then dropping it. "I owe you a favor, mister, and I'm a man who's conscious of his debts." He ground the cigarette butt out beneath his heel and gave Pierce a sharp glance.

"Honestly, I can't accept a lift."

"Why not?"

"Well, I can't."

"You mean you won't."

"I can't," Pierce said again, and then, seeing hostility gathering in the man's face, he added: "I mean I'm supposed to walk. I get paid for it." The man's expression didn't change. "I'm a professional walker," Pierce went on, wanting to clear himself of the unvoiced accusation but reluctant to make a full disclosure. "I've got a contract and in the contract it says I've got to walk and no rides no matter what."

The driver pulled out another cigarette and lit it with a match. He was taller than Pierce, and stared down at him so coldly that Pierce realized how false the walking story must have sounded.

"So where you walking to, then?" the man asked, in a contemptuous way.

Pierce decided to tell him, and did so.

The man opened the door of the car and eased himself inside. "That's an ambitious project you got there," he said, sarcastically.

"I can show you my contract," Pierce said, but the

man slammed the door, released the brake, and rolled off slowly down the hill; again the engine sputtered and caught, and again the car raced forward. Then it rounded a bend and was lost to sight behind a clump of trees.

An hour later Pierce once more saw the car parked at the top of a little hill with its driver waiting for him, cigarette in hand, leaning against a fender. The sun was lower now. It cast long shadows; the wind, rising steadily, was cool. The man watched Pierce approach. His gaze was stern and remote, but there was a hint of calculation in his manner, as though he'd arrived at some conclusion which he wanted to test.

"You mean you've actually set out to walk around the world?" he asked.

"That's right," said Pierce.

"And you say somebody's hired you to do it?"

Pierce told him about the Duluth agricultural company and the purpose of the project.

"Lord," the man muttered. "I've seen all kinds and sorts in my life, but never before a man paid to walk around the world." He seemed to be pondering the matter intently as he sucked on his cigarette, his eyes narrowed and his head slowly nodding. "You're kidding me, aren't you?" he said, giving Pierce a shrewd look.

"No, I'm not." Pierce wished he hadn't tried to explain the matter in the first place. Being a walker was bad enough, as he'd already learned, for in some peculiar way it irritated people. But now for the first time since he'd left Spark, he'd told someone what the purpose of his walking was—and already he could tell that the man was disturbed by it.

"Walking around the *world*," the driver said slowly, and he looked at Pierce with a flicker of disdain that implied he thought Pierce didn't measure up to such a task. "You really think you can do it?"

30

"Well, I don't know."

"Must be something that makes you think you can do it."

"I'm just starting out. I don't know yet."

"You've got a pretty humble attitude," the man said. "Seems to me that a man who sets out to do what you say you're doing ought to have a feeling of conviction about it, what do you think?"

"Well, the company thinks I can do it, I guess," Pierce replied lamely.

"Just another job to you, is it?"

"I said I get paid for it."

"And you can quit any time you get tired of it?"

"That's right."

"But the company, they don't want you to quit."

"Of course not."

"So they make it as soft and smooth and nice as they can for you, don't they, Mr. Walker?"

"I've got to do the walking."

"But they buy you new boots and pay for your meals and all that."

"Sure they do."

"Well, I guess you've got a desirable kind of position with this world-walk job of yours, don't you?"

"It isn't so easy."

"You're wrong," the man said impatiently, and he drew a cigarette from his pocket so swiftly that Pierce took a half-step backward. "You could do the walking right in your own living room, the way you're set up in this thing. You could just walk round and round all day in your bedroom slippers with time out for a nap and a shower and a nice nourishing supper."

"I don't know what you're driving at."

"What I'm driving at is that you don't suffer under your present arrangement."

31

"I've got blisters. My feet hurt."

"You don't *suffer.*"

"Why should I suffer?"

The man's eyes gleamed in the matchlight as he lit his cigarette. "You ought to suffer," he said decisively, indicating that this was a point obvious beyond argument. "You *got* to suffer. This world you say they got you started walking around, it's got bumps and lumps on it, mister, it goes way up high and it goes way down low, and anybody who's got the audacity to set his two feet on it one after the other, he's got to be a man suffering head to toe." He was staring at Pierce in a fierce, abstracted way, as if he were seeing not a fellow human creature but instead the inadequate embodiment of an idea that had caught in the web of his imagination and was strumming vigorously there. "What I'm telling you," he went on, "is that what you say you're doing, it's no small thing, you understand—"

"I never said it was."

"—I mean to say it's sizable, it's *large,* it's as big as the world itself," the man declared, "and you can't get bigger than that! No, mister—this business of walking around the world, it can't be done by just any fellow who happens to have a pair of legs under him, it's got to be done by a real man, a big man, a man who's been proved and tested by pain and trials and suffering."

"Well, I don't know," mumbled Pierce, shifting his feet uneasily.

"What I'm telling you," the motorist went on heatedly, "is that unless this walk around the world is done in the right way by the right man—and I mean a man who has *suffered*—then it won't work, it shouldn't be tried, and it can't be done." He glared at Pierce as he drew furiously on his cigarette. "And the thought occurs to me that maybe you are incapable of suffering, I mean the kind of suffering that a man has hammered into him like nails from the time he's a boy. I mean suffering to the bone, mister, and a man who hasn't trained up under that kind of suffering can't really suffer at all, for he doesn't have the background, and a man like that can't aspire to what you're aspiring to—"

"Hold it," said Pierce, anxiously. "You don't know me. You can't say things like that."

"I know you, Mr. Walker."

"I can suffer like anybody else."

"No, you can't."

"You can't tell."

"I tell by your color."

There was an uncomfortable silence. Pierce shivered as the wind caught the darkening hilltop.

"You don't suffer, Mr. Walker," said the other man. "Your feet hurt, but you don't suffer. You're tired, but you can quit any time, so you don't suffer, and if you get hungry you know you can eat—and suffering's when you can't quit and when you can't eat and when you got no place to go but go on, and that's why I say you don't suffer, Mr. Walker."

"My name's Davis, not Walker."

"Well, Davis, pleased to meet you." The man thrust out his hand so unexpectedly that Pierce started in surprise, and then, not wanting to be misunderstood, seized it quickly. "My name's Bonaparte, like that French emperor." He glanced at Pierce sardonically. "I'm not a walking man myself, Davis, but I did use to run some. That was before I got to smoking. The half-mile was my best distance," he added, his manner relaxing a bit, "though I wasn't too bad at the quarter-mile, and I ran the mile a few times, too. Say—what's so funny?"

Pierce had reacted to the sudden easing of tension by laughing.

"What you laughing at?" Bonaparte asked angrily.

"Nothing, I—"

"Something strike you funny?"

"No, no," said Pierce, gasping as he tried to stop laughing, "it's just a sort of h-h-habit I got—"

"You think maybe it's funny me saying I used to run or something like that?" snapped Bonaparte.

"No, no, it's not that—"

"You think it's funny just the sheer idea of these long black legs of mine running or something, is that it, huh?"

Pierce submitted to one final stuttering roll of laughter, trying at the same time to make apologetic gestures with his hands.

"Maybe you think a white man could beat a black man so easy it's funny even to think of it," Bonaparte went on, furiously grinding out his words. "If that's the case, maybe you'd better take a look at the record books, Davis. They show otherwise."

"I know it," said Pierce, his sides heaving.

"You think I couldn't run your white legs off at any distance you care to name, Davis?"

"No, no—"

"Even a world distance, Davis?"

"Look, I'd like to explain about my laughing, I wasn't laughing at you or anything you said, it's just a thing that comes over me sometimes that I can't help, you understand."

"Sure I understand." But Bonaparte was savagely aroused; his hands were clenched as though he were on the verge of attacking Pierce.

Pierce took a step backward. "Honestly, I think

34

you're a little too touchy, Mr. Bonaparte." To his dismay, he sensed the upward swell of more laughter, and speaking hastily before it could arrive, he said: "Anyhow, I've got to get going."

He turned and started off.

"You won't make it, Davis," came Bonaparte's voice from behind him.

Pierce bit his lips and kept on going.

"It'll take more than a pair of new boots to walk around this world!"

Pierce, striding fast downhill, glanced back over his shoulder and waved farewell.

"That white skin of yours, Davis, it'll shrivel in the sun." Bonaparte had an extraordinarily powerful voice. It reached Pierce easily. "When a real world-walker shows up, Davis, he'll put you in the shade for good!"

Pierce, not wanting to be unfriendly, waved again, getting a glimpse of Bonaparte on the hilltop outlined against the red failing light of sunset.

"You don't *have* to walk the world—that's your problem, Davis! First real trouble you run into, you'll turn tail home! Hey, let me tell you, Davis, a man with a home to go to, a man who doesn't have to do it, a man who gets a nice salary and new boots and all the rest—why, a man like that is going to go nowhere! You might as well quit right now!"

Pierce, pacing hard in the streaky shadows, heard the car door slam. He kept going, then stopped and turned, saw the black car swiftly bearing down on him, and in alarm, jumped off the road out of the way, tripped, lost his balance, and sprawled flat in the ditch. As the car sailed past, its motor burst out a gunfire racket, and Pierce heard an angry shout of laughter from the driver that trailed off in the distance like a curse.

* * *

It took Pierce one week to cross Indiana; Ohio required three. His pace lagged. Sometimes he dawdled. He'd lie half an afternoon under a tree watching gnats waltz in the April sunlight, or he'd numb his feet in a chill creek where minnows flashed above drowned beer cans, or, craving human presence, he might sit for hours in roadside diners listening to truckdrivers and waitresses. To them he was just a hiker, a nobody. When he wanted more coffee, he had to ask twice.

He was slowing down, but also he had problems. A bee stung him as he was relieving himself in a field three miles west of Lafayette, Indiana. In Kokomo he lost the heel of his left boot and limped around town for an hour before he found a shoemaker who would nail a new one on without delay. In Marion he was picked up by police on suspicion of vagrancy and was driven to police headquarters, where he was able to demonstrate his financial solvency and convince the sergeant of his right to walk the highways. Then, mindful of his contract, he went back three miles to the point of his arrest and resumed walking from there. On the outskirts of Dunkirk, Indiana, a boy hit him above the left ear with a stone, cutting him slightly; he spent a woeful day in Piqua, Ohio, a victim of diarrhea, and in the environs of Urbana he was bitterly rebuked by a woman who had offered him a lift in her car and, by implication, much more than that, and had been infuriated when he declined.

When he reached Columbus, Pierce mailed some postcards to his cousins in Des Moines, and then telephoned home. There was no answer, so he phoned his uncle's house (where his father had lived since Pierce's

mother had died) and was informed by his aunt that the
doctor and the judge had gone fishing for the day and
that Natalie had taken Stephanie up to her parents, in
Clarion, the week before, for a visit. Pierce asked his aunt
to say hello to everybody for him. He thought of telephoning Natalie in Clarion, but decided that a postcard
would probably do. He did, however, call Mr. Mordenstahl's office in Duluth, as it had been agreed beforehand
he would do when he reached Columbus. Mr. Mordenstahl was in Japan, but one of his assistants instructed
Pierce to stop at the newspaper office before leaving Columbus, a story having been promised there. Pierce went
to the newspaper, where he dutifully submitted to the
ironical questions of a skeptical reporter, and on the following day he was depressed to see, over a brief and frivo-
lous feature that was run on an inside page, the headline:
"Only 19,300 Miles To Go"—this being based on Pierce's
statement that he'd have to walk twenty thousand miles
in his circuit of the world, of which, since Spark, he had
disposed of about seven hundred.

In Newark, Ohio, he bought an odometer to measure mileage. He hooked it on his belt so that it rested
against his right hipbone, where it would, in theory, register his strides. But it never worked properly—it reported
either too much progress or none at all—and after a few
days he threw it into some bushes.

He was much wearier than he should have been.
Eastern Ohio was hilly, but not mountainous. After some
six weeks of walking, his legs were tough. His body had
long since become accustomed to the knapsack. His feet
hadn't blistered lately; they still ached sometimes, but he
found he could relieve them by changing from his boots
to a pair of walking shoes and back again several times a
day. His tiredness was psychic, he guessed. He suspected

37

that he didn't really believe in the world-walk—or, more exactly, that he was such a limited and ordinary fellow that he couldn't comprehend its implications nor imagine any of the possibilities that might be in store for him. In short, he was a misfit, an impostor—a fact which had been obvious to everybody except, until now, himself. In the countryside he was snubbed by the very cows and mocked by jays. In the towns he was saluted only by dogs and small boys. Where people were, in fact, he was lonelier than ever. His isolation was all the more apparent when he trudged endless concrete miles past diners, gas stations, billboards, motels, used-car lots, dumps, golf courses, factories, package liquor stores, model homes, and then more diners, gas stations, and billboards. Giant trailer trucks made the roadbed shake. Cars by the score blurred by. The air was sour with exhaust fumes. Pierce's eyes burned; he wept walker's tears unnoticed in a land all fenced and boxed and bounded, a poisonous populated world of glass and gas and steel and rolling rubber.

Once at a drive-in he was refused service. The waitress saw there was no place to attach the tray.

He reached Wheeling, West Virginia, on April 27. From there, again as arranged beforehand, he reported by telephone to Duluth, and was informed by an outraged Mordenstahl, back from Japan, that a onetime member of the Olympic track squad from Jamaica had accepted Pierce's challenge.

"What challenge?" asked Pierce.

"It's in the papers—don't you ever buy a newspaper? You challenged him to a footrace around the world, that's what it says."

"Challenged who?"

"A man named George Bonaparte."

"Oh, him. Well, I didn't challenge him, I just helped him get his car going," Pierce began to explain, but Mr. Mordenstahl cut him off.

"I don't give ten cowflops what you did, Davis. I'm telling you that he has publicly announced he is accepting your goddamned challenge for a footrace because you said a white man can out-world-walk a black man."

"I said nothing of the kind!"

"What are you trying to do, start a race war or something? Don't you realize that this is a business proposition intended to create good will among millions who are mostly non-whites and now somehow you've got this black fellow worked up and running his mouth off against us?"

"Honestly, it's all a mistake. He was the one who made racial remarks, not me."

"Well, at least you've got the decency to admit it, Davis. I'm not blaming you entirely, you understand, but you can see this has changed things considerably."

"You want me to quit?"

"God, no. You can't quit now. I mean you can't quit publicly, see what I mean? We've got to duck down and wait until we can see if this thing will blow over. He even got a paragraph in *Time* magazine!"

"I'll be glad to quit."

"Don't you do it!" exclaimed Mr. Mordenstahl. "Just lie low. I mean hide your knapsack and register in a hotel under a different name and under no circumstances say anything to anybody, particularly reporters, and call my office every day at twelve noon for instructions. Got that?"

"Got it," said Pierce unhappily, hanging up, but as

39

luck would have it, he'd worn his knapsack into the phone booth, and turning to leave, became wedged in the narrow space. His struggles to free himself put a fatal strain on the already rusted and worn support bolts, so that the booth swayed, tottered, and collapsed with Pierce inside, the force of the fall knocking him unconscious. He was removed and taken to the hospital, where an alert intern phoned one of his friends, a reporter. The reporter envisioned an amusing little piece—"Man Felled by Phonebooth"—but soon realized that the victim was Davis, the world-walker, who'd been sought ever since Bonaparte's press conference four days earlier in Cleveland. After interviewing his dazed and compliant subject for a good half hour, he had a photographer come to take pictures, and departed to write the story in which he deftly contrasted the ambitious goal of world-walking with Pierce's inability to make a safe exit from an ordinary public telephone booth.

The story wasn't so bad. It was the headline—"White World-Walker Denies Racial Bias"—which gave Mr. Mordenstahl the horrors, and, with minor variations, it was used that way by hundreds of newspapers across the country the next day.

"Now you're identified as the *white* world-walker!" Mr. Mordenstahl screamed into the telephone when Pierce phoned him that morning from the Wheeling hospital. Pierce tried to explain about his little misfortune, but Mr. Mordenstahl was too busy denouncing the situation to listen. "We're having a staff meeting this afternoon," he at length told Pierce. "Don't do anything, hear me? Just stay where you are until we call back."

But Pierce was shortly thereafter pronounced cured and fit by his doctor, and after he'd paid the bill he was discharged. He thought of taking a room in a hotel, but he decided that Wheeling wasn't a lucky town for him, so he set off again by foot on the Pittsburgh road, carrying his knapsack by the handle instead of on his back, to cut a less conspicuous figure. On the way he bought a newspaper and saw, next to the photograph of himself, grinning stupidly at the camera from his hospital bed, a wire-service picture of Bonaparte attired in a black sweatsuit, striding through a crowd of well-wishers in Youngstown.

When Pierce telephoned Duluth in midafternoon, Mr. Mordenstahl wanted to know why he hadn't remained in the hospital. Pierce explained why.

"You should have stayed there," said Mr. Mordenstahl.

"Well, the doctor said I was all right."

"You should have faked it. Headaches, backaches, anything. Listen, we got a public-relations man from Pittsburgh who'll find a doctor to declare you physically unfit to continue the walk, do you understand that?"

"Sure."

"So go back to the hospital and faint or something to get readmitted and wait for him there."

"Well, I'm not in Wheeling any more."

"Good God," said Mr. Mordenstahl. "Where the hell are you, then?"

Pierce wasn't actually sure. All he knew was that he'd followed the Pittsburgh roadsigns and that he'd walked about twenty-five miles. He thought he'd crossed the Pennsylvania line, but he wasn't positive of that.

"He doesn't know where he is," said Mr. Mordenstahl, as though he were speaking to a third party. "We've got a man walking around the world who doesn't know where he is."

"I could ask somebody," said Pierce.

"He doesn't even know what state he's in," said Mr. Mordenstahl.

"I've sort of fouled up," Pierce admitted.

Mr. Mordenstahl was silent for a while, although Pierce could hear him breathing.

"Listen, Mr. Mordenstahl," Pierce said. "I'll be getting into Pittsburgh before long, and when I do—well, then I'll know where I am."

"And where will that be, Davis?" asked Mr. Mordenstahl, with a note of sarcasm in his voice.

"Pittsburgh."

"All right, Davis. You go on to Pittsburgh—and that's the end, understand? When you get there, I want you to telephone that public-relations man, Roach." Mr. Mordenstahl spelled the name for Pierce. "If he isn't back from Wheeling by then, his office will tell you what to do and where to wait." Then Mr. Mordenstahl gave Pierce a telephone number to write down and made him read it back four times to be sure he'd gotten it correctly.

Pittsburgh was farther away than Pierce thought it would be. The sun set, night fell, and stars appeared, although he couldn't see them because of the glare of headlights along the highway. He trudged along, dispirited. The world-walk was almost over. He'd failed. Of course, the decision was Mr. Mordenstahl's, not his, and it really wasn't his fault the way things had gone, but he knew that everybody would assume that he just hadn't been up to the job.

The idea of the world-walk still tantalized him. There was something grand about it; something fearful, too. Walking was commonplace, but so was he. And if walking around the world was a repetition of the commonplace so prolonged and so far projected across unimaginable deserts and plains and range after range of mountains that it became, by sheer magnitude, some-

42

thing heroic, then wouldn't an ordinary man who actually did it—who really and truly and honestly walked around the world—wouldn't such a fellow be bound to become something of a hero?

Oh, maybe, he thought. And he was seized then by a curiosity not about the world-walk but about himself as a world-walker that was so forceful it made him grin in surprise, then laugh aloud.

And the thought occurred to him: Suppose, when Mr. Mordenstahl said *stop*, he kept on going anyway?

Pierce didn't walk much farther that night. At about ten o'clock he sat down to rest under a roadside tree, fell asleep, and woke at dawn, shuddering with cold and damp with dew. His feet were so swollen that he could hardly pull them out of his boots to massage them. Then he found he couldn't wedge them back in, nor could he get his walking shoes on, so he had to enter Pittsburgh in his socks.

He telephoned Roach from a drugstore.

"Where are you now, fella?" the public-relations man inquired, speaking in the patient and soothing tone one might use with a feeble-minded case (as Pierce guessed he'd been described by Mr. Mordenstahl).

Pierce told him the address of the drugstore.

"Wonderful," Roach said. "Now, listen. You just hop in a taxi and come right down to my office, okay?"

"I'm not supposed to ride in cars, Mr. Roach. It says so in my contract."

"Pierce, that contract is a thing of the past, and don't give it another thought. Mr. Mordenstahl himself would be deeply gratified if you took a taxi, and don't worry, you'll be reimbursed for the fare, I can assure you."

"Well, I think I'd better walk anyhow, Mr. Roach."

"I admire your spirit, fella, but on my honor as a human being you're not bound to walk another step, so just grab a cab, Pierce, and we'll see you shortly, okay?"

Pierce still wouldn't agree to take a taxi, so Roach, evidently fearing that he might go astray again, told him to wait where he was at the drugstore. In twenty minutes Roach himself arrived by taxi and bounded out to clasp Pierce warmly by the hand. He was an energetic little man with pouched blue eyes and curly hair, in the middle of which a bald spot nested like an egg.

"Pierce, I can tell right away that we're going to get along together like a couple of old Army buddies," he declared, displaying a sincere and winning smile that he managed to maintain even after a glance made it clear that Mr. Mordenstahl had not erred in pronouncing Pierce to be a halfwit, for the fellow was evidently trying to walk around the world in his stocking feet. "In we go," said Roach coaxingly as he held the door of the taxi open, but Pierce wouldn't enter it.

"I'm sorry, Mr. Roach, but I still don't think it would be right to ride in a car."

"Pierce, there is no law of man or God that forces you to walk," Roach began. Then, deciding it would be better to humor Pierce's obstinacy, he shut the door, paid his driver, and guided Pierce back into the drugstore for a cup of coffee.

"Pierce, I'll be absolutely frank and open with you," Roach said cheerfully as they sat at the counter. "The whole thing has been all arranged and worked out in detail, and the announcement has gone out this morning to the papers, so you are free to go back home as of this very moment."

"You mean I'm finished walking."

"Pierce, according to our little press announcement,

you have withdrawn as advised by medical authorities because of that concussion you suffered and your subsequent dizzy spells, on the grounds that it would be too much of a risk for you to continue this physically exacting and punishing world-walk thing."

"The doctor in Wheeling said I was all right."

"Fella, Mr. Mordenstahl is your doctor, if you know what I mean, but you'll be stunned when I inform you that he is going to pay you the lump sum of one thousand dollars in settlement of your contract, and you and your wife will get one week of vacation free of charge at Miami Beach, Florida, and how does that strike you?"

"It sounds very generous," said Pierce, much depressed. He sighed and scratched himself where insects had taken shelter during the night. "It doesn't seem fair, really," he added.

"Pierce, you've earned it."

"No, I mean if I've got to quit just because of Bonaparte."

"I'll level with you, Pierce," said Roach. "American business is ultrasensitive to social problems, by which I mean they don't want to have anything to do with them. Bad publicity is the root of the matter, Pierce, and nobody's blaming you, but I am in touch with Bonaparte and his people and we're working something out so that nobody gets hurt and nobody gets mad and Mr. Mordenstahl can sell lots of fertilizer."

"You mean he's hiring Bonaparte in my place?"

"In this world, anything's possible, fella," said Roach briskly. "But all you have to do is go back to your loving family by train, bus, or plane—your choice, our expense, Pierce—and the very minute your signed contract cancellation is in the hands of Mr. Mordenstahl's lawyers, the grand will be in the mail to you."

Pierce tried to force his feet into his boots, but they

still were too swollen. He reached into his pocket for some change to pay for the coffee. Roach forestalled him, however. Then, as Pierce swung his knapsack back on his shoulders, Roach whipped out a document from an inside pocket.

"Fella, there are two little things I am directed to do on pain of death," he said, thrusting a pen into Pierce's hand. "One is to get your John Henry on this highly advantageous and incredibly fair cancellation thing"—he paused, as Pierce obediently glanced over the document, then signed it and handed it back—"and the other is to see you safe aboard whatever means of transport you select, so you name it, Pierce, and we'll be on our way."

Pierce limped out of the drugstore and started walking along the sidewalk. Roach hustled along at his side. "You can be reunited with your loved ones this very night, I feel sure," he continued, panting a bit, as his legs were short and he was rather dumpy, "provided you go by air, how about it?"

Pierce continued walking, a gloomy expression on his face.

"Listen, Pierce," Roach said, changing tactics. "I've got another idea that may appeal to you." He winked up at Pierce and tried to nudge him in the ribs, but because of his shortness, nudged Pierce's hipbone instead. "I know a nice little hotel where they aren't too particular about how a man spends his time. You get yourself cleaned up a bit there, fella, and take a bit of a nap if you want, and then by and by—who knows? Your old Pittsburgh buddy Roy Roach might just drop by with a couple of live numbers who'll help you take your mind off your troubles!" He gave a wicked chuckle and nudged Pierce's hip again. "Pierce, we'll have a ball! I know just the sweet young thing you've been dreaming about while

46

you've been marching all those long and lonely miles. Pierce, this girl has a form on her that's got to be seen to be believed, and while I realize you're an honest, God-fearing married man, let me guarantee you that this charming little creature I'm thinking of will teach you such tricks for your own domestic use that your wife would thank her from the bottom of her heart if she knew—which I can bet she won't, isn't that right, fella?"

Pierce made no reply to this proposal. He kept plodding along in his socks, his pack on his back and his boots swinging by their laces from one hand. Roach, scuttling along beside him, was puffing and perspiring, but still game.

"Pierce, what I'm saying is that Pittsburgh's my town and you're my honored guest, so all you need to do is name your taste and it's yours. If you like 'em a bit more mature, there's a lovely lady just a phonecall away who practically wrote the book on the subject and I'd hardly dare introduce you without a medical certificate on your heart, as you might have a seizure—just kidding, Pierce—but if your inclination leans toward the exotic, I can take you over to McKeesport this instant to see a Chinese girl who can do things to your feet as a kind of warmup that will practically make you faint dead away, so you can imagine what happens later, fella. Besides that," said Roach, mopping his brow with his handkerchief, "we've got all different colors and shades of 'em able and willing to satisfy any known desire of man in whatever shape or form, singly or in pairs or even groups. I once had a very important client, Pierce, who requested no fewer than six at a time, dressed like nuns, if you can believe it. Say," he exclaimed suddenly, snapping his fingers. "I've got just the thing for you, fella, and it's a set of absolutely gorgeous twins, and they've got a little act

47

which is surefire every time, by which I mean that one is as shy and pure as the driven snow, Pierce, while the other is a regular slut, if you don't mind the word, so a little weekend with the two of them acting out these roles is quite frankly an unforgettable artistic experience which I wouldn't want you to miss—and all of it at Mr. Mordenstahl's expense, fella, needless to say, and don't worry, his company writes it off against taxes, so nobody loses, take my word for it."

"Listen, Mr. Roach, I appreciate your suggestions, but honestly I'm not interested in that kind of stuff."

"Pierce, I think I'm beginning to understand the situation," Roach declared, with slightly less enthusiasm than before, "and I can assure you that many another manly and virile young fellow has seen fit to follow the same path, and there's a certain bar right in the heart of town where I can introduce you to a group of individuals who will welcome you as a kindred soul, I have no doubt—"

"I didn't mean that, either," Pierce broke in. "I meant I'm not staying in Pittsburgh, that's all."

Roach seemed relieved. "Let me congratulate you on your decision, Pierce." He tugged Pierce's sleeve to stop him, and shook his hand. Around them the morning traffic cracked and boomed. "Pierce," Roach continued, "if I didn't have a vital meeting with Bonaparte's lawyer in less than an hour, I'd personally escort you to the air-port." He saw a cruising taxi and darted out a few steps into the street to hail it. "But I'll turn you over to my personal secretary—who incidentally is the kind of young lady who just might persuade you to change your plans, fella!—and she'll see to your transportation. So hop right in, Pierce, and we'll be on our way."

"I'm not hopping, Mr. Roach," said Pierce. "I'd really rather walk."

Roach gave Pierce a long, speculative look.

"It's gotten to be a sort of habit," Pierce added. "Don't worry, Mr. Roach. I can get along okay by myself."

Roach's busy little features remained immobile for a few more moments. "You signed that cancellation, fella. You realize that."

"I sure do, Mr. Roach. That's all over and done with, and maybe it's all for the best, I can't say."

"Just wanted to be sure there weren't any little misunderstandings," said Roach. He let bloom a magnificent smile and shook Pierce's hand again. "Pierce, it's been an honor and a privilege, and here's my card, so if there's anything you want or need at any time of day or night, don't hesitate."

"Thanks a lot, Mr. Roach."

"My pleasure, fella," said Roach, whereupon he hurried into the taxi to be driven off for his meeting with Bonaparte's lawyer, leaving Pierce to pad along the sidewalk as he pleased.

Pierce went on for a while without worrying about where he was going or bothering his head much on any subject whatever. He knew that he was still proceeding in an easterly direction, but he supposed that as the world-walk was over, a few more miles one way or another didn't matter. "I'm not walking for Mr. Mordenstahl now," he told himself. "I'm just doing a bit of walking on my own account, that's all. I'm walking for myself."

That reflection cheered him. He was glad to be alone

49

again and walking. He felt better that way. He admired what he could see of the sky through the city smog, and he smiled affably at everyone he met, undismayed by the scornful glances he received in return.

His night in the open had left him tired, though, and when the metropolitan area had thinned enough to permit trees to appear by the wayside, he took a nap under one of them. He woke in early afternoon. His feet had by then returned to their customary size, so he put his boots on again, got up, brushed some ants from his hair, picked up his pack, and set off once more.

"I'm supposed to catch a plane or something," he thought, but there wasn't any airport in sight, nor was there a railroad station or bus terminal; there was just the highway that ran east toward Johnstown, curling through hills that weren't really hills but were actually mountains. He glanced back toward Pittsburgh. "Well, I've been there already," he thought. "No point in going back." Besides, the day was brilliant, and the mountains looked interesting, so he kept going.

It was an hour or so later that he became aware that something was moving along behind him at slow speed some distance away. He heard the music first—jazz and folk-rock—and he assumed it came from a radio or record player in some house or gas station he'd passed, but he continued to hear it as he went on, and he realized that the music was moving in the same direction he was, and he wondered why a motorist would be poking along so sluggishly with his car radio blaring.

The highway wound in great snake-loops up a forested range. Pierce, looking down, caught a glimpse through the trees of what seemed to be the source of the music—a black van on the road below, just inching along. Pierce thought it might be a highway department truck, painting a new centerline, or possibly a hearse—except that such lively music wouldn't be appropriate from a hearse, and besides, a hearse wouldn't be driven so slowly except in a funeral procession.

Where the road curved sharply, the jazz was fainter; on the straight stretches, its volume rose again. Still, it seemed to be drawing a bit nearer, and Pierce judged that the van was moving slightly faster than he was. He decided to find out what it was, and so when he came to an overlook that provided a view of green furred mountains humping off east and south, he stopped, took off his knapsack, and sat down to wait.

A few cars passed by. A truck appeared, backfiring as it crested the grade, and then a brace of goggled motorcyclists sped by, leaning into the curve. No one paused at the overlook; it was as if they were anxious to put as much distance as possible between themselves and the music, which rolled up louder by the minute, its rising rhythms wringing birdcalls from the forest and echoing from the surrounding peaks.

At last the van toiled into view. Pierce saw that in front of it was a man on foot, a walker like himself, but a walker extraordinarily tall and lean, and totally black as well—black skin, black sweatsuit, black sneakers on his feet—a man who wasn't so much walking as marching, or rather strutting along with jazzy dance steps as though driven by the music that came out of two loudspeakers fixed on the roof of the van behind him.

It was Bonaparte.

He didn't notice Pierce sitting off to the side, but kept right on marching, his face glistening with sweat, his elbows jerking as his long legs scissored him ahead.

Pierce yelled *"Hey"* but he couldn't even hear it himself, the music was so loud. Bonaparte passed by, the van lumbering after him. Sitting on the tailgate was a pretty black girl, her legs dangling. She was manicuring her fingernails.

Pierce grabbed his knapsack, hoisted it to his shoulders again, and hurried off in pursuit, but since Bonaparte was going at a vigorous pace, it took Pierce several minutes of jogging to catch up.

"Hello there, Mr. Bonaparte," Pierce bellowed as he came puffing up to the other walker.

Bonaparte glanced at him, surprised, and then laughed. He didn't stop, though, nor did he signal to the driver of the van to turn the music down. With Pierce hustling along at his side, he kept on cutting his stork-legged strides, going around curves, down dips, up rises, and every once in a while giving Pierce a sidelong grin, which wasn't the kind of grin that made Pierce want to grin back, for it seemed to be derisive.

"Just wanted to say hi, Mr. Bonaparte," howled Pierce, in vain. Bonaparte couldn't hear him, and obviously wasn't interested in chatting with him anyway. Otherwise he'd have stopped walking and would have had that loudspeaker racket turned off.

The onetime Olympic runner was setting such a powerful pace that Pierce was hard-pressed to keep up, and apart from the physical strain of having to double his normal walking rate, he was made uncomfortable by the ambiguity of his position. Bonaparte hadn't challenged him to a race exactly, for Pierce had been the one to come hurrying up, but at the same time the challenge was present in Bonaparte's strenuous stride and in his bold sly glance. Pierce wished that he had simply given the Jamaican a friendly wave and let him go by. He'd had no particular wish to accompany Bonaparte, and he certainly didn't want to race him, but now here he was, pounding along the mountain highway, feeling foolish and humiliated, and at the same time being reluctant to fall back. "I'm in better shape than he is," Pierce told himself. He couldn't be sure of that, though, and besides, he had to bear the weight of his pack, whereas Bonaparte had nothing to carry at all.

Abruptly, the music stopped. The van driver evidently had gotten tired of it and had switched it off. Even so, Pierce was too winded to say anything, now that conversation was possible. His leg muscles, unaccustomed to such demands, were complaining, and his knapsack was becoming heavier all the time. Beyond this, he was depressed by the fact that they'd begun climbing a particularly steep grade, which Bonaparte was mounting with no slackening whatever. Pierce began to think he'd better quit. His disadvantages were too great. He was a cross-country man, anyway, and long-distance runners had no business competing with half-milers; it was bad for the legs and threw one's sense of timing off. The road seemed to tilt up vertically under his boots, making him wonder if he wouldn't have to grab trees to keep from falling off into some valley below, while beside him Bonaparte walked miraculously erect, as though for him the mountain were flat, and although this disparity was purely imaginary, it was true that Pierce had to take three steps to every two taken by his rival, and also Bonaparte was spraying sweat in all directions, including Pierce's, which dampening did little to add to Pierce's enjoyment.

At last they reached the top. The road plunged down. This, in a sense, was worse, for Bonaparte seemed to float and glide now, as if the highway shrank from his shoes, letting him drift down weightlessly in great soft bounds, while Pierce, still human and solid and heavier than ever, descended with painfully thudding feet that hammered outraged messages up his spine. He feared that everything was jarring loose inside him, his laboring heart and ballooning lungs flopping about as if displaced, leg bones unhinging at the hips, kneecaps detaching, while his knapsack threatened to overbalance him and send him cartwheeling down. Beside him, Bonaparte sailed like a shadow.

"I'll count to a hundred, then quit," Pierce thought, and when he'd counted to a hundred, he decided he'd keep going only as far as a billboard he saw down the road; then after that, he determined he'd wait until five cars had passed them and stop with the sixth, unless it turned out to be a truck, which it did, so then he thought of Natalie and Stephanie and Spark, and he thought of his days as a university runner trotting coltishly through springtime hills with steamy nostrils, and then his attention was directed to his left thigh, which was agitating painfully in a pre-cramp clench, and finally, just as he was really ready to bow out of this impromptu footrace, he realized that the road had leveled out into a narrow little valley, as though it, too, were tired, and that Bonaparte had slowed the pace.

"You're finished, Davis," the Jamaican said, or rather, croaked. All his sweating seemed to have paled him; Pierce, meanwhile, had darkened with his. "You're through," Bonaparte said. "How come you're still walking?" He looked down angrily at Pierce. "Didn't they tell you, Davis? *I'm* the world-walker now."

Pierce couldn't answer, he was so preoccupied with the physical problems of his protesting body. He lurched, he limped, he weaved and staggered once or twice, and there didn't seem to be enough air in that little valley to accommodate his lungs.

"You're fired, I'm hired, that's the story," Bonaparte informed him, in a slightly stronger voice.

The girl, having hopped from the van, came up beside them with quick mincing steps. She handed Bonaparte a towel, with which he mopped his face, and then a canteen, from which he took mouthfuls of water, gargled, rinsed, and spat.

"You're done, I've won," said Bonaparte. "You better take a bus home, Davis." He seemed refreshed, and lengthened his stride. "Mordenstahl has backed the black, you understand what I'm saying? You've mortified your white flesh all for nothing, so climb off the cross, now I'm boss." He gave a high-pitched laugh, handed the towel and the canteen back to the girl, then stepped out more smartly still, making poor Pierce pant keeping up. "They want a black man to spread their seed for them, Davis," Bonaparte declared. "They've seen the wave of the future, man, and that wave is not white! No sir, Davis! Your day is past, and now you're last!"

With this, he burst into laughter so hearty that it made him break stride, and then the girl, who'd been trotting daintily beside him, ran out ahead, her full hips straining her bluejeans. First she juggled the canteen in the air a few times, then she threw it playfully to Bonaparte, who caught it and handed it to Pierce. After that she began to dance backward, facing the walkers, using the towel teasingly as a veil, a skirt, a halter; then she drew it across her buttocks and sawed it to and fro as she swayed and shimmied, after which she stopped and held the towel cape-style while Bonaparte, his hands at his temples with index fingers erect as mock horns, charged her like a bull, and finally, tiring, she ran back to the van and climbed up on the tailgate again. All the while the walkers were proceeding along the curving valley road in mountain shadow, with the van a few yards behind them.

"You begin to get the picture now, Davis?" said

Bonaparte, resuming his full stride. He was strutting now, snapping his fingers, casting quick glances down at Pierce. "You're out, that's what it's all about. White's too light for this job, man, I mean to say, black's come back!" He was supercharged, as if walking energized him and cast up gleeful high spirits that sang calypso.

"I'm not racing," gasped Pierce. He lifted Bonaparte's canteen to take a drink, but it was empty, so he gave it back. "I'm just walking," he puffed. "The world's big enough. For two walkers. Seems to me."

Bonaparte gave him a sly look and increased the pace.

"You were talking. About suffering," Pierce said, laboring. "But honestly. That van. That girl. You're not suffering."

Bonaparte snickered and spat. His legs were whipping him ahead. Pierce had to jog, but he knew he couldn't do that for long. Walking he could manage, but not walking the way Bonaparte walked, which didn't seem to be walking at all, but some special mode of locomotion invented by Bonaparte for the world-walk, a sprinter's pace so extraordinarily swift and delicate that it implied supernatural properties, as if the walking runner were propelled not by the force of his legs but by the perfected realization of some ideal he'd achieved, so that, to Pierce's fogged observation, Bonaparte advanced without effort, less a man in motion than an element of motion, being dissolved and recreated instantaneously in a perpetual flow of movement.

"You can't," groaned Pierce. "Keep it up. This way."

The Jamaican didn't seem to hear him. He was gaining steadily on Pierce, mowing yards with feet as light as razors, while Pierce in his heavy boots ran and stumped and stumbled, trotted, waddled, his knapsack like a boulder wrenching at his shoulders, shoving him forward, bearing him down.

"This isn't. Walking," Pierce complained. "It can't. Be done this. Way."

Bonaparte, well out in front, turned all the way around to face him, but kept going, walking backward. He grinned, but he seemed angry again, as though the frenzy of walking had burned off his high spirits. "You're the one can't, Davis," he cried out. He spat, then he seemed to gray in the face, as if seized by a momentary agony, and he gave Pierce a ferocious look. "It's my walk now, Davis," he shouted. "Get off my road!"

Then he turned and strode on faster. Pierce felt faint, overburdened, ready to quit and lie down forever, and when suddenly from the van that was just behind him now there came a blast of amplified sound—the music again, full force, exploding doomsday proclamations across the landscape—he leaped, alarmed, and as though the van were an infernal machine bent on flattening him with its steamroller jazz, he dodged aside off the pavement and onto the pebbly shoulder, where he sank stunned to his knees, overwhelmed and fearful, his gasps like sobs, sweating as though his body wept.

On ahead went Bonaparte, the van trumpeting his path. Pierce, kneeling among weeds and stones, watched the girl on the tailgate, who sat in repose, eyes closed, receding as the van rolled on.

The original plan had called for Pierce to walk from Iowa to New York City, then to go by plane to Gibraltar, and from there, again by foot, across southern Europe to

Turkey, a country where Mr. Mordenstahl's company was seeking to expand its participation in a variety of agricultural projects, an effort in which the publicized appearance of the American world-walker could be advantageous. After Turkey, Pierce had been scheduled to traverse Iran, Pakistan, India, and Burma, and beyond that there were several choices—Indonesia, Australia, the Philippines, with perhaps side excursions to Japan and South Korea—but of course all this was null and void, for as far as Charles L. Mordenstahl was concerned, the world-walk of Pierce Davis had ended on April 29 in Pittsburgh, Pennsylvania.

Mr. Mordenstahl had switched walkers. He wasn't happy about it. He didn't trust Bonaparte and he didn't trust Roy Roach, who had negotiated the deal with Bonaparte's Cleveland lawyer, whom Mr. Mordenstahl didn't trust, either.

The world-walk idea, so noble and dreamlike in the purity of first conception, was threatening to become a nightmare for Mr. Mordenstahl. First there'd been that idiot car mechanic from Iowa, and now, perhaps worse, Mr. Mordenstahl realized that he'd been virtually blackmailed into sponsoring a man who represented a disturbing and unpredictable menace. "I shouldn't have done it," Mr. Mordenstahl would mutter in the privacy of his office or at night when he lay sleepless. "I shouldn't have. Should have left it alone. It's Roach's fault. Roach promoted this. Roach did it. . . ."

Roach had been recommended by one of Mr. Mordenstahl's Pittsburgh friends as being a quick-thinking go-getter able to come up with lightning solutions to public-relations problems. The solution Roach had worked out (and which Mr. Mordenstahl had approved) had sounded fine at first: Bonaparte would walk Africa and

South America as well as Asia, and his status as a black man from Jamaica would gain him sympathetic reception in places where a white American might not be welcome —yes, all that made sense, even though the price had been stiff, but Mr. Mordenstahl had been overtaken, too late, by second thoughts. He was tied to a black racist now. Instead of promoting American seeds, Bonaparte might start preaching revolution in every country he walked through, and this would put the Duluth company in an atrociously embarrassing position—and yet, to forestall this possibility by withdrawing sponsorship now would surely make matters worse, for Bonaparte had sworn he'd collect a nickel from every black man in America, if necessary, to finance his walk, and in that case, there might be retaliation against Mr. Mordenstahl's company. Roach had given assurances that he'd keep things under control, but Mr. Mordenstahl suspected that Roach had his own objectives in mind. A go-getter! Mr. Mordenstahl had enough go-getters right there in Duluth. He knew all about go-getters, and the chief thing he knew was that what these go-getters were determined to go and get was Mr. Mordenstahl's neck, scalp, job. And the infuriating part of it all was that the world-walk was such an insignificant aspect of his responsibilities. It was the sort of detail an administrative assistant should handle. He himself shouldn't be bothered. Yet he was bothered, bothered terribly. He was like a bull that has swallowed a pin, and despite all the preoccupations and diversions of ordinary bull life, is uncomfortably aware of the presence of the pin somewhere inside, working its way among nerves and organs and muscles. Superb organs and mighty muscles! Yet doomed should the pin find some vital spot.

He hadn't forgotten about Pierce Davis. Roach had assured him that the fellow undoubtedly would show up back home in Iowa sooner or later, but Mr. Mordenstahl had doubts. Still, as two weeks went by with no word at all from Pierce, Mr. Mordenstahl began to think Roach might be right. Then, on May 15, when he went to New York to see Bonaparte and his entourage board a plane for Africa, the Jamaican mentioned the footrace east of Pittsburgh. This confirmed Mr. Mordenstahl's earlier suspicion. Davis was still walking!

Mr. Mordenstahl was well aware of the irrationality that motivated men's thoughts and actions. He knew that Pierce was no particular problem—the problem was Bonaparte (or Roach, who'd flown to Africa to act as Bonaparte's advance man)—but he found himself, against his will, concentrating on Pierce. The world-walk had begun with Pierce, and everything had gotten worse from the time Pierce had taken his first step—and therefore, illogical though it might appear, wouldn't things improve if Pierce stopped walking?

"Why won't he stop?" Mr. Mordenstahl complained. "He's finished—doesn't he know that? He's signed his contract cancellation, so he's got no right to take another step! He's walking illegally!" In a fury, he ordered his assistants to discover Pierce's whereabouts by every means short of police intervention. "He's got to be found," stormed Mr. Mordenstahl. "He's got to be reminded of his legal and moral obligations, and, by God, he's got to be stopped!" The more he thought about Pierce, the more it upset him. All the burdensome realities of his executive existence seemed to count for little, compared to the maddening realization that Pierce Davis was still walking somewhere.

"I'm exaggerating the importance of this thing," Mr. Mordenstahl told himself. "I've got to put it out of my mind." But he couldn't. Pierce was becoming an obsession with him. "I am in responsible charge of many hundreds of employees in a score of countries," Mr. Mordenstahl would reflect. "Because of my decisions, millions of dollars are spent in one place rather than in another, and crops spring from the earth, one might say, at my command—and so why, in the name of God, must I be pestered and bedeviled by one little pipsqueak cretinous pissant from the State of Iowa who won't stop walking?"

But Pierce wasn't walking. He'd stopped, or at least he'd come to a pause on May 10, when he reached the city of Binghamton, New York. There he rented a room in a boarding house and got a job as a mechanic in a downtown garage. He wanted time to think about his situation, and as he'd discovered during his long tramp through Pennsylvania, he couldn't review the subject objectively while he was actually on the road, for when he was walking, one step led naturally to another and he couldn't seem to take seriously the idea that he wouldn't be walking any more.

He telephoned Natalie, who was still visiting her parents in north Iowa. After reporting that he'd been fired by Mr. Mordenstahl, he told her he had a job and would send her some money, and he promised to return home right away if she wanted him to. Natalie made haste to assure him that this wouldn't be at all necessary, and as far as money was concerned, he shouldn't worry about it, for her father had hired her as a receptionist in the clinic he shared with another doctor there in Clarion, which work she enjoyed very much and felt was useful, as it relieved the nurse, Mrs. Soames, for other duties. Then Natalie said that Stephanie was fine, having recovered from the measles under the expert care of her grandmother, who, as Pierce knew, had been a practical nurse in her day, and finally, Natalie said she'd sublet their apartment in Spark to a couple named Fingerling, and since she had supposed it would take Pierce at least a year to walk around the world, she'd made the contract for a year, so that if Pierce came home, there would certainly be a few little problems to iron out, but she went on to assure Pierce that whatever he decided would be all right with her.

So Pierce did nothing at all for a while except work at the garage during the day and go to the movies in the evenings. He told no one about his walking. He didn't feel that he would be able to discuss the subject usefully with his fellow mechanics or his landlady or a friendly coffeeshop waitress named Martha (who'd let him know she didn't care if he was married, for she wasn't particular about such matters). Besides, Pierce didn't have any pride in what he'd done. His brush with Bonaparte had humbled him. He still woke nights in a sweat from visions of Bonaparte striding tirelessly through his weary dreams, and once in a barbershop, while having his hair cut, he saw in a magazine a photograph of Bonaparte walking somewhere in the rural reaches of the Congo, amid blacks resplendently gowned (the one white face present being that of Roy Roach), which further depressed him, although he felt that Bonaparte's success was undoubtedly merited.

Still, he maintained his walker's purity. He refused to go on wheels. Even when it rained, he walked to work and back, although a city bus stopped right outside his boarding house. At the garage he declined to road-test cars, which eccentricity was accepted, for Pierce was a skilled and conscientious workman, and his boss didn't want to lose him.

Another kind of purity, however, was in danger. On the road Pierce had been untroubled by erotic fancies, but now he was beginning to be disturbed by them. His imagination, first occupied by the waitress Martha, expanded to harem size, providing space for female clients who brought in their cars for repair, actresses in the films he saw, women he glimpsed as he walked to work, girls he remembered from Spark, and even his landlady, who had chins and a wig. "I may fall," Pierce reflected with foreboding. His background excluded easy affairs. There weren't many adulterers in Spark, and those few preserved the nineteenth-century moral architecture of the place by going elsewhere for their forbidden joys—and they were more faithful to Spark even than that, for they knew it was a sin they were committing, and they undertook it in a spirit of guilt and dedication almost religious in nature (which no doubt elevated their passion to an ecstatic level unknown to more casual philanderers), but anyway, this attitude had marked Pierce profoundly, as it had marked all the other Pierces in the hundreds of Sparks throughout rural America, so that what might be a healthy release of animal energies to the complacent Easterner, Martha, presented itself to Pierce as a challenge to the communal gods that presided over his Midwestern soul. To put it another way, while he didn't exactly object to extramarital relations, he knew it was a damned serious business.

He began walking again, but not around the world. He simply started walking the streets of Binghamton in the evenings after work and on the weekends, instead of going to the movies. He found that this activity somewhat eased his perturbation, but at the same time it raised a rather perplexing point, namely, whether his walking was a sex substitute, and he wondered further whether he had been influenced in his original decision to take the world-walk job by an impulse to discharge in that fashion an accumulation of libido, and beyond that, he thought of various saints and hermits who'd gone to extraordinary lengths to deal with their horniness by isolating themselves in caves and on deserts, so it occurred to him that maybe a man capable of walking around the world (which combined the elements of isolation and strenuous activity) might be capable of amorous exertions similarly prodigious, and, in short, he became very much aware of the possibility that sex, too, was a factor in world-walking.

Pierce decided he ought to have a companion, a friend, someone to confide in—someone to walk with, in fact. So he invited Martha to join him in an evening stroll. He was forced to admit he had mixed motives, knowing that his passion for walking was somehow bound up with another form of passion, each of which Martha might help him satisfy (although not simultaneously), but he assured himself that walking would benefit Martha by giving her a hobby more uplifting than reading movie magazines and indulging in romantic adventures with men who, as she herself had told him, did not sufficiently respect her. Martha wasn't anxious to go walking. She told Pierce she had to stand behind the counter all day and in the evenings liked to get off her feet, at which remark she giggled and Pierce blushed. But she agreed to take the walk, her assumption being that Pierce wouldn't go farther than the nearest park. In this she was wrong. Pierce did have impure ambitions, but to him a mile or two was nothing at all, and he'd set as his objective a leafy glade outside of town where he'd walked alone a couple of times before. Martha couldn't make it. She managed the first few miles without complaint, but then she became tired and kept asking Pierce how much farther it was, and after this she started getting cross, and finally, when they were still well within the city limits, she announced she wasn't going another step, marched into a diner, sat down on a stool, and directed Pierce to call a cab. She had some coffee while they waited for the cab, and, feeling better, decided that her evening with Pierce might not be wasted after all. But when the cab arrived and Pierce told her that he couldn't ride in it, for reasons that weren't easy to explain, she lost her temper. "You must be crazy," she snapped at him. Then the cab drove off with Martha alone in back; Pierce, feeling like a fool, returned to his lodgings by foot.

He was humiliated by this experience. It worried him, too. He took it as a sign that walking had clouded his judgment, for he'd missed a real opportunity with Martha simply because he hadn't realized that no girl could have been expected to walk that far.

He decided that all the walking he'd done hadn't been good for him, as far as relations with other people were concerned. His stopping in Binghamton was an act of self-preservation, therefore, for if he'd kept on walking and walking, before long he wouldn't have been good for anything else, and a man couldn't make a career just out of walking.

He considered buying a second-hand car in order to drive everywhere he went, but he didn't. Nor could he bring himself to climb aboard the city bus to go to work. "I'll taper off bit by bit," he decided. "You can't expect to shake off a weakness like walking all at once." So he stopped taking his evening walks.

He walked less in reality, but in his imagination he walked constantly. For every waking step he didn't take, he took a hundred in his dreams. He was walking more than ever, it appeared, and his amorous desires kept pace, for the ghost of his walking obsession, striding along the endless highways of slumber, passionately pursued a female figure he sensed so strongly that he went to bed at night in shameful expectation, as if sneaking off to an adulterous assignation.

She didn't lie with him in his dreams. She remained upright, walking, and as he walked in her wake, it seemed to him that she was bidding him to rise by day as he had risen by night, bidding him to rise and walk, rise and walk. Which, in these dreams, he obediently did.

Her image was vast and vague. She towered like a cloud, supervising his pigmy steps from invisible heights. Her voice, when it came to him, was as enormous as the sky and as varied as the moods of weather, for sometimes it rang like maternal thunder, charging him to break the womb and walk life's world, and sometimes he heard it as an oracle's cry, urging him forward to an ambiguous destiny; then again, it was a female summons for male activity, but on a tremendous, impossible scale. The woman who invested his sleep seemed to break through all human forms and senses, yet still to be female somehow, as though she were the very earth itself, and thus he came to think of her: a mountain-breasted woman of a world with continental hips and thighs, with secret rivers that ran deep—a living world, his fate, where life itself demanded that he walk.

So it was, one day in early June, that Pierce felt he could resist no longer.

He quit his job, paid his landlady's bill, bought a packet of sandwiches which he stuck in the top of his knapsack, and headed east. At first he felt guilty, like a drunkard whose resolution has collapsed, but after a few

66

miles, as after a few drinks, the warmth of walking spread through his body, and he began whistling and humming as he went on his way.

By telephoning to Dr. Davis and Natalie in Iowa, Mr. Mordenstahl's staff assistants had been able to ascertain that Pierce had come to a halt in Binghamton, where he was working and not walking. They duly transmitted this encouraging information to their chief.

Mr. Mordenstahl wasn't satisfied. "What's he doing in Binghamton?" he grumbled suspiciously. "That's east of Pittsburgh, dammit—and how'd he get there, I'd like to know? Don't tell me!" he shouted. "Just get in touch with him and tell him he's got to go back to Iowa!"

When the assistants telephoned Pierce's rooming house in Binghamton, however, the landlady informed them that Pierce had put his pack on his back and gone off by foot, leaving no forwarding address. Which direction? East, said the landlady. Mr. Mordenstahl, told of this latest piece of insolence on Pierce's part, paled with rage. "Then go get him!" he spluttered. "Bring him here to me! I'll settle his hash!"

The two assistants flew to Binghamton, where they rented an automobile. For five days, they cruised along the highways leading east, making inquiries at gasoline stations and motels and diners, and patiently following up every report of a walking man until finally they found Pierce fifteen miles northeast of Albany, heading for the Vermont line. The assistants stopped their car, identified themselves to Pierce, and asked him if he wouldn't mind accompanying them back to Albany, where they'd take a plane to Duluth for a friendly conference with Mr.

Mordenstahl. This proposal Pierce politely declined. He told the two men that he realized the company wasn't sponsoring him any more, and he apologized for whatever trouble he'd caused, and then he said he'd always wanted to see Vermont, as it was said to be a lovely state, bid them goodbye, and went walking on ahead.

The assistants persisted, however. One of them stayed by Pierce's side, explaining that Mr. Mordenstahl felt he shouldn't be walking any more, while the other one drove the car behind them, in low gear. Pierce was courteous but firm. Whatever the company wanted to do was all right with him, he said.

"Then you'll stop walking?" the assistant asked.

"Well, no," Pierce replied. "I guess not."

At the next town, therefore, the assistants telephoned Mr. Mordenstahl; after an interval of profanity, he informed them that he would fly to the scene himself, to stop Pierce in person. In the meantime, he ordered them not to let Pierce out of their sight.

The two assistants spent the night in the same motel Pierce stopped at, outside of North Bennington, Vermont. In the morning, they advised him that Mr. Mordenstahl would arrive at noon at the airport at Rutland, where he expected to be greeted by all three of them, so obviously they'd have to drive up there, but Pierce said he couldn't accept a ride and besides, Rutland wasn't on his route. After some futile attempts to persuade him, the assistants separated—one driving up to Rutland alone and the other remaining with Pierce, walking east toward Brattleboro.

Pierce's companion was named John R. O'Brien. He was a slight little fellow with a shy and severe manner, but walking seemed to loosen his tongue, for before they'd gone more than a mile he began telling Pierce about his job, which frightened him, and his wife, who was lazy and sometimes cruel, and his mother, who in her old age had developed a passion for astrology and did nothing but consult various seers. Mr. O'Brien wasn't used to walking. He got pebbles in his shoes and a stitch in his side and the mildest uphill grade made him pant, so Pierce had to slow the pace for him.

"Why do you walk?" Mr. O'Brien asked at one point.

"Why doesn't everybody?" Pierce asked in return.

Mr. O'Brien replied that other people had jobs and careers and families, and he added that he wished he had time for walking, for it clearly was healthful, after which he requested Pierce to stop for a while as his feet were killing him.

It was midafternoon by the time the second assistant drove up in the car, with Mr. Mordenstahl seated in the back looking sullen, for he had been much put out by Pierce's refusal to meet him at Rutland.

"Climb in here, Davis, and let's talk this thing over," said Mr. Mordenstahl, but Pierce wouldn't even sit in the car, so Mr. Mordenstahl had to get out. He waved the two assistants some distance away, leaned against a fender, and gave Pierce a calculating glance.

Now, Mr. Mordenstahl was no fool, and he prided himself, with justice, on his hard-earned knowledge of human nature and his skills as a bargainer. During his career, he had handled virtually every conceivable kind of negotiating situation, and he had faced men of all colors and many nationalities. As a young fertilizer sales-man in Minnesota and the Dakotas he had striven to place his products with taciturn distributors of Scandi-navian descent, against whose rocky resistance his per-suasiveness had beaten and frothed like the waves of the sea. Later, as he rose in rank, he had confronted rascally equipment subcontractors in Chicago and haughty bankers in New York, and later still, overseas, he had trafficked with Arab sheiks and Moslem princes, with baronial Latin landlords, with African commissars, with Asiatic adventurers temporarily in control of various little nations, and one can hardly enumerate how many more slick and sinister human examples, but in any event, Mr. Mordenstahl was hardly a man to be cowed by the prospect of dealing with a twenty-eight-year-old garage mechanic from a small town in the State of Iowa.

Therefore, having sized Pierce up (and a very small size he judged him to be), Mr. Mordenstahl arranged in his mind the precise battle order of his attacking forces which would, he was certain, achieve the desired result in the shortest possible time.

He began by patiently explaining to Pierce the benefits of the settlement which Pierce had signed back in Pittsburgh, a settlement which was all the more magnanimous, he said, because Pierce, through his blunders, had violated the original contract in at least a dozen places, and, in the opinion of the company's legal staff, could be sued in several courts simultaneously.

"All you have to do is stop walking," said Mr. Mordenstahl in conclusion.

"But that settlement just means I can't do any more walking for your company, Mr. Mordenstahl," said Pierce. "I don't think it keeps me from walking altogether."

"Well, of course we couldn't forbid a man to use his legs, Davis, for it would be a violation of the Bill of Rights or some such thing," said Mr. Mordenstahl, "but the point of it all was that you'd simply go home and quit walking, as a sort of moral obligation on your part."

"But I don't want to stop walking," said Pierce.

Mr. Mordenstahl searched Pierce's face for signs of guile or greed or spite, but saw nothing of the sort there, and so turned his gaze briefly to the surrounding farmland, estimating its value per acre and classifying its soils.

"Look here," he went on, still in an understanding and patient way, "if you want to go around the world, we'll fix you and your wife up with a tour, first-class by air or ship, your choice, now how about that?"

"No, thanks."

"What is it you want, then?"

"Well, I just want to walk."

Mr. Mordenstahl's confidence in the outcome of this meeting was at this point slightly shaken, as it occurred to him that despite his vast experience as a negotiator, he might be facing something wholly new to him, in the sense that his previous adversaries, however much they differed in such characteristics as skin color and mode of dress, had all been men of some intelligence. But how did one deal with a blockhead?

"Now you're a smart young fellow," Mr. Mordenstahl began ingratiatingly—but the very words choked him. He frowned and mopped his forehead with his handkerchief. Then he tried to resume: "We ought to be able to reason this thing out together—" but again he was forced to stop short, for the sight of Pierce's open countenance profoundly discouraged him. He was reminded of what had been troubling him for weeks, namely, that his objection to Pierce's walking was an obsessive one, out of all proportion to the realities, and thus he had been drawn into a situation that bore the marks of fantasy: he was bargaining with an idiot to reach an irrational objective.

Why shouldn't Pierce walk? Mr. Mordenstahl asked

himself for the thousandth time—and, as always, the responses that arose were illogical, but nonetheless imperative.

Like every concept of generous dimensions, the world-walk idea had roots so deep as to be infantile. In conceiving it, Mr. Mordenstahl was grabbing for the world from the very cradle of his soul, with the mindless hunger of a baby. This he did not consciously acknowledge. From the beginning, however, he had been dimly aware that for him the world-walk would be a sort of conquest, for having been reared on a farm, he retained the fundamental instinct of the husbandman—that a man who walked a stretch of earth earned some claim to it. The world-walk would be a symbolic conquest only, it was true, but on a heroic scale, which had, every time he thought about it, raised in him an eager, megalomaniac sweat.

What disturbed and in fact enraged him now was not (as he supposed) Pierce Davis, but an insidious sensation of the impending loss of his own vital powers. It was as if the world-walk were the final optimistic shout of his creative manhood—"Yes, the world *can* be walked," he might have cried out, "and I, Charles L. Mordenstahl, will see that it is done!"—which, once uttered, had hung in the air to mock him. It was a young man's challenge— but a middle-aged man had foolishly given it voice, knowing (as middle-aged men know) that the world was not made to serve human egotism. Thus, confused and in torment, Mr. Mordenstahl fell victim to another subconscious illusion, that by stopping Pierce, he could arrest his own dissolution.

What gnawed on him more superficially was the knowledge that he was wasting his time. As he stood there amid Vermont's green hills, attempting to negotiate with this imbecile over something that really made no practical difference to him, he realized that important decisions were being postponed in his absence—or, worse, were being made by others.

Mr. Mordenstahl began seething with exasperation. He longed to beat Pierce to the ground with his fists, to dance upon his fallen body, and to twist those world-walking legs until they snapped and splintered. However, he managed to spread a smile of sympathetic concern across his handsome, pouchy features, and tried another gambit.

"You've got a problem, don't you, son?" he said to Pierce. "Tell me what it is. Maybe I can help. I want to help. I really do. You may not believe it, but I've been able to help a lot of young fellows work out their problems, and I was young once, too, so I realize how things are, whether it's money or women or family troubles, so just think of me as an older brother and let me know your problem."

"I don't have a problem."

"Everybody has problems," said Mr. Mordenstahl. "Sometimes the problems are so big we can't handle them except by running away. Or walking away," he added meaningfully. "But they've got to be faced, don't they? And it helps to have an older brother or an uncle around to confide in, so here I am, son," he concluded, patting Pierce's arm, "ready to help you, and just let me know what the problem is."

"There isn't a problem."

"Then roast in hell!" Mr. Mordenstahl roared suddenly, unable to repress his rage. "Don't you realize what a nutty thing it is you're doing? I could have you locked up in the bughouse for observation this minute just by snapping my fingers! There isn't a psychiatrist or a judge anywhere alive who wouldn't commit you as a total freak and menace, can you understand that?"

Pierce gaped at him. Mr. Mordenstahl's mouth was working furiously and his cheeks were darkly flushed.

"But of course I wouldn't do such a thing," Mr. Mordenstahl said, making an effort to recover his composure. "Unless I were forced to." He was breathing hoarsely. The veins on his forehead protruded. "Listen, Davis," he went on in an uneven voice, "you don't want to make us look like fools, do you? Officially, you're not walking. It's been published in the papers. But if you keep on going, then somebody's bound to find out, and—well, it'll make us liars, won't it?"

"Not if you don't sponsor me."

"Maybe not, but—" Mr. Mordenstahl looked distractedly around. The green hills disturbed him. He perceived that they hindered large-scale farming. "Bulldoze 'em flat," he muttered to himself, but he realized that the cost of such work would be prohibitive. Then he had a brainstorm. "What about a soil dam, Davis?" His manner was transformed. He became excited, almost joyful. He took a deep breath. "Here's how you could do it. Let Nature work for you free, that's always the secret! You build an earthfill barricade below your hill, see, and then you strip the hill of all vegetation. You can sell the timber, if any, and then put goats up there. Goats will do the job like nobody's business! Well, and then when there's nothing holding the soil any more, it gradually washes and slides down in the course of time, but you don't lose it because your soil dam is there to catch and hold it, and eventually you'd have a kind of plateau suitable for farming." He gave a little cackle of pleasure, whipped out a small notebook, and took rapid notes of his idea. "Might not be economic, but what the hell. You never know. Worth a gander anyhow." He thrust the notebook back into his jacket pocket and sized up Vermont again with keen, speculative eyes. "This place could be made as flat as Kansas!" he declared enthusiastically. "Of course, you'd still have the underlying rock formations left, but you could quarry them, maybe, or blast holes in them to make shelters for farm animals. In short, as I see it, Davis, you could wind up with a series of gigantic terraces, bounded by these soil dams, with certain rock structures rearing up here and there, and I'm sure these could be utilized in some productive fashion."

Mr. Mordenstahl nodded in satisfaction and regarded Pierce in an almost friendly way until he remembered why he'd come to Vermont in the first place, and his look changed to one of annoyance, as though Pierce were an obstreperous hill which wouldn't surrender its soil for agricultural convenience.

"Tell me honestly, Mr. Mordenstahl," said Pierce. "Why do you care whether I walk or not? I mean, it shouldn't affect you one way or the other."

"It does affect me, Davis. It may seem like a small thing to you, but—well, let me put it this way. I'm one of the last of a vanishing breed," said Mr. Mordenstahl, thrusting out his jaw and folding his arms across his chest. "I'm a fellow who's always carved out his own path. I'm a risk-taker, I'm an adventurer, I'm an idea-man. Now, it's true that most of my ideas don't pan out, and that's normal in creative thinking, but these young fellows who are coming up in the company now, they do everything by slide rule and committee, and they're afraid to think on their own, that's the truth of the matter, and they hover around like vultures waiting to feast on my mistakes, ignoring the fact that if I wasn't there to drive the company ahead, we'd still be a little jerkwater outfit with a regional business instead of being one of the biggest god-damned giants around!" He broke off with a sigh and let his arms drop to his sides. "The point is, Davis, when you've got an idea that turns out to be a clinker, then you liquidate it, but if it doesn't liquidate—well, then that implies a lack of proper control, and certain people may start whispering behind your back and suggesting that Mordenstahl doesn't have that old iron any more. But I do have that old iron," he said fiercely. He stooped to pick up a clod of dirt. "I've crushed men in my time for less, Davis," he declared, giving Pierce a hard look as he squeezed the clod of dirt in his fist. It wouldn't crumble, though, and he threw it down.

"You ought to take a vacation, Mr. Mordenstahl," Pierce said kindly. "Say—why don't you walk with me for a while? Just a few miles a day, it would do you some good."

Mr. Mordenstahl scowled. "If I were twenty years younger, Davis, I'd show you some walking! I could do it right now if I wanted!" He squared around as though about to march off that minute. Then he hesitated, his face sagged, his shoulders bowed, and he sat down heavily on the front bumper of the car. "I wanted to walk the world when I was your age, Davis," he said sadly. "I don't mean that literally, but in spirit that's what I wanted to do. I mean to say I wanted to do a worldwide thing. I thought in global terms, you see. I wanted to achieve something that would make the name of Charles L. Mordenstahl known everywhere, is that clear? Oh, I could have been a lawyer or a physician, but I went into agriculture because it provided me with a base common to all men, understand, and sometimes I dreamed that every time anybody ate a mouthful of food, they'd know it was because of me," he said, plucking a blade of grass and chewing on it, "as if the world were my family table, and all the people eating there my guests, my children, my sons!" He moaned and struck his forehead as though anguished, but he flashed a quick glance up at Pierce which made Pierce wonder if his performance were sincere. "I was strong, Davis, and I knew I was strong," Mr. Mordenstahl said in a feeble voice. "But I wasn't strong enough. I chased my dreams as far as I could, my boy, but the world is too big for any man, and that's a fact, and all you do is burn yourself out, and then it begins to slip and slide, and you know you won't make it, and you start thinking about the end of it all, where all you'll have of the world is a little plot six feet by two, and I'd do anything to spare a fellow creature from such disappointment, so have pity on an old man's gray hairs, Davis, and go back to your loved ones in Iowa." He gazed up wretchedly at Pierce, with tears in his eyes. "For your own sake, son, I'm asking you. I'm *begging* you. Look," he said, "I'm practically kneeling at your feet."

"You don't need to do that, Mr. Mordenstahl," said Pierce.

"Say you'll stop walking, Davis."

"I'm sorry, but I can't say it."

"You've got to say it," pleaded Mr. Mordenstahl.

"I can't."

"In the name of all you hold dear, stop walking."

"I'm not stopping."

"Look at me, you dimwit idiot!" Mr. Mordenstahl bellowed. "I've humbled myself before you! Me, Charles L. Mordenstahl! Evidently that doesn't mean chickshit to you, you ox-brained numbskull!"

"Well, anyhow, I'm going to go on walking," Pierce said, "and you might as well not waste your breath."

Mr. Mordenstahl struggled to his feet, panting with

wrath. "It's absurd, the whole damned thing is absurd," he muttered. He gave Pierce a furious glance. "There's only one explanation, Davis. You've got a new sponsor behind you, right?"

"No, sir."

"Don't lie to me. You've gotten yourself tied up with other interests."

"Nope."

"Of course you have! It's obvious!" Mr. Mordenstahl cupped his hands to his mouth and called to his assistants, who were matching pennies fifty yards down the road. "Look here, Davis," he said, "you might as well realize that you don't have the mental or psychological equipment to make a success out of this walk around the world. Face up to it. Even here in the States, where it's easy, you've fouled up. What do you think would happen to you where it's hard?"

Then he turned abruptly away from Pierce and got into the back seat of the car, shutting the door behind him. "It's all foolishness," he said, but he didn't seem to be addressing Pierce. "It's absurd, that's what it is," he grumbled, folding his arms and staring straight ahead. "Foolishness and absurdity!" He seemed to have forgotten about Pierce.

"Well, it may be foolish," Pierce told him through the window, "but a lot of things people do are foolish, but sometimes they can't stop doing them, and that's the situation with me, Mr. Mordenstahl. I mean, I don't seem to be able to stop walking, and as a matter of fact I don't want to stop, but even if I did, I couldn't."

Mr. Mordenstahl rolled up the window.

"And I've been wondering why I'm walking, just as you've been wondering," said Pierce, shifting to the window in front, which remained open, "because I've realized that walking around the world for no good reason is foolish, as you say, so only a fool would try to do it, but it occurs to me that something as hard as this can't be done without having faith in it—I mean, it may be a foolish thing to do, but if it can't be done without faith, then that's something in its favor, isn't it?"

Mr. Mordenstahl sat stonily silent, facing forward.

"And you don't get a thing like that overnight, Mr. Mordenstahl," Pierce continued. "You sort of earn it step by step, you might say, and that's what's been happening to me, not so much walking all these miles, but realizing that I'm moving toward some kind of faith, although I honestly couldn't tell you what it may turn out to be exactly."

The two assistants came puffing up. One glance at Mr. Mordenstahl informed them that they were to leave at once, so they climbed into the car without even looking at Pierce.

"I mean, a man who actually walks the world will be a man who's gotten hold of some faith or other, Mr. Mordenstahl, and that's worth a lot of effort—"

Pierce was forced to shout his last words, for the driver had started the engine.

As the car began to move, Mr. Mordenstahl turned his head toward Pierce. "Go home—go back to Iowa!" he yelled above the noise of the engine.

"I'm going to Iowa, Mr. Mordenstahl," Pierce yelled back. "I'm just doing it the long way around, that's all."

But Mr. Mordenstahl didn't hear him, for the car had pulled rapidly away. When it vanished around the curve, Pierce began walking again.

He felt lighthearted and expectant. The road was empty; so was the cloudless summer sky. "Well, I'm going on," he said aloud, to no one. And the green hills seemed to echo his words, as though the world he was walking wished him good luck—but Pierce knew that the world would change beneath his feet, he knew that the hills would soar and sharpen, that the sky would grow dark, the air chill, the nights dangerous. He guessed, too, that he might change as well, and he wondered what the world might walk up out of him, for he supposed that with every step he was leaving behind not only the life he'd known but also the self he'd been.

He was confident, though, and he stepped out smartly on his way. "Hey, world," he cried out, "watch me walk! Here comes Walking Davis!"

Part
TWO

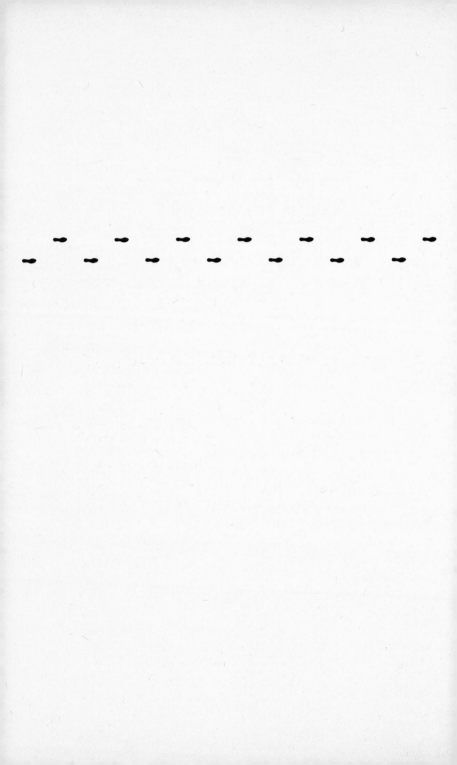

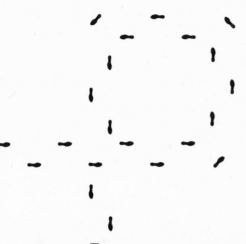

Bᴇᴄᴀᴜsᴇ of his accident (to be referred to later), Pierce's recollection of what happened to him in the following weeks was fragmentary and confused. He couldn't remember what roads he'd followed or which cities he'd gone through; he knew only that he'd headed east as always, and that his hopeful mood had slowly passed as the solitude of walking weighed down on him day after day.

Only once did he recall encountering a fellow walker, a man on the other side of the highway who was coming in his direction. Pierce approached him joyfully—but the fellow turned out to be a motorist whose car had run out of gasoline some miles back, and he hurried by impatiently, with an angry expression on his face, as though Pierce were somehow responsible for his difficulty.

Sometimes Pierce imagined that he wasn't completely alone—that behind him, just out of sight, was that same shadowy walking presence he'd divined back in Illinois and recurrently since then—but this sort of company he didn't care to have, nor was he encouraged by the fact that the people along his way either didn't look at him or regarded him in a hostile way. This made him feel guilty, although he wasn't sure why. "I've got a right to walk, don't I?" he'd ask himself, but sometimes he wasn't sure that he did.

Even the elements didn't seem to be kindly disposed after while. The rain beat down, soaking him, and the sun burned his face and hands. When he found no lodging at night and had to sleep in the open, the sight of the stars humbled him. His efforts were puny. He was creeping about one single small planet—but there were other worlds flung across heaven, worlds that blazed and swung and danced, worlds by the millions, so many that even in his imagination he couldn't walk them all.

On August 19, while having breakfast with his brother, Dr. Davis was surprised by a stroke, which paralyzed the right side of his body and deprived him of the power of speech. Even as he was collapsing, he reflected in bitterness as well as fear that this was Pierce's fault, for the very moment before, Judge Davis had asked if any letter had arrived in the morning mail from Pierce, and at the mention of his son's name, Dr. Davis had sensed a pulse of annoyance streak up like a bullet to explode some already weakened cranial vessel. He'd muttered "Pierce—" but nothing more, dropped his fork and slumped sideways against the wall, as the judge stared at him first in astonishment, then in dismay, and right away called for an ambulance.

The doctors at the county hospital could tell the judge only that Dr. Davis would either live or die, and that if he lived, he might remain crippled or, in time, recover, in whole or in part. In short, they knew nothing at all, so Judge Davis decided to summon the family to the victim's bedside. This meant, principally, Pierce. Now, although the judge realized that his brother was disappointed in Pierce, he himself had always liked the boy, and he felt that at such a crisis Dr. Davis would want to gaze once again on the face of his only child. In this, the judge was quite wrong. If there was one face the stricken man did not want to see, it was Pierce's, but he was too ill to be consulted on the matter even if his brother had thought of asking him about it.

Being a judge, Phil Davis was a person of limited but definite consequence in Iowa, and he had no hesitation in turning for assistance to his friends and colleagues in the public service. Therefore, after telephoning Natalie at her father's clinic up in Clarion and learning that she hadn't heard from Pierce lately, either, he got in touch with an occasional fishing companion who happened to be chief inspector of the state highway patrol. For the police it was a routine matter. The judge's nephew was off on a walking trip somewhere in the eastern U.S. and had to be located so he could fly home at once. Teletype messages were sent that afternoon to various Eastern authorities, and certain other inquiries were initiated, none of which produced any result whatever, for by that date Pierce was no longer in the U.S. at all.

The police in the New England states not only couldn't find Pierce, they couldn't even tell where he'd been. He had apparently pursued a circuitous and unlikely course, as though he deliberately intended to baffle them, although a more plausible explanation is that he wanted to avoid cities and main highways, preferring quiet roads through open countryside. In any event, the name of Pierce Davis was not found in the registers of hotels, motels, or rooming houses along what would have been the most direct routes northeast from Vermont, nor did his description jog the memories of waitresses or busboys or short-order cooks at the kinds of eating places he would have patronized. Pierce might have flown through the air like a wizard, for all the traces he left.

It is not known at what point he entered Canada, and the date of his entry cannot be fixed more precisely than sometime in the first week of July. However, it was almost certainly the world-walker who entered a marine equipment store in St. John's, Newfoundland, on either August 11 or 12 (the proprietor isn't sure which) to ask whether a man in a diving suit could walk the bed of the Atlantic Ocean to reach Europe. The proprietor, Mr. R. L. Craig, assumed that this prospective client was joking, so he obligingly laughed. Then it became clear that the question, absurd as it sounded, had been seriously propounded, so Mr. Craig composed his features and explained that while it might theoretically be possible for a diver to walk the Grand Banks—provided he had an extensive and costly support operation on the surface above him, and if the weather held calm throughout—once he reached the rim of the Continental Shelf, some three hundred miles out at the farthest, he'd have to quit. "Even a lobster couldn't walk beyond that," Mr. Craig recalled telling his visitor. "No, sir, to cross the Atlantic by foot, you'd have to be the Son of God Himself and walk the waves." All of which had much amused the clerks and other customers, particularly since the inquirer seemed quite taken aback by Mr. Craig's information, as though he couldn't believe that a man, properly equipped, would be unable to hike across the ocean floor.

"He was a tough one, by the looks of him," Mr. Craig recounted later. "A big ugly red-bearded fellow who smelled like a goat and had a nasty look in his eye"— which, given the probable effects of some thousand miles of lonely tramping from Vermont to the very tip of North America, might not have been too inaccurate a description of Pierce Davis at this point, except that Pierce's beard (when he had one, and he was customarily clean-shaven) was actually blond with reddish tints that glinted only in sunlight, and of course Mr. Craig's choice of the words "ugly" and "nasty" may have been influenced by the memory of the stranger's odor rather than by his appearance.

At any rate, the "red-bearded" stranger was noticed by others in St. John's in mid-August. The police questioned him a few times, as they did all suspicious-looking characters, but since he had some money and did not seem criminally inclined, they didn't take his name. A fisherman named Santos remembered that the bearded man had prowled around the wharves for several days, staring out at the harbor and muttering curses, once actually shaking a fist at the water, and there was a violent altercation in a tavern frequented by stevedores reportedly involving this same person, in which various noses were bloodied and a certain number of teeth dislodged, but according to the custom of such establishments, no complaints were made to the authorities, and so no written record of the event exists that might identify the surly red-bearded stranger as being the mild-mannered and cheerful Pierce Davis of Spark, Iowa.

* * *

How the world-walker crossed the Atlantic has never been satisfactorily established. His own recollection on this point was not only hazy but erroneous, nor do other sources provide an adequate explanation.

His first recorded appearance in Europe was on August 28, the date of his admission to the Royal St. Andrew's Hospital in Aberdeen, Scotland. (His passport number was duly noted in the file, leaving no possibility of doubt that Pierce was the patient concerned.)

While still under the influence of sedatives administered to ease his pain, Pierce asserted that he'd crossed the Atlantic by foot. Later he conceded that such an exploit was unlikely, and said he supposed he made the trip by air. This he most probably didn't do, however, for his name does not appear on any passenger manifests during August for flights to Great Britain from the major international airports in eastern Canada and the United States.

If he didn't fly, then he must have made the trip by sea. And yet here, too, there remains a perplexing lack of data. Only three vessels, all cargo ships, embarked from St. John's, Newfoundland, in the crucial mid-August period for ports in the British Isles, and Pierce Davis was not listed as passenger or crewman on any of them.

Two of these ships—the *Hudson* and the *Louisa B. Williams*—arrived in late August at Liverpool and Glasgow, respectively. The third, the *Happy Alice,* carrying a cargo of tinned codfish and pulped paper, a crew of twenty-one and a captain named W. S. McManus, reached the very bottom of the Atlantic on August 23, having sunk with all hands in a storm some nine hundred miles south of Cape Farewell, Greenland.

Now, if one accepts Pierce's presence in St. John's as late as August 15 (the apparent date of the tavern brawl), and if one assumes that he was able to board the *Hudson* or the *Louisa B. Williams* either under a false name or as a stowaway, then one still is faced by serious difficulties.

Pierce was without doubt in Aberdeen on August 28. However, the *Hudson* did not dock at Liverpool until August 26, and the *Louisa B. Williams* arrived at Glasgow in the late afternoon of the 27th. Since Aberdeen is three hundred miles north of Liverpool and one hundred and fifty miles northeast of Glasgow, it is obvious that Pierce would not have had time to make his way there by foot, but would instead have had to go by train or bus.

And yet not only was Pierce never known to use (except under duress) any form of transport on dry land other than his own two feet, but he would have had no reason whatever to go so far out of his way to the north, if he had indeed entered the United Kingdom at either of the ports mentioned.

Still, if Liverpool and Glasgow are excluded, one is left with the ill-fated *Happy Alice*, and the bizarre image of Pierce, dripping wet but a survivor alone in a lifeboat or on a makeshift raft of pulp-paper boxes, nourishing himself on tinned codfish while drifting at breakneck speed across half the Atlantic, past the Orkneys atop Scotland, and then into the North Sea, in order to reach Aberdeen on time.

In contrast to the mysteries and improbabilities connected with the crossing of the Atlantic, the facts of Aberdeen are beyond dispute, i.e.:

—That Pierce Davis, an American citizen, in possession of passport number such-and-such, did, at approximately four-thirty o'clock on the afternoon of 28 August, attempt to cross from the north to the south side of King

Charles Street near its intersection with Market Street.

—That this Pierce Davis, being an American, evidently looked instinctively to his left before stepping off the curb, unmindful of the fact that in Britain traffic proceeds in a direction contrary to that elsewhere.

—And that this same Pierce Davis was consequently struck by a taxicab, from which he suffered a clean break of the right femur, a hairline fracture of the right tibia, and multiple contusions and abrasions on the rest of him, including a head-knock on the pavement that left him senseless for a full two hours, during which period he was taken to the Royal St. Andrew's Hospital and placed under treatment.

Roy Roach was in London, occupying a suite in a posh hotel. George Bonaparte, on the other hand, was in jail in Johannesburg, Union of South Africa, having been arrested August 24, shortly after he had crossed the border from Zambia into Southwest Africa, and charged with illegal entry and inciting rebellion, for he had brought in a satchel of subversive pamphlets which he would have distributed if the police hadn't seized him first.

Roach, who'd been in Kenya making arrangements for Bonaparte's later appearance there, flew to Johannesburg, where he found that the problem of obtaining Bonaparte's release was complicated by the fact that the ex-Olympian was a Jamaican, and Jamaica had no diplomatic relations with South Africa. Roach then took a plane to England, to seek help through the British government.

For Mr. Mordenstahl, Bonaparte's arrest was the

public-relations disaster he'd feared. For Roy Roach, it was an opportunity of the kind he'd had frequently in the past, for Roach knew how to reach for new clients while standing on the ruins of old ones. His position had improved in all respects, in fact, for he had actually been able to increase his fee from Mordenstahl, as compensation for the extra burdens of minimizing the Duluth company's sponsorship of Bonaparte, while at the same time he was free to exploit the various possibilities which Bonaparte's arrest presented. Before he had even left Kenya, he had telephoned a British press agent friend of his and directed him to begin a publicity campaign, to organize protest rallies among the many liberal groups traditionally opposed to South Africa—and to gather funds, the first uses of which were to pay Roach's expenses. Once in London, Roach supervised these projects from his hotel suite, and developed new ones. He hired a hack journalist to whip out a series of articles in Bonaparte's name, which were sold for a stiff price to a London weekly that wasn't too fussy on such matters as authenticity. Then, with an eye to the future, Roach began trying to line up commercial sponsors to replace Mr. Mordenstahl's company (an activity he didn't bother mentioning during his almost daily transatlantic phone conversations with Mr. Mordenstahl, in which he assured his client he was keeping a tight lid on the whole affair).

But he couldn't sell Bonaparte. The British, French, and West German companies he approached showed an initial interest in the publicity potential of associating their products or services with a world-walker. In each case, however, this interest faded, and Roach's efforts to force conclusions were politely rebuffed. The advertising and publicity directors of these firms did not explain why, nor did they need to, for Roach had suspected from the beginning that they would balk for the simple reason that their customers were white and Bonaparte was black. The image would therefore be wrong.

"I need a white one," Roach told himself. The thought of Pierce Davis passed several times through his mind, for Pierce did have some credentials for the job, in the form of newspaper clippings, but Roach assumed that Pierce was back in Iowa, and besides, the fellow had shown himself to be both dimwitted and unreliable. Still, Roach realized that if he were going to mine the world-walk further, he'd need a white walker. He began interviewing prospects: amateur track runners, unemployed actors, stunt men from film studios, refugees from Eastern Europe, circus acrobats, and American college dropouts. He also interviewed the bellboy who brought up his mail, and, on the recommendation of his chauffeur's sister, he even had a talk with a husky-voiced woman who did male impersonations in queer nightclubs. None of these candidates seemed right to him, however. Besides, his earlier efforts to market Bonaparte had made matters worse, for he had persuaded the potential sponsors on one key point: that Bonaparte's commercial value rested largely on his publicly established reputation as a world-walker. What the sponsors wanted now was what Roach couldn't provide—a white Bonaparte. For an unknown newcomer, be he as white as a frog's belly, they'd pay little or nothing at all.

Roach finally had to conclude that he'd made as much money out of the world-walk as he could, and with characteristic practicality, he put Bonaparte out of his mind. He informed the London lawyers who were working on the Jamaican's case that any further efforts to obtain the prisoner's release were up to them, and that in any event they should send their statements of account to

Duluth. As for Bonaparte himself, Roach didn't so much as mail him a postcard.

The prospect of leaving London depressed Roach, for he'd had a fine time there. He'd denied himself no pleasure or convenience. By day he was driven to appointments in a chauffeured limousine, a comely stenographer by his side to record his thoughts, and by night he toured the nightclubs and gambling casinos in the company of the same young creature or of others equally attractive and attentive to his needs. He'd completely restocked his wardrobe with costly suits and shirts. He'd refurbished his personality, too (which was the only item he'd been unable to list on his expense account). He felt himself to have expanded in scope and scale. Pittsburgh didn't define him any longer. He was internationalized—but to no lasting purpose, if he had to go back to the U.S.

In early September, as he was reluctantly making plans for his departure, he chanced to learn something which encouraged him to prolong his stay. He had dropped by the American Embassy one day to pay a poker debt to a boozing companion who clerked there. "Here's something that'll tickle you," his friend remarked, handing Roach a folder. "Talk about your walker down in Africa—well, here's a fellow who claims to have walked across the Atlantic Ocean."

Roach chuckled, but as soon as he saw that the material concerned Pierce Davis, he read it attentively, thus learning of Pierce's accident and hospitalization in Aberdeen. "I know that poor boy," he exclaimed. "He's an old and cherished friend of mine." He began thumbing through the report. "What's the phone number of that hospital? I want to call up there and make sure he's getting the best treatment so his leg will heal up in a hurry."

"He's not there," said the Embassy clerk. "That's the odd part of it. Nobody knows where he is now."

"What do you mean?"

"Five days after they brought him in, he skipped out—well, I guess with a broken leg he didn't skip—but anyhow he disappeared. Oh, he'll be picked up soon enough, though. A man with one leg in a cast can't get far. They'll find him any day now."

Roach decided to wait.

As Pierce was an American citizen, the report of his accident had been duly made to the U.S. Embassy in London, which in turn had relayed the information to Pierce's family in Spark. Judge Davis, receiving the message in Natalie's absence, had thereupon cabled the Embassy, asking that arrangements be made for Pierce to fly home as soon as he could. This request was transmitted promptly and accurately to the Royal St. Andrew's Hospital, but the staff grapevine got it all wrong, as often happens, and so the first Pierce heard of it was on the evening of September 3, when a friendly nurse dropped by his bedside and sympathetically informed him that the authorities were going to extradite him to America the very next day, and that she, for one, would always believe him innocent of whatever he'd been accused of.

This misinformation shouldn't have given Pierce cause for more than a moment's alarm, as he'd broken no law. On the other hand, the knock on the head he'd suffered in the accident had played hob with his memory, so he may have imagined that he'd committed all sorts of atrocities. A further possibility is that he sensed instinctively that his return to the States, for whatever reason,

94

would put an end to his walking—and that, above all, he couldn't accept.

In any event, at some time between eleven that same evening and six the next morning, Pierce Davis made his exit from the Royal St. Andrew's without troubling to seek a release, leaving behind the boot to his right foot, two dirty undershirts, and an unpaid bill.

It is not difficult to imagine that with great effort and much caution Pierce could have left the hospital undetected during the hours of darkness. It is quite another matter, however, to understand how a man with one leg encased from hip to ankle in a heavy plaster cast would have been able to walk—or rather, to swing himself along one-footed with the aid of a pair of crutches—for hundreds of miles through a countryside for the most part heavily populated, where he was bound to be noticed and talked about by dozens of persons every day, without having been reported to, picked up, and identified by the police, who'd been put on notice at once, and so were on the lookout for him.

And yet this is apparently exactly what Pierce Davis did.

There were, granted, certain advantages he must have had. The search for him centered initially on Aberdeen itself, the police assuming that a man with a broken leg couldn't go more than a mile or two. In this they underestimated Pierce's physical strength and endurance, powerfully developed by this time, and they also took no account of his remarkable determination. He must have made steady progress south, crutching his way through the sparsely settled regions of northeast Scotland while the authorities were peering into toolsheds and warehouses in the back alleys of Aberdeen.

Secondly, the police never imagined that he might

walk. They kept an eye on the port, the bus terminal, the railroad station, and the local airfield, and while they did make a few patrol-car checks of the roads, thinking that Pierce might try hitchhiking, this was done only on major, heavily traveled highways—i.e., precisely those which he would have avoided.

Finally, it must be admitted that the search for Pierce was a routine and minor matter. He was wanted, but he wasn't wanted very badly, and so only token efforts were made to find him. Still, an official circular had been put out, and as it was rather unusual for the police to be seeking a man fleeing on crutches, the public imagination was stimulated to produce a considerable number of reports concerning crippled fugitives seen hobbling along the roads of the island, in which more than the customary proportion of contradictions was mixed in with what may have been reliable material.

For instance, Pierce was seen twice on the morning of September 17, once in Manchester and once in Hull, and obviously, as these cities are one hundred miles apart, one (and perhaps both) of these supposed Pierces must have been false. To cite another example, he was reported to be in Dover, on the English Channel, on September 12, which he could not possibly have reached by foot at such an early date. Then again, he was noticed in the city of York on September 15, which would have been plausible except that the witness, a dental surgeon, swore that the walker's plaster cast was on the left leg, not on the right, so that this testimony must be rejected.

Despite the profusion of his supposed appearances, the real Pierce was never once stopped by the police. This does not mean that the authorities failed to follow up the reports, for in some instances this was rather promptly done. So it was, during the early part of September in various villages and towns and cities throughout Britain, that a certain number of one-legged war veterans found themselves unexpectedly quizzed by police, and that some arthritic pensioners, limping along the streets, were annoyed by official expressions of interest in their identities, and that even a few gout-ridden citizens propelling themselves about in Bath chairs were subjected to brief scrutiny.

At some point Pierce managed to rid himself of his plaster cast (it is not known whether this was done by some agreeable doctor, or whether Pierce did it himself with a hammer and chisel), and he disposed of the crutches in favor of a stick. Even so, reports of the ubiquitous cripple continued, and spurious Pierces were sighted long after the real walker had left the British Isles entirely. He was seen in Oxford the following spring, for example, creaking along past the Bodleian Library, and he turned up, too, at the Henley Regatta that summer, outfitted not only with cast and crutches but with an eyepatch as well, and although the search for Pierce received scant press attention, and was not widely known among the public in general, it is at least an interesting coincidence that the "crutch races" which have become such a popular feature at county fairs date from this same period.

Pierce Davis's crutch-walk through Britain was an unusual achievement, even if the walker himself was unable to remember having done it. Beyond this, it may be taken as Pierce's tribute (albeit an unconscious one) to the great English walkers of a bygone age.

In England, Pierce was on hallowed walking ground. It was there, in early Victorian times, that modern walking was invented. That is, for the first time in history, men walked who didn't have to. It is true that English gentlemen took up walking only when the development of the railway system permitted common people to begin traveling by wheels; still, the important point is not why these early walkers started walking, but that they liberated walking from its lowly status of sheer pedestrian necessity.

The English founders of walking would probably not have considered Pierce a true walker, however, partly because the knapsack on his back would have indicated that he was nothing but a damned hiker, and partly because he quite simply was not English, and even if he had been English, he wouldn't have been their sort of English, whereas (to gloss over a complex ethnic difficulty) an Englishman of the right sort could wear a pack on his back and qualify as a walker rather than a hiker—which attitude, incomprehensible as it may be to outsiders, was nonetheless a fundamental tenet of those gentlemen of the last century who were, in a walking sense, Pierce's spiritual ancestors.

The Victorians were powerful walkers. They thought nothing of a ten-mile stroll before breakfast, and a jaunt of twenty-five or thirty miles was barely enough to maintain a proper muscle tone, or, in winter, to freshen up a stimulating case of frostbite. They walked the roads, the lanes, and the paths, and if trodden ways were lacking, they walked all the same—through the forests and the valleys, through marshes, bogs, and fens, up mountains and over frozen lakes, and, as occasion presented itself, they walked across half of Europe to climb the Alps (although in this activity they verged perilously on mere hiking), and then they walked back again. For them, the modest pace that Pierce Davis set in his American period would have been a frightful bore. Indeed, had a Mordenstahl existed at the time to launch such a venture, an entire regiment of bewhiskered and iron-legged Victorians could have walked the world in short order, pausing only to plant the flag of Empire here and there.

Legends of these walkers abound. There is the story of an Anglican reverend from Swindon who, having gone out one winter night to walk his mind clear of Darwinian doubts, vanished in a blizzard and was found next morning near Wigston Magna, no fewer than seventy miles distant, frozen stiff upright and in mid-stride. Then there was a certain Captain Piers-Struther, who, after being captured by the Russians at Balaklava in 1854, escaped from his Siberian prison that winter and walked a thousand miles across the frozen Barents Sea to Norway, where he arrived quite fit and ready for further service to the Crown. Pierce's broken-legged trek would have received the approbation of another noted walker of those times, Professor Clandragon of Cambridge. This learned don took special pride in mastering his physical handicaps, these being lumbago, rheumatism, and the inability to bend his left leg at the knee. Professor Clandragon refused to travel by wheels, but walked wherever he went, which trips included frequent and, for him, arduous journeys to the Continent for professional meetings; in his will he directed that his body be vertically supported by two friends so that it could be "walked" to the graveyard. Another inveterate walker, Sir Weston Godspeed, was said to have tramped fifty miles every day of his life from his twelfth into his ninety-third year, until, betrayed by failing eyesight, the aged knight erroneously walked into the North Sea near Harwich, and perished when, assuming it was but a cow pond, he attempted to cross it.

For weeks Dr. Davis had maintained a stationary condition. He was not badly off. He could eat, perform bodily functions, watch television, and reason in his mind. With this latter faculty he concluded that Pierce remained the greatest threat to his life—the mere sight of his son's face would kill him, he was convinced—and hence, at the first opportunity, he painfully printed with his left hand the message: "I do not want to see Pierce," and gave it to his brother.

This had little effect, as Judge Davis assumed that the sick man merely meant he was reluctant to let Pierce see him in his present forlorn state. At this time, of course, the question of whether Pierce would come home or not was far from resolved, for only a few days after the family was informed of Pierce's hospitalization in Scotland, came the news that he had vanished. Judge Davis at first supposed that Pierce was on his way back to Spark. Even later, when it became clear that this was not the case, the judge was not particularly worried. The sense of urgency had passed, the doctors having assured him that Dr. Davis would survive at least for months, with perhaps some gradual improvement.

Natalie had come down from Clarion at once. After a few days she'd gone back, for there was really nothing she could do, and she had, in her hometown, a life that interested her. She was now not only managing her father's clinic but also studying toward qualification as a nurse. With her family connections and her own energetic drive, she thought it quite likely that by age forty she would be the head nurse at the hospital there in Wright County.

She had found more happiness than she'd ever had with Pierce, and she was determined not to give it up. If Pierce did come back, she vowed she'd divorce him. At the same time, not being a vindictive woman, she felt sorry for him, and a bit guilty, too, if only because of little Stephanie, who would know no other father. As Natalie realized that she was finished with Pierce, be he alive or dead, she began to regard him with affectionate regret. "He was really a good fellow," she thought. "He never did any harm to anyone. He was kind and sweet-tempered. . . ." The world-walk, too, she began to see as a truly heroic adventure, for after all it had been that quixotic undertaking which had unburdened her of Pierce. When Stephanie inquired (as she did at decreasing intervals) when Daddy was coming home, Natalie would reply that Daddy had gone away on an important trip, and that it would still be a long time before he was finished, because he was trying to do something no one else had ever done before.

So she told Stephanie, and so she began half-consciously to persuade herself, and as the busy weeks went by with no further word of Pierce, she was able more and more to think of him (when she did think of him) as a fellow of noble qualities, the chief of these being a decent respect for the convenience of his family.

It was in the northern approaches to London that Pierce, emerging from the amnesiac fog caused by his accident in Aberdeen, began to take stock of his situation, and although he now was fully aware of who he was—Pierce Davis—and what he was doing—walking—he had no idea where he was or how he'd gotten there.

He was tired, hungry, and miserable. His right leg ached at every step. The boot to that foot was missing; in its place were wrappings of rags and newspapers, clumsily tied up in string. Apart from the clothes on his back, his only possessions were his passport, a few British coins, and a stick which he used as a cane as he limped along the highway.

From the evidence of the coins, and by reading scraps of the newspapers on his right foot, he concluded that he was in England, and as the road signs were succeeded by street signs, he realized that he was entering London itself. These deductions were of little interest to him, though, for he was possessed by the conviction that something was pursuing him, and that he dared not stop to rest or eat.

Someone had warned him; that he remembered. "The police are after me," he thought. "I've done something wrong somewhere. A crime of some sort." He couldn't recall what it had been, but the fact that his memory refused to acknowledge it made him afraid that it wasn't a minor one. He began to use little sidestreets, and kept glancing back to see if he were being followed. It was a chill autumn afternoon, already darkening. He was glad enough of that, for it made him less noticeable. In the distance the dome of St. Paul's could be seen rising gloomily above gray surrounding shapes, but Pierce barely gave it a glance. "I've done something wrong," he kept muttering as he limped along the greasy pavement. "What was it? A real crime, maybe—but what?"

Whenever he glimpsed a man in uniform ahead of him, he ducked aside. He shrank from postmen, street-sweepers, sailors on leave, and even from messenger boys on their cycles. The sight of an elderly hotel doorman made him turn off into an alley and pick his way among garbage cans to find an exit on a safer street.

He knew he wasn't a criminal type. He'd never done anything worse than stealing apples when he was a boy, and he couldn't remember having done a single thing in recent months except walking—and he was the only one who'd suffered because of that. If any crimes had been committed, they'd been committed against him, he thought, but he couldn't shake off the feeling that he was guilty of something, and that, since the police were looking for him, they undoubtedly had good reason.

The deeper he went into the city, the more confused he became. His common sense suggested that he was exaggerating the matter. Surely if he'd committed some felony, he'd remember it. Of course, he might have done something minor, a misdemeanor of some kind which could easily have slipped his mind. In that case, he ought to get off lightly. Then again, it occurred to him that he might already have been tried, found guilty, and jailed. He'd lost a few weeks somewhere. He might very well have spent them serving a sentence. If so, fine. He'd be in the clear. On the other hand, if he didn't know what he'd done, he might go and do it again, which would be contempt of court or some such thing, and he'd be treated harshly a second time.

"I'd better talk to a lawyer," he thought. But he didn't know any lawyers in London. He didn't know anybody there. In fact, he could think of only two persons in the world he might rely on to advise him in such cloudy circumstances: his uncle, Judge Davis, and Mr. Mordenstahl. He'd have to telephone collect—but to which one? He fidgeted in front of a public phone booth, pondering the matter. Finally he decided on Mr. Mordenstahl, on the theory that his former employer, as an international businessman, would be more likely to know of a good London law firm, even though Pierce recalled that Mr. Mordenstahl had been rather annoyed with him the last time they met.

Pierce's call to Duluth was accepted with great reluctance by John R. O'Brien, the executive assistant who'd accompanied the walker for several miles back in Vermont, but as Mr. Mordenstahl had directed his staff never to mention the name of Pierce Davis in his presence again, Mr. O'Brien decided to dispose of Pierce by referring him to Roy Roach, so he gave Pierce the name of Roach's hotel and hung up.

Pierce was greatly relieved to know that Roach was there in London, too, for he remembered how friendly Roach had been in Pittsburgh. When he phoned the hotel, Roach's stenographer answered, but she was giggling so much that Pierce could barely understand her. Then Roach himself took the phone, breathing rather hard. He was delighted to hear from Pierce and commanded him to come to the hotel at once. After a brief negotiation (Pierce once again declined to use a taxi), it was agreed that Pierce would walk to the hotel, which wasn't far. Roach would meet him out in front.

When the public-relations man saw Pierce's filthy and woebegone condition, he hustled him around to a side entrance. "Pierce, you're looking a bit frazzled at the moment," he said, propelling the walker toward a service elevator, "but you're a sight for sore eyes, I can tell you, and we'll get you cleaned up in no time at all."

Pierce wouldn't enter the elevator.

"Pierce, I honor your principles as a dedicated walker and all that," exclaimed Roach, "but this thing isn't a wheeled vehicle and it doesn't go anywhere but straight up and straight down, so I can't see your objection to it."

Pierce replied that what Roach said was undoubtedly true, but just to be on the safe side, he'd climb the stairs.

Roach was aghast. "That's twelve flights, fella," he said, but Pierce insisted on using the stairs, so after tipping a bellboy ten shillings to walk up with him and see that he got to the right floor, Roach took the elevator alone.

In the suite Roach ordered a meal to be sent up, while Pierce took a shower. (The stenographer, whose services weren't needed any more that evening, picked up her things, including her douche bag, and departed.)

"Pierce," Roach announced, as the walker sat down hungrily to his supper, "I've got terrific news for you, fella, and in a word, you're back on the payroll—*my* payroll, Pierce, which means you'll be walking for none other than yours truly from here on in."

As Pierce glanced up in wonder from his plate, Roach proceeded briskly to explain that, since Bonaparte had been forced to give up world-walking for political reasons, he was now arranging new sponsorship on Pierce's behalf. "We'll make a million, Pierce," he concluded, with a snappy smile, "and I only hope that walking's still your bag."

"I'd like to do it, Mr. Roach," Pierce said, "but I don't think I can."

"Pierce, I don't blame you," Roach said. "After what you've been through, fella, Jesus Christ himself would want to quit, but I can promise you that things will be different from here on out with Roy Roach at the helm, and there'll be plenty of money and a roof over your head every night, and when it rains, not a step will you be forced to take; we'll play cards and go to the movies instead, provided the towns we're in have movies, and if they don't, well, they'll always have some female companionship, eh, Pierce, so I can assure you that when you walk for Roy Roach you'll think you're in Paradise itself, and the only danger and discomfort will be a potential dose of the clap, so I'll put some penicillin in the suit-case, right, fella?"

"That's not what I meant, Mr. Roach."

"Pierce, I was just joking," Roach declared, switch-ing tactics, "for I know you're a serious young man with ideals and lots of them, and what I really want to tell you is that this time you'll be walking as a symbol of America, with maybe a replica of Old Glory sewn on the back of that new walking jacket we'll order made up to your measurements tomorrow morning at one of the finest British tailors, just to make it absolutely clear to every-body in all the countries you pass through that if the world is going to be walked around for the very first time ever, by God it will be a fine young strong American boy who'll do it, and I can promise you one thing, and that is that in those places where Communist agitation has stirred up anti-American sentiments, I will personally arrange for police escort and protection, and maybe we can order another jacket with the Swede emblem for your use on such occasions."

"No, Mr. Roach, I wanted to say that I think the police are looking for me."

"Pierce, I'm sure that's a minor misunderstanding which can be cleared up in an instant," said Roach, who knew through his friend at the U.S. Embassy that Pierce was wanted for little more than his unpaid hospital bill up in Scotland. From the same source he also knew about Dr. Davis's stroke, but had decided not to mention it, as this distressing news might cause Pierce to go home.

"I don't know whether it's minor or not," Pierce went on. "I don't know what it is at all, but I've done something, that's for sure."

"Pierce, don't worry about it," Roach said.

"I can't help worrying, Mr. Roach. It's a strange thing, not to know what you've done that would set the police after you, but lots of strange things have happened to me since I started walking that wouldn't have happened if I hadn't, for there's a vast difference between people who walk and people who don't, in my opinion. For one thing, you see things when you walk that you wouldn't see otherwise. For example, have you ever seen a tree that walks, Mr. Roach?"

"Not lately, fella, and would you mind explaining what you mean?"

"When you walk, you go slow, Mr. Roach, and let's say you see a big tree in the distance. Well, every step you take changes your position with respect to that tree, so very gradually it gets a little bigger, and it moves off to one side or the other, depending on where it is, so pretty soon you get to believing that it's the tree that's doing the walking instead of you, and it's the kind of thing you don't have time to see if you drive by in a car."

"Fella, I understand what you mean, and I'm relieved to hear your explanation, for you had me wondering about your brains there for a minute."

"The hills walk the same way, Mr. Roach," continued Pierce, who was glad to have the opportunity to talk to a sympathetic listener about his walking experiences, "and sometimes when the sun hits them, boulders jump up like eyes opening or something, and the rivers, well, you can see them slowly twisting and shifting around like snakes, so when you're walking, you realize that all these things have a life of their own."

"Those are very poetic thoughts, Pierce, and it occurs to me that you could use a good night's rest, so I'll have them bring a cot in for you right away."

"The point is, Mr. Roach," Pierce went on eagerly,

"that a walker sees the land the way people saw it for the first time, and the way they saw it for most of history, too. Why do you think the Indians worshiped trees and mountains?"

"It was their kick, I guess," said Roach, eyeing Pierce doubtfully.

"They worshiped them because they saw that they moved, you see, and they figured there were spirits inside, that's why, and that's what I've seen, too, Mr. Roach. Oh, I don't mean I believe in spirits," Pierce said, noting the expression on Roach's face, "but maybe it's a mistake my trying to tell anyone about it who isn't a walker, too, for I guess you don't understand."

"Pierce, get it all off your chest, as it's wrong to keep stuff like that bottled up," said Roach with some foreboding.

"Well, you see, walking like I've done, Mr. Roach, I've seen sights that nobody else today can see, for you only see them if you're walking, so naturally I've thought about the same things that all the old dead walkers thought about when they walked, and so my thoughts have been ancient thoughts, Mr. Roach, for my world has been an ancient one, and who knows, maybe it's the real one after all?"

"Pierce, that's a tremendous concept, all right," said Roach, who was becoming more and more concerned, "but if you let loose any such notions to our sponsors, fella, they'll think you're an oddball, so my advice is forget it."

But Pierce wouldn't stop. "Listen, Mr. Roach," he said, in some excitement, "can you imagine all the millions and millions of walking men who did what I've done and thought what I'm thinking for all those centuries in the past? And yet today I'm the only one in the world, maybe, who can honestly say he's in touch with them by doing what they did, and that really sets me off from everybody else. And people feel that, Mr. Roach, and they don't like it."

Roach nodded, but uneasily, for his dismay was mounting with every word Pierce uttered.

"I mean, they sense that I can see what they can't see—the trees that walk and the hills that move—and they feel in their bones that they're out of touch with the earth, and that they've lost the vision of the world as their home which walking men had even before history began," Pierce declared earnestly, tapping Roach's knee for added emphasis, "so when I walk by, Mr. Roach, everybody suddenly gets a little homesick."

By this time Roach was beginning to fear that his hopes to profit from Pierce's walking were doomed, as he could hardly expect potential clients to sponsor anyone who might at any moment start spouting such stuff.

"Listen, Pierce," he said, pacing about the room and rubbing his plump little hands together, "you've been by yourself too much, fella, and while I admire and respect your thoughts and ideas, it's obvious that you need a change, so we won't even mention the subject of walking for a few days, and I here and now guarantee you, Pierce, that you're going to have the time of your life right here in the greatest city of them all, and you'll forget about those dead people you referred to, because I'm going to introduce you to some living people—and by people, I mean the kind of people who've got breasts and hips and thighs, fella, if you get my meaning, and they're here by the thousands just waiting for you, Pierce."

"Mr. Roach, I sure appreciate your consideration of me—"

"In a word, Pierce, you badly need a good lay."

"—but when I'm walking, I don't get bothered about women, and I've sometimes thought that walking the world is like having a woman in a way."

"Pierce, I thought I'd heard them all but this is a new one," said Roach, despondently.

"Anyway, I'd like to walk for you, Mr. Roach," Pierce added, "but I've got to clear up this business with the police first. That's what I hoped you'd help me find out about. But you don't have to wait around for me. There are lots of fellows who could walk for you."

"There's only one Pierce Davis, fella," said Roach, thinking of Pierce's clippings. Then he froze in place, his agile wits at work. "Pierce," he exclaimed, his voice cracking in agitation, "I won't rest until that cloud of doubt is lifted from your mind." He rushed over to the corner where the telephone was. "I happen to be acquainted with one of the top men at Scotland Yard, Pierce, and I can immediately clarify whether you're in dutch or not, so here goes." With one hand he kept the receiver pressed down as he pretended to place a call. Then he went through a long and involved imaginary conversation, at the end of which he turned sadly to Pierce. "Fella, I don't know exactly what you did, for they wouldn't tell me, but it's a serious matter, and the only thing for you to do is get out of the country fast."

Pierce was thunderstruck.

Roach hustled over and seized him by the shoulders. "Pierce, don't worry. Roy Roach is standing by to help you, and have you got your passport and any other documents? Hand them over, fella, for the first thing is to conceal your identity."

Pierce hastily gave Roach all his papers.

"That's it, Pierce," said Roach, examining the documents carefully. "Now listen, fella. I'm going out for a while to make the arrangements—and don't bother thanking me, as I wouldn't desert you in your hour of need—so don't answer the phone or the door and just lie low and trust old Roy."

By the following evening Roach was able to supply Pierce with a pair of second-hand boots that almost fit, a suit of patched but serviceable tweed, a few pounds in cash, and a forged Canadian passport issued to a nonexistent Pierre Delacroix. As he guided Pierce out of the hotel and into the dusky street outside, Roach provided a few last words of counsel. "Fella, you cross over to France as fast as you can and get down to Marseilles, where you can work your passage back home, and have no fear, I won't mention your real name to a living soul." With this, he shook Pierce's hand and for a few moments remained watching him hurry anxiously off. Then Roach turned in the opposite direction, hailed a taxi, and was driven to a theatrical casting agency to interview prospects.

It was little more than two weeks later that Roach, with a briefcase full of sponsor contracts, presented to the public a husky and amiable young fellow whom he was able to identify to the full satisfaction of anyone who cared to know as the famous American world-walker, Pierce Davis, and it was this same Pierce Davis that Roach launched on the European leg of his global journey, giving him a ceremonial sendoff from the steps of St. Paul's Cathedral (a departure thrice repeated for the benefit of advertising cameramen who wanted to be sure they got a proper shot of the distinctive rainwear which had been supplied to the walker by a well-known maker of such items).

*   *   *

Ever since his mid-June meeting with Pierce in Vermont, Mr. Mordenstahl had sensed himself in decline. He was beginning to bungle things. When quick decisions were called for, he sometimes faltered. When a calculated deferral of action was in order, he often brought matters perilously to a head. He was subject to odd moods of anger and depression. His suspicions of his potential rivals mounted to the point where he was afraid to leave Duluth lest he be ousted in his absence. Hence he postponed vital business trips, refused to send deputies in his stead, and only at the last moment himself departed, ill-prepared, to make hurried and usually disadvantageous deals and then fly back as soon as possible in a sweat to make sure there was no one seated behind his desk.

He was aware of his errors. He knew what he was doing wrong, and he knew he had better stop. But somehow he could not. A certain fatality had possessed him. The company itself was not doing badly. Its sales were above those of the previous quarter, and despite his fumblings, there were more foreign contracts than ever. However, these facts did not reassure him. The business might be prospering—yet Mr. Mordenstahl whispered to himself, "Expand or die," no longer, but rather, "Expand *and* die."

He expected disaster. He almost yearned for it. He still, irrationally, blamed the world-walk for his troubles, and he was not surprised when, after he had failed to halt Pierce, there followed Bonaparte's publicized imprisonment in South Africa, a matter which was the subject of a most uncomfortable half hour at the September meeting of the board of directors. Outwardly, Mr. Mordenstahl was aghast at his failure to deal effectively with his problems. Inwardly, he accepted them with the alienated calm of a man who, having taken a seat at a poker table to play a hand or two, discovers that he is being systematically fleeced by professional gamblers and yet cannot rise and leave but remains clutching his cards in a condition of psychic shock, only remotely aware of the fact that he is being ruined.

It was in the last week of September that his immediate and only superior, the president of the company, suggested that he take a vacation. Mr. Mordenstahl hastened to agree that he needed one, and he promised to arrange it without delay. Back in his own office, he was horrified. Yes, this was how it would end, he thought. First the proposed vacation, then there'd be a leave of absence—and after that he'd be pensioned off or kicked upstairs to be the vice-president of nothing.

He squirmed in his chair, fearful and humiliated. His mouth was dry. He wanted a drink, and he took one. On his desk, as a memento of his boyhood, was a handful of soil from his parents' farm—soil he himself had plowed, seeded, fed with manure and watered with his sweat. But it had been preserved in a transparent casing of poured plastic, and he could not, as he wished then to do, open it to refresh his senses with its earthy odor. "Am I finished?" he whispered. "Finished?" He began, pathetically, to attack the plastic with a letter-opener, a vain task. His hand slipped, and he cut his thumb. He cursed, dropped the letter-opener, saw a thin line of blood appear, and thrust the thumb into his mouth. It was comforting.

"Finished? . . . Nonsense!" He stood, resolute and angry. "I'm not finished yet!" And still, as he paced his office, sucking his thumb, he could not rid himself of the feeling that doom had entered into him, where it might not have troubled itself over a more cautious man. "Maybe I should have stayed on the farm," he thought. "A farm is all a man needs. A farm is world enough. . . ."

He wondered if he had not reached too far; perhaps he was being punished for his overweening ambitions. The very agility of mind and inventive energy that had hitherto distinguished his career might be turning against him now. He felt threatened by his own creations, as though all the millions of seeds sown in his name were thrusting forth vines to throttle him, and as though the countless acres of soil plowed at his behest were rolling mountainously in to bury him—yes, and as though the very tempo of his racing heart might be governed by the steps of the walker he'd so foolishly launched.

"Finished? Not on your life. I'm not finished." But his voice was uncertain, his eyes anxious. "All I need is a rest, and then I'll take charge again as before." He wasn't sure of that, though. He didn't seem to be sure of anything. It took him the better part of a day even to decide what he'd do on his vacation (he settled finally on fishing), although, oddly enough, he seemed from the very beginning to have known that he'd go to Iowa to do it.

Pierce reached the English Channel on October 10. He knew he couldn't walk to France, but he resolved to pace off the equivalent mileage on the deck of the ship as it steamed across, and thus keep his walking accounts balanced. This was no easy task, as the passage was rough and he at once became seasick. But he kept staggering wretchedly along the tilting, slippery deck for the duration of the trip; when the port of Calais was reached, the crew had to admonish him repeatedly to disembark, for he calculated that the ferry had gone faster than he had, so that while it had finished its voyage, he was still theoretically a couple of miles behind in the water, and had quite a few more deck circuits to do.

He didn't walk through France; he sneaked through. He couldn't believe that his fake identity had given him more than a few days' grace. The British, he was convinced, would soon be on his trail again, and they'd get the French authorities to help find him. So he did his walking mostly at night, and by day he kept a sharp lookout from the haystacks and hedges where he hid.

Pierce found that walking in France was a reckless and foolhardy thing to do, and that a man who voluntarily went about by foot in that country ought to be arrested for attempted suicide, for the French motorists seemed pledged to stamp out pedestrianism by running down and killing its practitioners. Pierce was nearly murdered several times in every mile he walked. Some drivers would cut their ignition systems and coast up silently behind him before launching their mad attack. Others would lie in wait at crossroads with engines idling at the ready, or would hide around corners, whimpering with berserk eagerness, and sometimes the drivers craftily worked in pairs, so that Pierce, leaping out of the way of one juggernaut, would find that he had dodged into the path of another, bearing joyfully down on him from the opposite direction. The fact that these fanatics often slaughtered each other seemed to make little difference; as long as their hoods and radiators were splattered with pedestrian gore, they died as proudly as Vikings.

What with his hair's-breadth escapes on the French highways and his stealthy nighttime walking, Pierce lost whatever intention he may have had of following Roach's advice and heading south to Marseilles. His only purpose was to get out of France alive. He thought he was heading east, toward Belgium, but in the darkness he frequently missed his turns, so he blundered about for quite some time in a southeasterly direction, and as his pace was slow anyway, he soon exhausted the modest funds Roach had given him. He was, in short, reduced to the status of a tramp. But when he stopped at sleek and prosperous Lorraine farms to beg a meal or at least a drink of water, the sight of him so infuriated the good people there that they drove him away with curses and threats and sometimes a stone or two, and once the dogs were loosed on him, requiring him to run several miles with these curs gnawing at his calves. He arrived at the German border gaunt from hunger, his clothing in tatters, and so demoralized that the toot of an automobile horn even at a distance would make him skip in alarm and stare wildly about, his facial muscles twitching.

His appearance rekindled old Franco-German rivalries, the French border guards being determined to get rid of such an unprepossessing tourist, the Germans being loath to accept him. Pierce, fearing that any prolonged delay would bring to light his real identity, left his forged Canadian passport in the hands of the guards, and as they passed it back and forth like a hot potato, each side unwilling to accept it, he slipped quietly off into the darkness and entered Germany on his own responsibility, without the benefit of any official permission whatever.

At the theatrical casting agency in London, Roy Roach had flipped through scores of photographs. From these, he had set aside a dozen or so. After interviewing the owners of these faces, he had finally chosen a husky young fellow with burnt-blond hair and protruding ears, who looked enough like Pierce Davis to be, if not a brother, at least a first cousin.

Roach's new walker was an American tennis bum named Ellsworth "Dusty" Lynes, one of those athletic drifters who exist at the margins of the sporting and entertainment world, always hoping for a bit of prize money or a film job, and in the meantime giving tennis lessons (or ski lessons, if they are ski bums), and providing escort services to ladies wealthy enough and needful enough to pay for them.

Roach didn't expect Lynes to walk around the world. Even if he'd harbored such an ambition, he would have abandoned it after the first meeting, for Lynes was obviously an indolent sort of fellow who wouldn't stoop to pick up a tennis ball unless a quarter were lying beside it. All Roach wanted him to do was to walk in Western Europe until the sponsor contracts ceased to bear fruit; then he and Roach would go their separate ways.

Lynes readily agreed to this modest plan. He had no interest in walking a step more than he had to. Nor did he object (as Pierce might well have objected) to the way in which Roach commercialized the walk. Lynes advertised not only the raincoat on his back but every other garment he wore (and some he didn't), and he was photographed at various later stops in the act of refreshing himself with a certain type of tea, obtaining energy from a celebrated candy bar, smoking cigars and cigarettes of well-known brands, pausing to rest on a special make of shooting stick, blowing his nose on a particular kind of disposable tissue, etc.

Roach was in high spirits. He was convinced that the real Pierce wouldn't turn up for months (if at all), by which time the bogus Pierce's walk would be finished. To calm the fears of the family back in Iowa, he thoughtfully dispatched a cablegram there reading RETURNING HOME IMMEDIATELY and signed PIERCE, the effect of which was to reassure Judge Davis and dissuade him from any notions he might have had of prosecuting more vigorously the search for his missing nephew.

"Dusty" Lynes (or Pierce Davis II, as he might be

called) left the steps of St. Paul's in the midmorning of October 24. The newspapers, viewing this venture as an advertising stunt, took only token notice of it. The walker was escorted by the Roach limousine as far as Greenwich, so that more pictures could be taken with the Royal Naval College in the background. Roach and the advertising photographers then drove on ahead to Rochester, some twenty miles distant, where hotel reservations for the night had been made. Pierce II had, of course, remained behind to walk, the assumption being that he would arrive in the late afternoon at the end of a brisk five-hour ramble. Roach was surprised, therefore, when Pierce II appeared in Rochester only two hours after he'd been left in Greenwich, a promptitude that caused Roach to take his protégé aside for a few words of pointed counsel.

Despite this advice, Pierce II continued, on the following days, to exhibit a most remarkable swiftness of foot. He traversed the twenty-five miles from Rochester to Canterbury in a mere hour and a half, a rate of progress that would have amazed even the old Canterbury pilgrims, who were used to miracles, while for the fifteen-mile stretch to Dover this modern Mercury required but fifty minutes. Nor did he slacken his pace in France, for, to cite but one example, he walked the fifty-odd miles from Beauvais to Versailles between two and four o'clock on the afternoon of October 28, a rate of some twenty-five miles per hour.

Far from being proud of this prodigy, Roach continued to manifest signs of annoyance and concern, an attitude which proved to be justified when, on November 3, a Paris newspaper published a series of photographs, supposedly taken outside the city of Orléans on the road south toward Bourges, showing Pierce Davis II approaching, entering, and being driven off in a little red British sports car operated by a young woman identified as Sally Summers, a California tennis player of minor note, who had in the past year been frequently seen making the rounds of tennis tourneys in Europe in the company of her co-national, Ellsworth "Dusty" Lynes.

Mr. Mordenstahl, having motored south ostensibly for a fishing trip (although the fishing would have been better in Minnesota), found himself, to his surprise, coming to a stop in the town of Spark, Iowa.

He'd had no conscious wish to go there. He certainly didn't want to see Pierce (although his animosity toward the walker had faded, as he was preoccupied by his own problems). Nor, had he wanted to see Pierce, would he have expected to find him there, for as far as he knew from the last reports he'd permitted to reach his ears, the crippled walker was still wandering somewhere in England. Indeed, Mr. Mordenstahl had no idea why he'd come to Spark at all, except that somehow he couldn't help it. "Here's where it all began," he thought as he sat bemusedly sipping coffee in Biedler's drugstore on Main Street, watching through the window the autumn leaves whirl about on the very spot, perhaps, where the first world-walking step had been taken.

After finishing his coffee, Mr. Mordenstahl looked up Pierce's address in the telephone directory and went there. He had never met Natalie and of course was unaware of the fact that the apartment had been rented to another family, and therefore he greatly alarmed Mrs. Fingerling by asking her, in a sympathetic and even lugubrious manner, if any word had been received concerning her missing husband. Once matters had been straightened out, Mr. Mordenstahl apologized, noted down Natalie's address in Clarion, and took his leave.

He remained in Spark the rest of the day, strolling about the town and striking up conversations with various citizens on the subject of Pierce Davis and the world-walk. He had supposed that Pierce would be a figure of some note in Spark because of his ambitious undertaking, but he learned otherwise. It was true that no one had a harsh word to say about Pierce, and that he seemed to be regarded as a decent fellow (although a disappointment to his poor stricken father), but these remarks had a dim and distant ring to them, as though Pierce had been absent for seven years instead of seven months.

This in itself did not trouble Mr. Mordenstahl, for he had no reason to suppose that Pierce's personality would have made a permanent dent in the communal consciousness. However, he was surprised and perturbed and finally made somewhat angry by the fact that the world-walk seemed to mean so little to these people. Few of them remembered anything at all about why Pierce had left town, and even these few got the reason wrong. George Gorman, the plumber, said Pierce had gone on the road as a traveling salesman. Mr. Marlin, the town clerk, recalled that Pierce had set off walking, but he was certain it was on some surveying job for the state highway department, while Grady L. Suits, who ran the hardware store, informed Mr. Mordenstahl that Pierce had gone camping on the Little Sioux River and was presently employed in a bottling plant in Council Bluffs. Even Judge Davis, visited briefly by Mr. Mordenstahl in mid-afternoon at the courthouse, was discouraging on this point, for he kept referring to Pierce's effort as "a hiking trip," and when Mr. Mordenstahl ventured to expand this definition to its proper global scope, the judge looked at him disparagingly, as though he were a badly drawn will, and made no comment.

"It isn't fair," Mr. Mordenstahl said to himself, "it isn't right." He felt personally rebuffed and reproached. True, there'd been little publicity on the world-walk, but here in the walker's own hometown, one had the right to expect that people would remember what Pierce had set out to do, and that they'd take a little bit of pride in it. "He walked blisters on his feet for nothing," thought Mr. Mordenstahl. "He broke his leg in vain." He was sorry for Pierce and also for himself. "The world-walk was a failure," he admitted, "but there was something fine about it anyhow. Even failure ought to be remembered, if it's failure in a cause worth failing for." Icarus, he knew, had fallen gloriously into legend when the sun melted his waxen wings, yet here in Spark not so much as a cat's shadow remained of the world-walk, similarly noble, similarly doomed. (Himself he likened to Icarus; Pierce was the faulty pair of wings.)

"Men must have recognition," thought Mr. Mordenstahl. Without it, he reflected, their identities wither, they crumble into dust, and they might just as well not have lived at all. So he was greatly downcast to realize that the seed of his mind had amounted to nothing, just as the real seeds he had caused to be planted had ripened to wheat which people ate not knowing whence it came, nor caring. What he had done was, so to speak, flushed blindly through their bowels.

Pierce's fate and his own thus became somewhat entangled in his mind, and he began to regard Pierce simply as an aspect of the world-walk idea. And since this idea, having been so easily forgotten, might never have existed, likewise it seemed to Mr. Mordenstahl that

Pierce's reality was in doubt. It was as though he had disputed, on that sunlit Vermont road, with a ghost whose steps had left no trace.

"It isn't fair," he kept muttering. "It isn't right." In his wanderings about town, he returned from time to time to the Main Street intersection where beneath the spiraling leaves there should have been a little bronze plaque, but wasn't.

The only person who gave Mr. Mordenstahl any satisfaction that day was the last one he saw before his departure—Mrs. Muncie, the retired schoolteacher who lived at the edge of town. "Pierce Davis?" she remarked, cocking her head at her visitor. "Of course I remember. He set off last March seventeenth to walk around the world, that's what he did."

Mr. Mordenstahl sighed in gratitude.

"I told him not to," Mrs. Muncie continued briskly, "but he went on anyway. He's a plain country fool, that boy, and twice a fool to try a thing like that." Mr. Mordenstahl began mildly to protest this harsh judgment, but something in Mrs. Muncie's eye gave him to understand that she would not shrink from delivering a similar verdict on him, so he merely thanked her for her trouble, and then obliged her by carrying her garbage out to the road as he left.

Pierce Davis I was at this time creeping through Germany with the same nocturnal stealth he'd used in France, and for similar reasons. He feared every man and car he saw—and in the latter case with justification, for German drivers were fully as dangerous as the French, the only difference being that whereas the French had tried to murder him out of malice, the Germans did it on principle.

Having no money and no papers, Pierce could neither pay for his food nor work for it, and so he begged and thieved and went hungry in equal proportions until November 17, when he was placed under arrest as a vagabond by two patrolmen in the ancient city of Nuremberg. As often happens with captured fugitives, Pierce was pathetically grateful to be released from the wretchedness and uncertainty of a life in flight. He burst into tears and tried to shake the hands of his benefactors. But when they marched him to their patrol car, his old instincts surged up. Weak as he was, he resisted their efforts to get him to enter it. Every time they stuffed him in, he managed to get at least a leg or an arm back out, so that at length one of them tapped him on the skull with a pacifying instrument and he was transported unconscious to the stationhouse.

Pierce was a balky prisoner. He wouldn't say a word in response to questions (which he didn't understand anyway, for he knew no German), and as he had no documents, the police were at a loss to know who he was. His fingerprints, circulated as a matter of routine, produced no information (except in the negative sense that he was not known to be a crook), and his clothing was so soiled and shredded that its origin could only be guessed at. Moreover, Pierce refused to walk, on the supposition that this telltale activity might identify him at once. He was reluctant even to stand.

After a few days of this the police judged that he was a mental defective, and turned him over to the medical authorities (since he wouldn't take so much as a step on his own, he was trundled to the detention center in a wheelchair, pushed by a fuming and resentful assistant jailer). The doctors treated Pierce to a full physical examination, and then they sent him along to the psychiatrists.

It should be noted that, so highly advanced is the art of psychoinvestigation in Germany, the subject's cooperation is no longer considered necessary. In fact, the more modern practitioners, understandably sick and tired of having to listen to ill-organized neurotic ramblings, insist that patients maintain a rigid silence during analysis, so as not to hinder the business at hand. For this reason, Pierce's refusal to speak, far from being a handicap to German science, was positively welcomed by the experts, who happily set to work on him at once, subjecting him to a succession of tests and cures, including immersion in frigid baths, electroshock therapy, hypnosis, brainwave charting of his dreams, etc., and altogether every technique short of outright dissection.

When poor Pierce could stand no more, he broke down. "I give up," he whimpered one day as he lay wrapped in an ice-cold sheet while two bearded professors flashed photos of nudes on a screen before him, meticulously noting the varying dilations of his pupils. "I'll confess the whole thing," he gasped, much to the annoyance of the psychiatrists, who tried to pretend he hadn't spoken at all. "I didn't realize what my crime was," he moaned, shuddering with the cold, "but I've figured it out now, and I'll make my confession." He was so insistent that the two psychiatrists (whose English was considerably more polished than Pierce's) reluctantly concluded that they'd have to listen to him.

"Very well," said one of them. "What's your crime, then?"

"It's pretty bad, doctor, and in fact I'll bet you've never heard of it before," said Pierce, sitting up on the examining table and trying to massage warmth into his frosty limbs, "and I hardly know how to mention it, really."

"Go ahead," said the first psychiatrist, resigning himself to being bored by another windy confession. "It's something sexual, I suppose."

"Well, you might say there's a bit of sex in it," said Pierce, blushing despite his chill.

"You did something nasty, did you?"

"Nasty's not the word for it, doctor."

"Been diddling around in the family circle, eh? Come, come, my boy," urged the psychiatrist. "Out with it. You can't surprise us. We've heard everything here."

"Well, it's walking," said Pierce.

"Walking?"

"That's right, doctor. I'm a walker."

The two psychiatrists glanced at each other.

"I'd be ashamed to tell you how much walking I've done," Pierce went on, "for you wouldn't believe it, and I don't know whether that's a hanging matter in Germany, but if it is, get the rope ready."

"You say you're a walker?" asked the second psychiatrist, uncertainly.

"That's what I am, gentlemen," said Pierce, "and I feel better already having admitted it, even though I can tell you're both shocked by the news."

The psychiatrists once more exchanged glances.

"I'm a hardened case," Pierce continued, anxious not to spare himself. "They've tried to reform me a dozen times and more, but I just went on and did it again, and if you let me go this minute, I'd go walking all the same, so you see it's hopeless and I can't help it."

"Are you referring to ordinary walking?" asked the first psychiatrist. He rose from his chair and walked across the room. "Like that, do you mean?"

"Like that, doctor," Pierce replied. "Oh, a little of it

can be tolerated, I guess. A man can walk a couple of blocks to buy a newspaper without getting arrested, maybe, just like he can go into a bar for a drink or two. But suppose that same fellow drinks all day and all night right out in the open where everybody can see him? Well, that's an offense to public decency, so they arrest him and put him in jail. It's the same with walking, except walking's worse. A lot of men get drunk, but nobody walks— nobody walks like I walk, I mean—so it's a crime without parallel, you might say."

"What makes you think walking is a crime?" asked the second psychiatrist.

"It's obvious," said Pierce earnestly. "If a man does something nobody else does, and if people don't like seeing him do it, then it'll be made a crime against society sooner or later, even if it doesn't actually hurt anybody. For example," he went on, scratching the itchy places where they'd put electrodes on him the day before, "suppose you liked to carry a pair of stuffed owls around with you wherever you went, on buses and in elevators and stores? Well, people would begin avoiding you and giving you dirty looks, and some of them would warn you not to, but if you kept on carrying those two stuffed owls around, in defiance of public opinion, you'd find yourself behind bars quick enough, I can tell you. And that's been my experience walking."

Then Pierce told the psychiatrists about the state trooper in Iowa, who'd gotten angry at the very idea that he wanted to set foot on the superhighway, and he told them about the police in Indiana who'd arrested him for vagrancy, just because he'd been walking, and then he went on to explain that he'd had to flee England under an assumed name, for Scotland Yard itself was after him there, seeking to put an end to his walking, and finally, he reported the terrors he'd suffered on the Continent, where the French and German motorists had expressed the general antagonism toward walking by attempting to flatten him under their wheels.

"So you can see, gentlemen," he said in conclusion, "that I'm in a terrible fix, because while society is determined not to let me walk, I've got a compulsion to do it." The recital of his walking troubles had stirred his sense of grievance, and he gave physical vent to his feelings by pacing about the room. "I can't say I'm ashamed of it, for I'm not," he told his two listeners. "It doesn't hurt a soul in the world, so why don't people stop persecuting me and let me alone to do it? But I don't care, gentlemen. I've got one of those uncontrollable desires you write books about, and in my case it's walking. If you cut off my legs, I'd do it on my hands," he went on defiantly, "and if you chopped those off, too," he added, while the psychiatrists toyed uneasily with their beards and kept an eye on the alarm buzzer, "I'd manage to roll myself along like a ball, because when a man gets himself mixed up with something like walking that works into his skin and won't let him alone, then he'll do it no matter what." Pierce was striding about the examination room with one length of the cold sheet flung over his shoulder, toga-style. "You can lock me back up if you want to," he declared, "but it won't do you any good, for I'll keep going anyhow!"

Which prediction proved to be true, for although Pierce was returned to his cell, having been judged a paranoid personality, possibly violent, suffering from a peculiar variation of the common foot fetish, he took advantage of the first opportunity that came his way, and in the late afternoon of December 4 made his escape.

It had been snowing heavily since noon that day,

which had delayed but had not prevented an official tour of inspection on the part of a parliamentary committee from the Bundestag. This visit naturally preoccupied the staff of the detention center, and while it was in progress, the normal schedule of security checks could not be followed. All prisoners were in their cells, however, and all the cells were locked, so that not even a mouse could get out, if mice had been permitted in such institutions, which they were not.

The parliamentary committee (consisting of three men and two women) arrived, went the rounds, listened to the explanations of the doctors, examined the equipment, peered at a sample prisoner or two, asked questions, etc., and then, after resuming heavy outer garments against the whirling blizzard outside, departed. During this time, the group remained together with one single exception, that being just at the end, when one of the women, Frau Hoffmann (a Christian Democrat of Wagnerian dimensions), excused herself for personal reasons, and although her absence was a protracted one, her colleagues were not concerned, as they were familiar with the size of the meals that this good woman was accustomed to consume. Still, they were already late, and so, when they perceived her approaching along the hall, they wasted no time in doorway discussion, but hastened out to their limousine to be driven to the railroad station.

It was later remembered that Frau Hoffmann seemed even more sullen than usual in the car, that she hunched herself deep in her coat and scarf in one corner and kept blowing her nose in her handkerchief, saying not a word to anyone. At the station, as she clambered onto the train with the others and was not observed getting off, her companions assumed for some time that she was safely aboard. Subsequently, at about the same time that it was discovered that she was not on the train at all (a search of the conveniences having been made with the assistance of the conductor), Frau Hoffmann herself, stripped to her corset, was located on the floor of the laundry closet attached to the visitors' bathroom of the detention center back in Nuremberg, her mouth gagged with one towel, her hands and feet tied with two others, and as the trousers and shoes of the English-speaking madman were found beside the unfortunate lawmaker, and as his cell was empty (the lock having been crudely but effectively picked from the inside), with the prisoner himself nowhere present, one can only conclude that Pierce Davis had seized what chance had so bizarrely offered him, and had resumed his walk around the world in the guise of a modern Valkyrie.

At approximately the same time that Pierce Davis was creeping through the snowdrifts behind the railroad station in Nuremberg, West Germany, improbably but effectively clothed in the ample garments of Frau Hoffmann, the other Pierce Davis was bringing his brief career to a close.

The public exposure of his walker as a rider had greatly worried Roy Roach. But his luck held fast. The revelation of the Paris newspaper did not come to the attention of his major sponsors (the only company to cancel its contract was a minor producer of foot salve, which had, by that time, already paid half the stipulated amount), so that after upbraiding and threatening Pierce II in a stormy meeting at Bourges, Roach directed his star to proceed on the agreed route, but at a more plausible pace.

Now, there was a streak of impishness in Pierce II which the original Pierce never had, and in fact Pierce II was something of a wiseacre and a smart-aleck, as well as being lazy, and, as Roach commented later, "a good-for-nothing bum." If Roach wanted him to walk, very well, he'd walk. From Bourges onward (until he got bored with the whole thing), Pierce II exhibited none of the hotfooted haste he'd shown before. On the contrary, he crept at a snail's pace, he dawdled, he delayed. Schoolboys trudging reluctantly toward their schools passed him like whippets, and arthritic old-timers overtook him with ease. For Pierce II at this time ten miles a day was a stupendous achievement; for the seventy miles from Bourges to Moulins he required no fewer than seventeen days.

From time to time Roach's limousine would roar into sight from the direction of one of the châteaux where the walker was supposed to have appeared for photographic purposes, and Roach's flaming face would be thrust out of a window.

"Walk faster!"

"I can't. My feet hurt."

"Hop in, then, dammit. I can't keep those photographers there all afternoon."

"What—ride in a *car*? You want me to *cheat*? *Me*?"

Sometimes, in order to meet commercial deadlines, Roach had to ferry the photographers back to the spot where his laggard walker strolled, so that certain products held up by Pierce II for the cameras were shown with backgrounds not of splendid Renaissance constructions but of simple fields and humble barns.

Infuriating Roach was not Pierce II's only pastime. He took the opportunity to sample the wines of the area, and in fact he often did more than sample them, and was observed quite frequently reeling and staggering on his way, a bottle in his hand, bellowing old college songs over the French countryside. On two occasions posed photographs were rejected because of a slack and foolish expression on the walker's face.

When the obliging Miss Sally Summers appeared, as she did several times, Pierce II indulged in pursuits less dangerous to his liver, one of these being tennis. Miss Summers would park her little red car in a field, and, using the car itself as an impromptu net, the two of them would volley as keenly as the uneven ground would permit, often drawing quite a collection of rustic onlookers (who were attracted chiefly, one may conjecture, by Miss Summers, who was known in the tennis world less for her forehand than for her backside, i.e., she was celebrated for her daring court attire, and was the first to proclaim by personal example public support for "topless" tennis).

However, the attention span of Pierce Davis II and his amiable consort was not great, and they soon grew tired of rural pleasures. One early December afternoon when the exasperated Roach made yet another limousine expedition to locate his slowpoke model, Pierce II was nowhere on the assigned highway or on any of the adjoining roads, neither was he in the fields nor was he found (as he had once been found) in vinous slumber in a ditch. Through an interpreter, Roach was informed in a nearby village that a little red sports car of British make had passed by an hour earlier going south at high speed, and that from this vehicle, jarred loose by the bumps and jolts of the cobbled street, there had popped out, as a sort of souvenir of the abbreviated world-walk of Pierce Davis II, one fuzzy grass-stained tennis ball.

"Your husband is a dedicated man," Mr. Mordenstahl said to Natalie.

"Pierce always wanted to do something important," Natalie responded.

The two of them were sitting in the parlor of Natalie's parents' home in Clarion, where Mr. Mordenstahl had come calling on his way back to Minnesota. On the mantel stood a photograph of the world-walker, looking uncommonly intelligent.

"I admire his conviction," said Mr. Mordenstahl.

"Spark was too small for him," said Natalie.

"He wouldn't stop walking."

"He had to go and try it."

They had readily fallen into the past tense, as though Pierce were dead, and what they said about him collided only by accident with the truth, for they were talking not so much of Pierce as of themselves.

"He wanted to make a lasting imprint," said Mr. Mordenstahl.

"He needed to develop his capacities," said Natalie.

"He had ideas and energy!"

"He was determined to be free."

"You don't find that spirit nowadays," said Mr. Mordenstahl.

"He went after what he had to have," said Natalie.

Thus Mr. Mordenstahl and Natalie were, unaware, murdering whatever was left of the memory of the real Pierce. It was there, in the Leonard family parlor in the town of Clarion, that the poor fellow was nailed to the cross so that his very substance could drip out of him, and his empty skin could be stuffed with other people's hopes and desires. That is the way public heroes are made, though. Pierce himself, had he known, probably wouldn't have complained.

"There must be recognition," declared Mr. Mordenstahl, flushing at the thought of the injustices done to him. He envisioned a marble monument on which his own name would appear in letters slightly smaller (or maybe no smaller at all) than those used for Pierce's. At the unveiling he would make a speech. He began, in his mind, to compose it. *Ladies and gentlemen, it is my privilege here today to speak to you about a man who set forth in this world, alone, unknown, and to all appearances ordinary. . . .*

He hesitated, and then revised this to: *Ladies and gentlemen, once in every generation there appears in America a man who. . . .*

And Natalie, who also fell into silence, thought: *He won't come back. Heroes don't come back.*

Ladies and gentlemen, once in a hundred years there bursts onto the stage of world events. . . .

They glanced into each other's eyes, and for an instant they realized what they were doing—but only for an instant.

"It was an honor to have known him," said Mr. Mordenstahl.

"He was a good man," said Natalie.

"His achievement must be recognized publicly."

"It really should be."

"I won't rest until it is," vowed Mr. Mordenstahl, with a paternal smile—and thus modestly was laid the foundation for what later became the effort to enshrine Pierce Davis in the pantheon of Iowa heroes, alongside such notable sons of the Hawkeye State as Herbert Hoover, the Ringling Brothers, and Maytag, the washing-machine king.

During the three-month period from December to March, Pierce Davis I walked from southern Germany through Austria and Yugoslavia to northern Greece, a distance of some thousand miles, mostly through mountains which were heavy with snow and bitterly cold. How he survived this arduous winter journey (which apparently included brief excursions into Hungary, Rumania, and Bulgaria as well), he did not explain later in detail—which is understandable enough, not only because his subsequent long illness undoubtedly washed much of it from his memory, but because the way of life he had been forced to adopt was one he took no pride in.

At the outset Pierce's position was unenviable. He knew that the Nuremberg authorities would shortly discover Frau Hoffmann, and that they would immediately begin searching for a hulking transvestite last seen in the vicinity of the railroad station. He needed to resume male attire right away, and then to make his departure from the German Federal Republic, or at least to find some refuge where he would be temporarily safe.

His handicaps were extraordinary, however. He had no documents (except for a Bundestag member's parliamentary pass), nor had he any money apart from the few marks which Frau Hoffmann kept in her purse along with some bonbons, breath sweeteners, and tweezers. He knew not a word of German, he had not the vaguest idea of where to direct his steps to seek help, and in appearance, he was, to say the least, a most conspicuous figure, bound to attract attention wherever he went.

In the short run Pierce's prospects were dim, nor in the long run were they much better, for, as both a foreigner and a fugitive from justice, he could not hope to provide for his needs by any legitimate economic activity. At the same time he did have one considerable asset, Frau Hoffmann's fur coat, which he was able to sell the very evening of his escape.

Drawn by its maze of crooked streets and dingy buildings, Pierce made his way into the most disreputable quarter of the city. There he readily came to the attention of a brisk little multilingual pimp who, out of curiosity and an instinct for business, followed him as he lurched along in the snow in Frau Hoffmann's galoshes. On hearing this furred, ungainly lady mutter curses in English, the pimp assumed that she might well be nothing less than a British peeress in search of some exquisite and therefore expensive form of pleasure, and so he lost no time in introducing himself. He was not disappointed when he learned that Pierce wanted not to buy but to sell, for the fur was a costly one, and the pimp shrewdly judged that the supposed noblewoman was in no position to drive a decent bargain.

Pierce undoubtedly obtained not the twentieth part of the value of the coat. Still, his immediate requirements were satisfied, for he emerged from the transaction with a man's suit on his back, a pair of worn but sturdy boots on his feet, and a modest amount of money in his pocket.

Later he met his recurrent needs for cash by acting, in his words, as a "commercial representative" who provided occasional "messenger services." He was unwilling to define his activities more explicitly, but what this work amounted to is not too troublesome to figure out.

Despite the growth of the European Economic Community, with the lowering or abolition of customs barriers, there still is international trade in a number of items, the profits of which are conditioned on the avoidance of vexatious import duties. In such commerce, transportation is the nub of the matter. Where border guards and customs inspectors cannot be bribed or deceived, they must be circumvented, and so the merchandise is floated in by sea or parachuted by air, run in strapped to the bellies of dogs, flown in by homing pigeons, catapulted by slings, fired by cannons, or, most commonly, carried in by hardy hikers who cross in rugged terrain that is not heavily patrolled. The seasonal snowdrifts that forbid mountain passes to the ordinary smuggler would hardly have daunted a man who had traversed Britain despite a broken leg and had endured the thousand tweaks and goosings of a German medical inquiry, nor would the wading of an icy border stream or two have troubled a walker who would have crossed the very bed of the Atlantic had the technical means available so permitted. If Austrian merchants wished to furnish Yugoslavian clients with relatively inexpensive cigarette lighters, or if some Yugoslavian entrepreneurs wanted to bestow Swiss watches on their Bulgarian cousins, in exchange for herbal extracts of Oriental provenance, Pierce could well have assisted them in his zigzag winter wanderings, and those who may be inclined to criticize him for doing a bit of underworld walking at this point might remember that no less a traveler than Marco Polo also paid his way east by trade, and his achievement was in no wise tarnished by that fact.

Pierce's winter trek through southeastern Europe came to an end on March 5 as he was passing through the Rhodope Mountains in northern Greece, just below the Bulgarian border.

He himself was ignorant of his location. There'd been a track through the mountains, but he'd strayed from it somewhere, or it had ended. Far below he could see valleys, although he couldn't seem to find a way to go down to them, for the mist kept rising in his way. Sometimes it hung about him thickly, making him stumble in the gloom. Sometimes it glittered like a veil of suns, and he was blinded.

It was warmer. The snows were melting. He heard the occasional hushed booming of avalanches, and he feared that one would rush down to drown him. He was drowning anyway, though, for the fever was working in him. He was climbing as the fever climbed, and descending as it receded. It scrambled his senses; he heard the mist and saw the cry of snowslide, and the mountains became deserts, or seas, or they fell away to nothing and left him walking chasms, or they reared up to enclose him within a world of rock, where each step cost him centuries.

He kept falling. He'd get to his feet and go on a few steps, and then he'd slip and fall again. For a time this annoyed him, for despite the fever, he could feel the pain of cuts on his hands and face, and besides, he knew it would take him a very long time indeed to walk around the world that way. And then he found it funny and began laughing, and even when he didn't fall he managed to make himself fall; it occurred to him that perhaps this was, after all, the best method of traveling, as it broke the monotony.

The last time he fell, he fell quite a long way. He went rolling and tumbling down a slope, picking up the damp heavy snow as he went, so that when he finally stopped, he was more snow than man. Opening his eyes (for he'd taken a short nap while he'd fallen) he saw

137

through his dizziness a comical white animal face peering down at him. It baaed at him, and he baaed back. He heard a man's voice calling to him, but he couldn't understand the words. He tried to raise his head to see who it was, but he couldn't, so he simply said: "I'm Pierce Davis. Glad to meet you," and lost consciousness.

With considerable difficulty, the goatherd who found him lying there was able to carry him down from the heights to the nearest village, where there were people to take care of him, and it seemed at first that he wouldn't trouble them more than a day or two before dying.

It was in Greece that Pierce, in a manner of speaking, fell in love. How this came about can be explained partly in world-walking terms, for with the exception of his sojourns in Aberdeen and Nuremberg, this was the first real pause he'd made in his travels since Binghamton, New York, where, through his courtship of the coffeeshop waitress, Martha, he had sensed that walking was not unrelated to sexual expression, inasmuch as when he didn't walk, he got horny. Sometimes, in fact, he thought of sexual relations as horizontal walking, in the course of which the two partners sought to walk into each other, but he didn't care to pursue this line of reasoning very far, as it implied that walking alone, as he did, was a kind of masturbation, which he'd been taught to regard as an unhealthy activity.

In Greece the object of Pierce's interest was his nurse. At first she was no more than a shadow that roamed through the field of his fever. Then, progressively, she became a pair of hands, a supporting arm, a distinctive but not unpleasant earthy odor which he missed when it was absent, and finally, as the fever fell away altogether, he was able to see her in totality as a dark, strong woman of about his own age, with a mournful expression and a quiet step. Her name was Daphne, and he judged that she was a widow, for in both manner and attire she resembled the village housewives rather than the unmarried girls, and yet she evidently had no husband.

In the house where Pierce stayed a couple of rooms had been set aside as a communal clinic where sick persons without families could remain until they recovered or died. The patients were mostly herdsmen, and during his convalescence, Pierce shared his quarters with a succession of these rustics, who imparted powerful intimations of goat to the place. A doctor arrived each week from the valley below, but he was principally a dealer in commodities. He spent more time negotiating purchases of goats and wine than he did examining patients. Anyone who had to have a leg amputated or a broken limb reset was loaded into the back of the doctor's little truck with his acquisitions to be taken down into the valley.

When he felt better, Pierce ventured outside to take stock of his surroundings. The sun was hot, for it was now mid-May, and the huddled huts of the village were so white against the blue noon sky that it hurt his eyes to look at them. The mountains were bare. There were no trees to speak of, except for certain gnarled and desperate-looking ones which he guessed bore olives, although they bore nothing then. The soil, where there was soil, was thin. He knew that the people of the village had a struggle to wring a living from such a meager landscape, but when he tried to pay for his food and care (his capital consisting of an array of Swiss watches strapped from the wrist to the elbow of his right arm), his offer was refused by everybody in the house, these being Daphne and her relatives, including several rather hard-faced but courteous men.

Pierce's gratitude had from the first been centered on the figure of his nurse, who after all had virtually prevented the very life from leaking out of him. In time this sentiment was overtaken and submerged by the flow of an emotion that rose with the return of his strength but which Pierce, in his simplicity, supposed was merely the return of his will to walk. He became restless and moody. Sometimes he went out with the men of the house to work in the vineyards, and sometimes he stayed in his room all day or sat immobile in the sun outside watching the village children play.

As frequently happens in such cases, the true nature of his feelings was disclosed to him with the assistance of the lady concerned. One evening after supper he returned to his room to find her tidying up there. He began helping her in these labors, during which their hands made contact more than once, evidently by accident, and when in some mysterious fashion the candle got knocked over and extinguished, their gropings about in the darkness kindled a different sort of flame entirely. In short, one thing led to another, and what Pierce had failed to carry out with the waitress Martha he bountifully succeeded in doing with the nurse Daphne.

Pierce awoke the following morning eager to renew and expand the experience. But he found that matters had changed. Daphne no longer presented herself to perform any services, nursing or otherwise, and her attitude indicated that it would be highly improper for her to maintain any close contact with him. At the same time the manner of the other members of the household likewise underwent an alteration, and Pierce found himself to be the object of a reserved and measuring judgment, chiefly on the part of the men. Pierce didn't notice this for a while, however. His perceptions were too hotly focused on Daphne. At night he'd wake flushed with yearning, and by day the sight of her even at some distance would make him perspire. She passed him by with averted eyes, thus managing to convey to him the idea that he was uppermost in her thoughts, too, which inspired a greater devotion on his part, and altogether he mooned about like a lovesick schoolboy.

He was troubled about how matters were to be resolved. As time went on it became clearer to him that such affairs were not left solely to the discretion of the two principals, but concerned the family, which in practice meant the entire village, as everyone seemed to be related to everyone else; his intentions were therefore of public importance, a proper subject to be reviewed by every soul in the place. If at first Pierce had imagined that he and Daphne could slip off to some remote cabin for a joyful little weekend, he now saw that such a solution was unthinkable, for the general attitude, silently conveyed by brooding, watchful faces, informed him that a man's desire for a woman was held to be a weighty business indeed.

Pierce's passion, far from being diminished by all this gravity, grew stronger. The very air of the village seemed charged with what was stirring in him. Daphne herself, withdrawn into her family, became the more desirable as she was less visible. The force of the community's concentration on the matter recreated her, in Pierce's imagination, as the essence of female power, and thus the whole affair became enlarged and elevated. Poor Pierce, having only just emerged from the private fires of his fever, now was publicly roasting in his sexuality.

"I guess I could settle down here, all right," he'd mutter to himself. "I'd have to stop walking, it's true, for I couldn't expect her to go with me, but it isn't such a bad life they've got here, and I wouldn't be lonely any more." And even as he said it, he had the impression that he had already settled down in the village, that he had given up walking forever, and that he was simply following a course which had been decided on some time earlier, by whom he wasn't sure.

The problem burdened him. He felt guilty, but he wasn't sure why. "I'm married already," he thought, but this fact seemed to matter little. He knew Natalie didn't care. Why should he? He did care, though; not so much about Natalie as about something else he couldn't quite define.

He no longer went off with the men to work in the vineyards. Instead, he sat in his room to avoid the searching glances he encountered everywhere outside, yet this didn't ease him, for he was at the mercy of his own thoughts still. "I'm married already," he kept thinking, but he began to suspect that the woman he was betraying was the one he'd known only in his dreams, where she'd hauled him to his feet once before to set him on his way again. That was his marriage, then. He'd bound himself to her, and if in dedicating himself to something that existed only in his imagination he was as big a fool as any man who wore himself out for the sake of some notion or other that took hold in his mind, he was nonetheless wedded, sworn, and pledged.

He knew he hadn't really stopped walking then. No, he'd walk some more. That thought brought him alertly to his feet, and he went out strolling through the village. "I was sick, that's all," he thought. "I was sick and I was tired, but I'm not any more." For the first time in weeks he felt lighthearted. His legs tingled, as though urging him to get them busy walking again, and then he did what he hadn't done for so long he could barely remember the last time—he laughed.

Pierce's laughter rang along between the tiny houses as though it were a public announcement of his renewed intentions to go walking off. It brought women to the windows and children running outdoors, and when the men returned from the fields, the laughter seemed still to be echoing in the village, and they knew what it meant. The emotional atmosphere got dark at once. The glances Pierce received were sterner than before; he knew that he was being harshly judged and generally condemned.

"Well, maybe I deserve it, even though she sort of led me on," he reflected, "so now the only thing to do is apologize and be on my way." He renewed his earlier attempts to pay the family for his care with Swiss watches, but his offer was rejected with less courtesy. Gazing from one severe male face to another, Pierce began to wonder whether the real cost of his treatment wouldn't prove to be a good deal higher than a few watches, for, as these people had certainly saved his skin, they might consider that it belonged to them. This thought worried him, for soon there were unmistakable indications of their proprietary attitude, the chief of these being the fact that whenever he sauntered off from the house, he found himself accompanied by two or three of Daphne's relatives, who did not particularly bother to conceal the knives that hung from their belts. At the same time, he was alarmed to notice that the women of the house were busily engaged with their needles, creating what he feared was a trousseau, so he decided that as explanations were impossible, he wouldn't waste time trying to provide them, and one morning just before dawn, he left two watches under his pillow, eased himself out through a window, and departed the village on tiptoe, hoping that the dogs wouldn't bark.

He hadn't left unobserved. The first time he stopped to rest, he saw not one hundred yards behind him on the road the swiftly advancing figure of one of Daphne's brothers. "He isn't coming after me to give me back my watches, that's for sure," thought Pierce, and he hastily got up and went on his way. Whenever he glanced back, which was often, he saw his pursuer with a glint of metal winking at his waist in the sunlight, but try as he might, Pierce couldn't lengthen the distance that separated them, for his legs had been too long unaccustomed to hard walking, and it was all he could do to keep from losing ground.

"Maybe he's just going to the nearest town to do some shopping," Pierce thought, but they passed through two towns amply equipped with stores, and Daphne's brother displayed no interest in any of them.

It occurred to Pierce that the fellow might hail a policeman to arrest him for breach of promise (although no promise had been made), and then he guessed that in Greece, domestic matters were probably settled by the family itself, without reference to public authorities, which thought didn't cheer him, for he strongly suspected that the kind of settlement the brother had in mind would be both quick and permanent. "They sure are touchy about their women here," he grumbled as he labored along the stony road, "and for my part, I didn't get anything out of it except that one time, so I'll get my throat cut mostly for daydreams."

He wondered whether he might not appeal to the police for protection himself, which, however, caused him uneasily to reflect on his situation, for he didn't have any papers whatever, and he wouldn't be able to account for his remaining Swiss watches properly; besides, for all he knew, there might be a law in Greece which penalized people for making love to widows.

He hoped that the brother would get tired and quit, or at least stop for a meal, but the man kept marching grimly after him, so Pierce had to keep going, and the two of them skipped breakfast and lunch as well. Once the brother made an unexpected dash forward, closing the gap to fifty paces before Pierce chanced to glance back. Pierce had to break into a run, too, which exhausted him further, but he couldn't resume walking until the other man had done so first, and they trotted quite a few miles before this happened.

"That little fellow's got a lot of stamina," Pierce thought, "and in fact he's probably got more than I do." He almost decided to stop and fight it out, if that had to be done, but then he remembered the knife and how deft all the village men were in the carving arts, and he guessed that his chances of surviving by walking were better.

His mistake had been to stop walking in the first place, he reflected, even though his illness hadn't given him much choice. When he'd stopped, right away he'd found himself surrounded, and he'd started expecting things of people, and they'd started expecting things of him, and he thought that Greece wasn't too different from Iowa in that regard, except that the Greeks seemed to take everything more seriously.

All day long the two men walked. Pierce had never walked so far or so fast before, as he'd never had such a compelling reason to do so. He had only a hazy notion of where he was. He was heading east as usual, and he supposed that sooner or later he'd reach the Turkish border, but he doubted that he'd get there before night fell or he collapsed. By late afternoon, when his hasty steps brought him into the port city of Alexandroupolis, he was in a desperate condition, for his legs were threatening to give way, his empty stomach was roaring for nourishment, the Swiss watches hung like stones on his arm, and he had a frightful crick in his neck caused by his constant backward glances.

He tottered along the waterfront, sifting plans for escape. He thought of jumping in the water to swim away, but he feared his legs would cramp and he'd drown. Nor could he climb into one of the dories and row off, for the owner would raise a cry and set the police after him. He might rent one, though. Unstrapping a watch, he thrust it at the nearest fisherman, gesturing urgently toward the line of little boats. The man assumed he wanted to be taken fishing or sightseeing, in either of which cases the next day would be preferable. He tried to explain this to his eager client, but Pierce, glancing back, saw Daphne's brother, much winded, stagger into sight around the corner, his knife out and clutched in one hand.

Pierce hurried the fisherman down to the boats. He unstrapped another watch and pressed it on the man. "Which one?" he shouted in his ear. The fisherman seemed mesmerized by the sight of two watches in his horny palm, so Pierce gave him a third one, clambered into the closest dory, untied it, pushed off, and began rowing out into the harbor. By the time Daphne's brother reached the wharf, Pierce was beyond knife-throwing range. He didn't feel easy, though, until he'd circled around behind a couple of larger vessels that were moored in the harbor, and then he realized that his antagonist might have commandeered another boat and be pursuing him still, so he kept rowing and rowing while his hands blistered and his arms numbed.

Pierce spent the night on the Aegean Sea, sometimes drifting along in the darkness, sometimes rowing, more frequently being sick over the side, for the water was choppy and he was a poor sailor. "I'm still walking, in a sense," he told himself hazily. "I'm just doing it with my arms instead of my legs." A storm rushed over him, flattening him with wind and drenching him with rain. Bailing out the boat with his cupped hands, he let an oar slip and lost it, so afterwards he could do no more than paddle a bit and let the waves shove him about as they pleased.

When morning came, he was terrified to discover that he was out of sight of the shore. A walker ought to die on land, not at sea, he kept thinking, and as the day wore on and his thirst made his tongue swell and his hunger led him to nibble at seaweed, he began hallucinating mountains and valleys and forests where there were only waves, and he wished he'd brought along some earth in his pocket just for the feel of it, as he knew it would have given him a bit of security.

His last hallucination that day was of a hospital ship hurrying toward him out of the sunset. This vision persisted and became real, except that the vessel shrank in size and changed color and purpose as it approached, and instead of being the great white ship of mercy he'd imagined, it turned out to be a police patrol boat, combing the coastal waters for political refugees attempting to flee the country.

The police not unnaturally assumed that Pierce was one of these enemies of the state, particularly when his

147

swollen tongue prevented him from responding to their questions after he was hauled on board. To bring him to reason, they interrogated him with fists and boots for a while, and stood a guard over him on the deck when he collapsed. Pierce, concluding that he'd fallen among madmen, adopted what seemed to be the only course open to him. At his first opportunity he upended his guard, rushed to the railing and dived overboard into the sea, swimming off underwater as the bullets churned all around him. Luckily for him, an early-evening fog had gathered, so the police were balked in their efforts to spot him with their searchlights, but they assumed, reasonably enough, that if he hadn't been riddled by their guns, he'd drown.

Pierce was a buoyant fellow and had no trouble staying afloat. He even took naps. He figured he'd starve to death before he sank, but he worried about man-eating sharks and about storms and about getting caught in the propellers of ships that might cruise across him during the night, and so instead of merely drifting, he summoned up his last reserves of strength and swam as much as he could, despite the fact that he had no notion whether he was headed toward land or away from it. Although he didn't know it at the time, he swam the Hellespont that night, like the legendary Leander, fetching up near dawn on the coast of Turkey, not far from the site of ancient Troy. Thus he put Europe behind him, and dragged himself onto the continent of Asia.

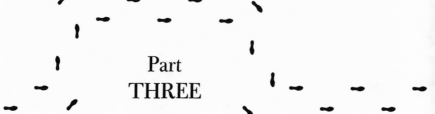

Part
THREE

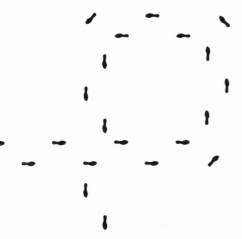

During the winter and spring Mr. Mordenstahl's managerial functions at the Duluth agricultural company had been gradually diminished. They fell away one by one, like the hairs of his head, in a process barely perceptible, and only lately had he come to realize that, administratively speaking, he was growing bald.

In the old days, he would have been fired outright or informed in plain language what he'd have to do to hold his job. But such simplicity was evidently impossible for a large modern international business; instead, Mr. Mordenstahl was subjected to bureaucratic tortures so delicate and prolonged that they would have excited the admiration of a Byzantine monarch.

He still retained his powers, but when he sought to exercise them, he found that decisions had already been taken, and that there was nothing left for him to do but ratify them. His directives to the staff were frequently circumvented, his suggestions in conferences were politely ignored, important visitors often came and went without his knowledge, and he had the impression that his telephone was being monitored and his mail reviewed. There was little positive evidence he could seize on. Even if there had been, his vital forces had become so enervated that he could not have acted on it. He was withered and wretched, and likewise confused, because his executive fangs had been drawn with such subtlety that he felt he still had them, though he knew he did not.

What particularly depressed him had been what he believed to be the ignoble end of Pierce Davis's walk. The last message from Roach had reported that Pierce, having gotten involved in some unsavory troubles in Britain, had fled to France, settled down there, changed his name, and applied for French citizenship. Mr. Mordenstahl had felt it his duty to relay this information to Pierce's family, but, as he was by then accustomed to having his duties performed by others, he did nothing about it. He also did nothing to forward the idea he'd broached to Natalie the previous fall. Pierce had disappointed him and didn't deserve a memorial. "He tried," Mr. Mordenstahl reflected, "but he didn't try hard enough." He resolved to forget Pierce, which cost him an effort, for the world-walk had been the only thing left which seemed to have any meaning for him.

In June he was required to visit his company's projects in Turkey at the time of an important contract renewal. He went for purely ceremonial reasons, however. While a junior executive stayed in Ankara to conduct the negotiations, Mr. Mordenstahl humbly allowed himself to be driven some seventy miles south for the dedication of a new irrigation project. "I'm just a ribbon-cutter now," he thought moodily. Glancing around at the other official personages gathered there, he saw by their doleful expressions that they, too, were the victims of time and chance, and that their sonorous titles mocked them, inasmuch as the real authority resided elsewhere. "We're a useless lot," Mr. Mordenstahl decided. "If the earth itself were to swallow us up, it wouldn't matter a pinch of moose dung."

His own company having taken a leading part in the project, Mr. Mordenstahl had been assigned the honorary task of cutting the ribbon—or, in this case, of turning a silver-plated tap which would permit water to flow into the fields beyond. When all the speeches had been finished and the commemorative gifts bestowed, he obediently stepped forward to execute this simple duty. As he placed his hands on the tap, he happened to glimpse, out of the corner of one eye, the figure of a man striding along the public highway that bordered the project, and since there was something remarkably familiar about the fellow—although he was too far away for his features to be distinguished—Mr. Mordenstahl paused and frowned and looked keenly in that direction. Then his eyes widened and his mouth fell open.

"It's not possible," he muttered. He was astounded. The walking man seemed to be none other than Pierce Davis. How could that be? Mr. Mordenstahl remained bent above the silverplated tap, gaping at the walker, whose identity was becoming more unmistakable with every step. "He didn't stop," whispered Mr. Mordenstahl, in agitation and excitement, while behind him rose polite murmurs of concern at his delay. "He kept on going, I'm damned if he didn't!" he exclaimed. "He walked through Europe! He's in Asia now!"

Although Pierce was still at a considerable distance, Mr. Mordenstahl straightened up and began waving at

him, and he would have completely forgotten his ceremonial function had not a Turkish bureaucrat hastened
to his side to remind him. "The tap?" inquired Mr. Mordenstahl, who'd been about to utter cries of welcome at
the approaching world-walker. "Oh, yes, the goddamned
tap." And so, impatiently, he bent again and gave it a
powerful twist.

The result of his action—or what seemed to be the
result of his action—was extraordinary. Not only did the
water gush forth toward the land, but the land itself, as
though crazed by the prospect of refreshment after centuries of thirst, rushed forward to meet it, or so it appeared, for great fissures opened in the earth and ripped
wildly across the plain toward Mr. Mordenstahl and the
assembled dignitaries, engorging a pair of dusty villages
that stood in the way. The ground shook and roared. The
sky darkened. With cries of "earthquake" in several languages, the various ministers and contractors and pleni-
potentiaries fled for their limousines, shedding hats and
briefcases.

Mr. Mordenstahl remained where he was, mesmerized by this terrific spectacle. "I turned the tap too hard,"
he thought in the first moment of confusion, and then he
speculated that his recent forebodings had come true, and
that the soil he'd sought to improve in a lifetime of labor
was ungratefully attempting to murder him. If it had not
been for his courageous chauffeur, who dashed up to seize
his arm, he might have stayed there until the rising
storms of dust had suffocated him. It was only with difficulty that the driver managed to haul Mr. Mordenstahl
off to the car, for he was virtually inert with shock. "The
earth did open up," he kept mumbling, "but not for
me." As the car sped perilously away across the dancing
fields, Mr. Mordenstahl stared dumbly at his hands, still

gripping the silver-plated tap, which had been wrenched from its coupling. He wasn't aware of this trophy, however. Tears had beclouded his eyes. Mr. Mordenstahl wept, but not in thanksgiving at his escape; he wept rather for the final glimpse he'd had of the vindictive earth, split in wrath at man's presumption; he wept as Charlemagne wept over Roland, he wept as age weeps for youth lost in time's chasm—he wept, in short, for Pierce Davis, whom he had most clearly witnessed, beyond any possibility of doubt, at the moment in which the walker was devoured by his ambition—that is, Pierce had plunged into one of those gaping crevices and so had been swallowed down forever by the very world he'd so bravely sought to walk.

As Mr. Mordenstahl was returned to Ankara by car and from there to America by plane, an international effort was organized to bring food and medicine to the devastated zone. Such bodies as could be found were laid out in rows to be identified and buried; the injured were treated by crews of doctors and nurses, flown in by helicopter, and the homeless were housed in tents.

A delegation of notables soon arrived to inspect the ruined land and to cheer the survivors and rescue workers by their presence. These visitors included authorities from the Turkish government, a United Nations official or two, and representatives from the relief organization itself, together with an American specialist in fund-raising and public relations who'd gotten himself hired by persuading the dispensers of mercy that he could raise half a million dollars through his European contacts alone.

Roy Roach had remained in Europe, and he had prospered there. He had an instinct for scandal and disaster; no sooner was a cabinet minister found in the wrong bed or a currency menaced by speculation than Roach was on the scene to wangle a commission from the panicky principals, and such was the convincing glibness of his tongue that not only were his promises to hush things up believed, but when matters got worse (as they usually did), he was able to redouble his efforts and quadruple his fees, and quite frequently, when the ruin was total, the final act of his clients before killing themselves or being hustled off to jail or into shameful retirement was to write Roach a letter of warm recommendation.

The earthquake, having gobbled down Pierce Davis and several hundred peasants, had thereupon, in a manner of speaking, excreted Roach. His professional assumption had for some time been that the greater the human misery involved in an event, the greater the potential profits, and so he was staggered by the possibilities that appeared to him on the inspection tour. While the relief officials, hardened as they were to suffering, blanched at the mangled corpses and winced at the screams from the medical tents, Roach felt a surge of optimism, and an interesting scheme leaped into his imagination. Certain European suppliers would make handsome contributions to the relief work, in exchange for which Roach would see that they received contracts for rehabilitation and reconstruction, a process that would require some bribery here and there—and if they did not in fact receive such contracts, it would not matter much to him, as by then he would have pocketed his honorariums and be elsewhere altogether.

So speculating, Roach walked jauntily amid the

groaning human wreckage on the Anatolian plain, accompanied by his latest secretary, a young lady from Istanbul hired the day before, who he hoped before long would respond to his interest in folklore by demonstrating some native dances. From time to time the delegation would pause for a few words with the surviving inhabitants, in which exchanges Roach's secretary acted as interpreter. This was no easy task, as the dialect was difficult and occasionally impenetrable.

"That chap back there I couldn't understand a bit," the secretary confided to Roach in her neat British accent. "It sounded almost as though he were trying to speak English, actually." Roach took a casual look in the indicated direction. "Pathetic case, really," the secretary continued. "I suppose his larynx was injured in the quake." Roach took a second look, and a third, and then he excused himself and hurried back to a mass of medical dressings from which protruded a pair of familiar ears.

"Pierce Davis, as I live and breathe!" declared the fund-raiser in amazement, after studying such portions of the figure before him that were unbandaged. "I swear to God above I can't believe my own eyes, fella, so you'll have to tell me you're not a mirage or a ghost or something."

"Hi, Mr. Roach," said Pierce.

"This is incredible and beyond belief and let me know right away how come you're in such terrible condition."

"I fell into the earthquake," said Pierce, whose voice was about his only undamaged faculty (the Turkish girl had never heard Iowa English before). "I got chewed up by a bunch of rocks down there and I hurt all over, but I climbed out again, and here I am."

"And what the hell were you doing in this country

anyhow? Don't tell me! You were walking, right?"
Roach's little eyes gleamed; he broke into a winning
smile of admiration, and gave Pierce a friendly clap on
the shoulder, which made Pierce scream. "Sorry, fella,
but do you mean to tell me you've been walking all this
time on that little venture of yours I don't know how
many hundreds and thousands of miles, and do you happen to have any press clippings or sworn statements from
public officials and the like to prove it?"

"I don't have any clippings, Mr. Roach."

"Doesn't matter. Those are easy enough to get,
fella." Roach paused, once more struck by a brainwave.
"Pierce, I can guarantee you right now on my honor as a
fellow American that your fortune is as good as made, but
first of all I'd like to assure you that I've been working on
this world-walk project just about as hard as you have,
and I've invested my time and energy in it with hardly
any recompense worth mentioning. In fact, I've reaped
many a heartache from it," said Roach, pressing the
breast pocket of his Italian suit, where several Cuban
cigars were tucked in a silver case, "but what I'm saying is
that I'm fed up with working for nothing, and so after I
tidy up a few odds and ends here locally in my current
undertaking, and you get yourself mended from your injuries, I'm prepared to make you rich beyond your wild-
est dreams and famous as well, and how would you like
that, Pierce?"

"I don't get you, Mr. Roach."

"Pierce, I'll be frank with you. You can't make
money unless you've got something to sell, and I mean
something tangible. Now before I left New York last year
I had a chat with a onetime associate who has a business
in New Jersey making athletic equipment—I don't mean
jockstraps, I mean exercisers and trampolines and such—

and I had a revelation, fella, which I didn't mention to this old buddy of mine as it was premature, but what I'm going to do to guarantee you and me our proper cut in this thing is to phone a lawyer of mine back in New York to draw the contracts to be ready when we fly back—"

"Listen, Mr. Roach, I'm pretty thirsty. Could you get me a little water?"

"Pierce, you'll be drinking champagne soon enough, and let me draw the rest of the picture. We are banking on the fact that the American public is conscious of being fat and flabby and investing millions in getting rid of it, and also that they are naturally attracted by the product with the most memorable gimmick, so in a nutshell, fella, you will publicly advertise an exercising treadmill operating on ordinary house current and retailing at maybe forty-nine dollars, and we'll sell them by the thousands."

"There's a tent over there where they hand out drinking water in canteens, but my legs are so swollen I can't walk there myself, so if you—"

"Pierce, this little treadmill will be called something like the World-Walking Treadmill and we will sell the American people on the theme that they can walk around the world right in their own homes by setting the thing up in the family room, let's say, and it's quiet, so it won't interfere with television viewing, so you'll have all these overweight Americans walking their way to health on these sturdy and handsomely designed little electrical treadmills that you plug right into the wall—and maybe we'll have have a battery-powered model for outdoor use, in the case of family picnics—and as for your part, fella, I envision you doing a real walk around the world on this selfsame commercial treadmill right in Macy's window overlooking Thirty-Fourth Street, let's say, or maybe in Abercrombie and Fitch, but anyhow with full publicity and signs in the window, so everybody passing by can stand for hours if they want watching you walking on this thing in your world-walker's sports costume (which is another sales possibility right there, Pierce!) and maybe having refreshments brought in by cute little models also appropriately attired—"

"I'm dying of thirst."

"—and we can tone the thing up to full authenticity by having a placard in there with you announcing your daily mileage and total mileage and all that, and even a world map which will chart your progress as you go from one continent to another, so all in all, Pierce, you'll still have the satisfaction of walking around the world while doing it for a handsome salary (which we'll square away on as to numbers soon enough, I promise you), plus the knowledge that you're helping lead thousands and maybe millions of your countrymen into sweating off unsightly fat."

"Water," Pierce croaked feebly.

"Pierce, I can tell you're still too shaken up by this earthquake to decide everything down to the last detail, but I'll be back in a couple of days and in the meantime, I'll make sure these people give you everything you can possibly need."

"Water—!"

"Water and medicine and whatever, fella, for I want to get you well as soon as possible as my new partner," said Roach. However, he noticed that Pierce had lost consciousness, which raised in his mind such doubts as to Pierce's stamina that he decided on the spot that he'd be better off hiring some sturdier athlete to walk around the world in Macy's window. So he tucked one of his business cards among Pierce's bandages and rejoined the visiting notables to be driven back to Ankara for lunch.

How far into the jaws of earth Pierce had descended, and how long he'd remained there, he didn't know, but the experience roused dreams which gave him something to think about while he waited for his injuries to heal.

He dreamed once that he hadn't fallen at all, but that he'd merely changed the direction of his world-walking from horizontal to vertical. He dreamed, too, of having walked vast subterranean regions, where he'd raced demons across fields of burning coals, and of having somehow fallen up to heaven, where he found God and the angels with packs on their backs and boots on their feet, walking clouds.

Pierce realized that the other victims of the quake held him in special regard. Those who had the use of an arm reached up to take off their caps when he hobbled by, and at mealtimes the choicest morsels were pressed on him. At first he supposed this was a traditional courtesy toward foreigners, and then he wondered if the people held themselves responsible for the disaster and were trying to make amends to him for the trouble it had given him. In any event, he felt obliged to his companions in misfortune, and as soon as he was able, he entered fully into the work that had to be done. Whenever a machine broke down, he repaired it. Sometimes he made new ones out of spare parts. He organized expeditions to trap the sheep which had fled at the time of the quake, and he devised a public latrine which became a model for other refugee settlements in the stricken area.

His efforts were all the more necessary because of the dwindling of relief activities. By the end of August the funds had been exhausted, the medical staff had departed, the top executives (including Roy Roach) had gone to India because of a famine there, and Pierce and the peasants were left largely to their own resources. Once a week a government truck would arrive with a load of foodstuffs, but there wasn't enough to eat, and Pierce, who took charge of rationing and distribution, left himself to the last, which often meant that he skipped meals altogether.

He was at this time an impressive figure. His hair and beard had grown long and were bleached gold-white by the sun. On his substandard diet he became gaunt. Above his wasted cheeks his blue eyes seemed enormous. He stood a head taller than any of the men, and strode about the camp wrapped in a sheepskin robe that swung majestically above the remnants of his torn and tattered boots.

For the Turks he had great respect, not just because of their reverent attitude toward him, but because they were walkers—better walkers than he was, he knew, for while he'd been walking for little more than a year, they'd walked all their lives, being too poor to have even a donkey to ride on. And although he was reluctant to part company with them to go on his way, he took comfort in the knowledge that virtually everywhere he went in Asia he'd be among people who walked, and that therefore he'd have a strong common bond with them, even if he couldn't understand a syllable of what they said. It seemed to him that he was closer in spirit to these ruined, impoverished peasants than he'd been to anyone before, including his own family, whom he could barely remember now. Walking was his world, he thought, and any man who walked was his brother.

The plight of the refugees got worse as the weeks went by, for the nights were colder and the dust that blew up from Mr. Mordenstahl's abandoned irrigation project was about the only thing that covered anybody. The food supply decreased, too, and Pierce felt ashamed at eating the little he took. He finally decided that he'd do his comrades more good by leaving than by staying, being determined that at the first town he chanced to reach he'd get together some provisions to send back to them.

One morning at sunup, therefore, he shook as many hands as he could, bid a general farewell by means of respectful bows and friendly gestures, and went walking off in a southeasterly direction. He was aware of the fact that his departure caused considerable excitement, but he assumed that was only natural after such a long ac-quaintanceship and cast no backward glances. At noon, however, he was greatly surprised, on hearing some com-motion behind him, to see that he had been followed by all the people from the camp, who came trudging along carrying their few pitiful possessions.

Pierce was overwhelmed by this demonstration of their attachment to him. At the same time, he knew that they'd be better off back at the camp, for he had no idea how long it might take to reach a populated place, so he urged them by signs to return. They wouldn't, though. They clustered about him with smiling faces, patting him on the back and nodding encouragingly up into his emaciated, gold-fringed features, and when he turned to walk on, hoping they'd decide to go back, they began walking along with him.

What this meant, Pierce had no idea, but he was in no condition to reason properly, as hunger made him lightheaded. He sensed that his companions expected from him what he couldn't provide—some relief from their misery—but at the same time he was glad they were there. Walking always raised his spirits until loneliness overtook him; now, for the first time, he knew he wouldn't be lonely. The farther he went, the happier he felt. Others had chosen to share his steps, perhaps his life as well. They'd walk the world together! He kept turning around to smile at his ragged companions, encouraging them to walk on. Sometimes he carried one of the children or helped support an old man whose legs were unsteady. "I'm walking with my own people now," he'd say to himself. "I'm walking with my own true family." And tears would work their way down his cheeks.

It was at night that he became troubled. "They shouldn't have followed me," he'd think. "They should have gone back. It's too late now, though." He didn't know what lay ahead, nor how they would manage to live once their meager food stores were exhausted.

As the walk continued the number of Pierce's followers steadily swelled. From each inhabited place on the way, some three or four onlookers would suddenly stop gawking at the procession, run inside their hovels to stuff their belongings in a sack, and hasten to join the marchers. Soon there were several hundred men, women, and children walking behind Pierce, and the greater the number of walkers, the more persuasive a sight it was to the village bystanders, and consequently more of them were seized by the impulse to walk as well. They began coming by the dozens from other directions, too, for the news had gotten around the area, and in some cases whole village populations packed their movables and hurried to catch up.

Pierce's hundreds grew to thousands. How many there were he despaired of estimating. His original followers were all but lost in the crowd. Only rarely did he glimpse a familiar face. Deprived of the comradely presence of his acquaintances, he began to feel isolated again, being alone with strangers who were not so much accompanying him as driving him ahead of them, toward an unknown destination.

Each day more arrived. The mass of Pierce's followers seemed to stretch for miles behind him—thousands of black-garbed figures struggling along in the dust raised by tramping feet, carrying their sacks and boxes, clutching hens and pigeons, and urging along a few lambs or calves that were as lean and pitiful as their miserable masters.

"It isn't a walk, it's a march," thought Pierce, glancing uneasily back at his ragged army. Half of Turkey seemed to be at his heels, a great mob of fervid, desperate faces urging him on—toward what? He didn't know, but he greatly feared that, as they considered him to be their leader, he would be held responsible for whatever came to pass.

As the supplies of food and water diminished, arguments broke out. The disputants often brought their cases to Pierce for judgment, but as he couldn't understand a word they said, those decisions he ventured to make were frequently unfair, which led to further wrangling.

Soon he realized that there was grumbling against him. When it rained, he saw that some evidently blamed him for it, and when it didn't rain and dust clouds raged through the multitude, angry glances were cast in his direction and some fists were shaken at him. One night he sought to slip away in the darkness, but a dozen men gathered around him at once, blocking his way, and when he lay back down again, they crouched nearby, watching him.

He became so apprehensive that he ate little and slept hardly at all. His earlier feelings of brotherhood had vanished. He was virtually a prisoner, and his position was deteriorating daily as the marchers grew hungrier and more dissatisfied. What did they want from him? He knew only that where once he'd been the symbol of their mysterious hopes, he now was the focus of their increasing disappointment, and he walked alarmed and despairing, not knowing what to do or where to turn.

One day what looked from a distance like another village turned out to be a British archaeological camp where tents and trucks were posted near an excavation in the plain. The sight of Pierce marching up with his horde of peasants brought one of the archaeologists hurrying out, waving his hands in agitation. Pierce stopped, so everybody behind him stopped, too.

The archaeologist told Pierce he'd have to keep his followers away from the site, as he didn't want people stepping on his shards. Pierce broke in to say that the peasants were following him against his will, and that he didn't know why. The Briton cast him a suspicious glance, but then began questioning some of the people in their dialect, which he understood well enough.

Finally he was able to explain to Pierce that on the day of the earthquake none of the surviving peasants had noticed Pierce approach along the public road nor had any of them happened to see him topple into the fissure. A sizeable number of witnesses had observed him climb out of it, however, amid sulphurous belchings of smoke, and with his blond hair and blue eyes he had thus fulfilled an ancient legend that foretold the emergence from the earth of a mighty prophet who would utter unintelligible incantations, and word of the arrival of this formidable personage had spread rapidly throughout the region.

"They think you're some sort of messiah," concluded the archaeologist, "and when you set off walking, they assumed you were starting on a crusade, so of course they followed." He gave Pierce a rather sly glance. "At least, they began by thinking that," he added. "Now they're apparently swinging around to a different viewpoint."

"What's that?" Pierce asked, much troubled by the archaeologist's report.

"They now strongly suspect that you're really a demon sprung loose from Hell itself, intent on leading them to perdition—in which case they'll deal with you rather severely, I dare say."

Pierce was horrified by this information. "Look," he said. "You've got to help me get out of here. I'll just jump in one of your trucks and you can drive me to the nearest city."

"Are you mad?" cried the British archaeologist. "I can't jeopardize my dig. Those people might destroy months of painstaking labor in their rage."

"But they may murder me!"

"You should have thought of that earlier. You CIA chaps are all alike. You go about stirring up trouble and meddling in politics without the faintest notion of the consequences."

"I'm not in the CIA!"

"Oh, obviously you're sworn to deny it, but I've run into your type before and I'm not easy to fool. I can promise you that if you come within fifty yards of the dig with that rabble of yours, I'll shoot you first and apologize to your government later."

Pierce had little choice. His crusade continued.

Each day things got worse. The multitude of Pierce's followers kept growing. Pierce himself was literally a prisoner now, for four husky men had undertaken the job of being his bodyguards. Not only did they remain alertly at his heels, but they knotted ropes to the corners of his robe, holding the free ends in their hands. Thus Pierce plodded along like a leashed dog, reflecting bitterly on his earlier hopes for a world-walk *en masse*, for he knew now that walking with others was even worse than walking alone, and that walking was something that couldn't be shared, so he resolved that if he had any future at all, he'd use it more wisely.

Disputes became more frequent, more savage, and violent, but Pierce was no longer called on to act as judge, which didn't ease his mind, for he took it as a further sign of his fall from authority. He sensed a heightening of fury in the people, and when his bodyguards hauled him to a halt one day near a village and produced a wicked-looking pair of sheep shears, he thought his time had come, and fell into a faint. It turned out, however, that they were advertising him to the local inhabitants as a genuine prophet, and merely intended to trade clippings from his holy beard for bread. This traffic proved successful, and Pierce's standing somewhat improved. Still, he couldn't grow hair as fast as it was being scissored off. When his beard was gone, his barbers began harvesting his locks; in a few days he was as bald as a basketball and of no further commercial value.

He hoped they'd recognize his uselessness by letting him go, but they didn't, and he kept scanning the horizon anxiously for some indication that a town might be near, but he saw only the endless, vacant stretches of dusty landscape. Then one morning he noticed that some of the men had managed to acquire two long pieces of timber, which they carried to the base of a knoll that rose forty feet above the plain. Pierce got up from the place where he'd slept and started walking as usual, but he went two steps only before his guardians yanked hard on his ropes, flopping him to the ground. Then they wrestled him out of the robe. The next thing he knew, his boots were being pulled off. "Well, they're just robbing me, that's all," Pierce thought as he lay in the dust. He didn't want to be left completely destitute, however, so he reached quickly into the pocket of his trousers to grab the handful of coins left from the sale of his last Swiss watch, and clapped them into his mouth for safekeeping, and just in time, too, for the trousers were stripped from him next, then his shirt and underwear, and in a matter of seconds, he was stark naked.

They hauled him to his feet and pushed him forward to where the timber lay. Pierce saw that the two pieces had been nailed together in the form of a cross, which fact greatly disturbed him, but he had little time for reflection, as the men lifted the cross, loaded it on his back, and forced him to lug it up to the top of the knoll, where several other men waited, one of them holding a hammer and some long, narrow spikes.

Naked and hairless, his mouth bulging with coins, Pierce stood gazing in horror all around. The cross lay at his feet. Nearby a man was finishing the excavation of a hole where the base would be planted. On the slopes of the knoll and gathered all around it were the masses of peasants, sending up howls of vindictive rage. Pierce searched the land and sky for some sign of deliverance, but the plain lay empty beneath the morning sun, and there was not so much as a cloud overhead. Then he was seized by the shoulders and knees, swept off his feet, and dumped on his back onto the cross. The man with the hammer stepped forward, knelt, and produced one of the spikes, as another man held Pierce's right wrist against the arm of the cross.

In anticipation of the agony, Pierce moaned, or tried to moan. He exhaled no sound, however. Instead, a coin appeared from his mouth and lay on his lips. The hammer hung in midair. Then the man who held it put it down, and in great wonder reached out to take the coin. Pierce produced another one, and the man who'd been clamping his wrist down let his arm go in order to pluck up what had so strangely flowered forth from his mouth. Pierce moaned out a third coin, and a fourth, fifth, sixth. When he realized that no one was holding him down, he sat up and saw that the men were staring at him, awestruck. He spat out yet another coin. The hole-digger approached it gingerly, stooped, and picked it up.

Pierce got to his feet. They didn't charge at him to throw him down again, but backed off, bewildered and apprehensive, and one of them fell to his knees, clasping his hands together, an example the others decided it was prudent to follow. In the meantime the crowd had become impatient, and those highest on the slope pressed up to see what was going on. When the executioners were seen to be kneeling prayerfully around the naked, silver-spitting prophet, word of this extraordinary event spread rapidly.

Pierce went to the edge of the downward slope and mouthed out a couple of coins. The throng there melted back from him, kneeling and praying and letting the coins lie where they'd fallen, as though afraid to touch them.

Pierce began going down. Wherever the way was jammed by people, he let fly a coin, whereupon a path opened before him, as believers by the score fell on their faces. He counted the remaining coins with his tongue, and so was able to ration them out properly as he completed his descent of the slope and passed through the rest of the multitude. With his last coin, he reached open space. There he wasted no time on farewells, but immediately displayed that long, steady stride which had won him his modest cross-country reputation at the University of Iowa, and in that way he abandoned the Moslem crusade he'd been unlucky enough to lead, and fled bald and bare across the Anatolian plain.

The news of Pierce's death in the earthquake was conveyed to the family by Mr. Mordenstahl in person soon after his return to the United States.

On being told she was a widow, Natalie clutched her throat, turned pale, sat down, and closed her eyes. Mr. Mordenstahl, standing blacksuited before her, had been the one to burst into tears. He then drove from Clarion down to Spark, where he wept some more while telling Judge Davis, and the judge, himself genuinely shocked and saddened, was rather annoyed at such a display of grief on the part of an outsider. For the time being, at least, it was decided to keep the information from Dr. Davis, who had improved to the point where he could walk to the hospital recreation room unaided and shoot a game of pool.

Mr. Mordenstahl had hoped that his company would pay Natalie the indemnity stipulated in Pierce's contract, but the lawyers refused to do so, pointing out that the contract had long since been canceled, and that in any case, proof of his demise was lacking, as there was no corpse. Mr. Mordenstahl pleaded, he cajoled, he raged, but when the lawyers proved implacable, he rushed out vowing he'd pay the indemnity from his own pocket if he had to. It occurred to him later that such funds would better be spent on the Pierce Davis Memorial, which the walker's heroic death had revived in his mind. He telephoned Natalie to explain this notion. The fact that she made no comment on it did not lessen his enthusiasm. He began writing letters to every important person he knew, soliciting contributions. He raised the matter repeatedly in company conferences, and plagued the directors with memoranda.

In time his persistence on this subject accomplished what his earlier incompetence had not. Mr. Mordenstahl was replaced as executive vice-president. He was given the title of senior vice-president for international relations, by which means the directors got rid of him for weeks at a time, as he had to fly all over the world to carry out the ceremonial functions of which this new job solely consisted.

Forward movement on the Memorial was imperceptible, except in Mr. Mordenstahl's zealous imagination. There he constructed it a thousand times, and a thousand times dismantled it, unsatisfied. At formal dinners, while other speakers dutifully penciled improvements in their speech texts right up until delivery time, Mr. Mordenstahl sketched Memorial designs on his. (Should it be in the shape of a globe, he wondered, with a walking figure on top? Perhaps a giant pair of legs? One magnificent bronze foot? No, a statue would be better— but how high? Fifty feet? A hundred?) And not infrequently, during his addresses, he would manage to interpolate references to the Memorial, which irrelevancies made little difference to his somnolent audiences.

Mr. Mordenstahl pressed on. In spare moments between planes and at night in faraway foreign hotels, he drafted letters to Senators, Congressmen, philanthropic foundations, historical commissions, university presidents, and touring clubs, and once he telephoned the

Governor of Iowa. The responses he received were vague. Even Judge Davis was evasive when Mr. Mordenstahl asked him to approach the mayor of Spark, to have a suitable site earmarked for future construction.

Although it should have been clear to Mr. Mordenstahl that he was perhaps the only person anywhere who gave the matter any serious consideration, he was undaunted. Possessed by his dream of the Pierce Davis Memorial, he was, for the first time in years, a happy man.

Pierce's flight from the Turkish peasants took him all the way into northern Syria, where he came upon a Christian monastery, anciently established in the rocky wilderness. The monks were accustomed to offer hospitality to the occasional wayfarers who passed by, so they readily took the naked walker in, treated him for sunburn, blisters, and general exhaustion, and gave him an old habit to wear. With his mechanical aptitude Pierce made himself so handy around the monastery that he was invited to undergo a conversion and remain there, but he told the monks that he'd been a Methodist in America, which hadn't been too useful to him, and that lately he'd been a sort of Moslem evangelist, which hadn't worked out at all well, so he'd concluded that the religious life wasn't for him. Then he helped the monks dig a new cesspool, which was badly needed, and went on his way.

He headed south to Lebanon, for he needed money, and the monks had advised him he'd be more likely to find a job there. He also decided he'd better get another passport to replace the forged Canadian one he'd left back at the French-German border. When he reached

Beirut, however, he learned that the U.S. diplomatic establishment had been dynamited by terrorists the previous week, nor could he obtain employment, for garage proprietors were hiring Arabs only and looked askance at Pierce in his monk's robes and sandals. On the other hand, Pierce benefited by his religious costume, as Christians assumed he was a mendicant friar and pressed alms on him, so that he collected more that way than he could have by working. He was bothered by those who asked him to administer such sacraments as marriage and extreme unction. He told them he wasn't really a priest, but they wouldn't believe him, and finally, thinking that he ought to provide some services in exchange for his alms, he relented to the extent of hearing a few confessions along the way to Israel, and generously forgave a host of sins.

In Jerusalem he bought a proper outfit of clothing to wear. He also bought a camera, and while he was waiting for the American Embassy to process his passport application, he made sidetrips to various places of historical interest, snapping photographs. On one of these excursions, he walked to Jericho, which lay east, and as it was dark when he left that ancient town, he mistook the road back to Jerusalem and went farther east instead. He discovered his error only when he walked into what he later learned was the River Jordan. It was low at the time and he forded it with no difficulty, and indeed, with surprising speed, for when he was halfway across, a burst of machinegun fire sent the sacred waters frothing all around him, encouraging him to complete his passage with no delay.

The next morning he kept on going into Jordan, intending to stop at the next town for information on how he could return to Israel by a safer route. Whenever he came upon an interesting sight, he unlimbered his camera and took a picture of it, so that by nightfall, when he reached the outskirts of Amman, he had used up all his film and it was ready to be developed by the authorities who arrested him there. As Pierce had no papers whatever, and as he had taken photographs of military fortifications as well as of pastoral scenes and camels, he was found guilty by a military court of being an Israeli spy (albeit a clumsy and obvious one), and in consequence, after spending a night in jail, was taken off to a remote place outside the city at dawn the next morning to be executed by a firing squad.

His trial having been conducted in Arabic, Pierce hadn't understood a word, and even when he was shoved up against a wall alongside three other convicted spies, he failed to grasp the situation. When he was offered a final cigarette, he declined, for he didn't smoke. While the other condemned prisoners sucked despairingly at their cigarettes, Pierce gazed about complacently, causing the guards to marvel at his coolness. He recognized the military judge who'd sentenced him the night before, and smiled affably in his direction. He also noted with interest a uniformed group of military observers from African and Asian countries, some sporting ornate battle decorations on their tunics. When his hands were tied behind his back, however, he began to feel ill at ease, and when a squad of soldiers marched briskly up before the waiting prisoners, halted, knelt, and loaded their rifles, he realized what was in store for him, took one step forward, and fainted.

Two soldiers ran forward to haul him upright

against the wall, and as they were slapping him back into consciousness, Pierce dimly perceived that a tall, lean officer had left the group of observers and was striding toward him.

The officer seized him by the shoulders and stared piercingly down at him. "I know you, man," he exclaimed harshly. "You're that walking fellow, right?"

Pierce, too dazed and frightened to speak, blinked up into a severe black face framed by a white Arab-style headdress.

"You're Pierce Davis," the officer went on, shaking him roughly. "That's your name! So what the hell are you doing here, Davis? How come you're in a mess like this?"

Pierce recognized the officer as George Bonaparte, but this fact had no meaning for him. His eyes were fixed on the row of kneeling soldiers, whose rifles glinted in the sunlight.

"Can't you understand me, Davis?" Bonaparte asked. "What's the matter with you, can't you say anything?"

Pierce opened his mouth, but instead of speaking he burst into laughter, his eyes rolling from Bonaparte to the soldiers and back again.

"Stop that damned laughing," Bonaparte snapped, in disgust, but Pierce couldn't stop, so Bonaparte shoved him back against the wall and went off to speak to the military judge and the captain of the firing squad.

"Listen to me, Davis," he said when he returned to Pierce. "I've got no business interfering in this thing, but they let me have a couple of minutes to talk to you, and for my own satisfaction, I want to know how you got yourself involved spying for the Jews."

Pierce swallowed his laughter. "Doing what?" he managed to ask.

"Spying, you damned fool. They're going to shoot you for spying."

"That's a lie," said Pierce, trembling from head to foot. "I'm not a spy. I've never spied in my life and you can tell them that."

"I'm not going to tell them anything, Davis," Bonaparte replied sharply. "Your life doesn't mean a damn to me one way or the other, but you've been tried and convicted as a spy, and you might as well know it."

"I'm a walker, not a spy, and you know that better than anybody, so why don't you tell them the truth?" Pierce cried out desperately. "That's what I've been doing all these months—walking! That's why they've been after me in every country I've been through, and I swear to you they've tried to kill me in a dozen different ways, and now they're going to do it with bullets!"

"Shut up, you idiot," Bonaparte ordered. "They say you were sneaking around taking photographs of camouflaged installations."

"I wasn't sneaking, I was walking, and let me inform you that you're wrong about the charge. It's walking I'm guilty of, not spying, and you're lucky you quit walking yourself, for it's a capital offense everywhere, as you can see," Pierce said wildly. "I'll die for walking if I have to, but I'll be damned if I die for spying, and as for the Jews, I've got nothing to do with them, and the only one I'm even acquainted with is Mr. Shapiro who runs the drygoods store back in Spark."

But Bonaparte had returned to the other officers, who were impatiently pacing about. He began conversing with them rapidly in Arabic, from time to time jerking his thumb in Pierce's direction and then tapping the side of his head. The officers were obviously annoyed and unwilling to delay the executions, but they listened to

Bonaparte's explanations. Then they approached Pierce and quizzed him, with Bonaparte as the interpreter, and at one point they unbound his hands and had him lower his trousers so they could see if he were circumcised, which fortunately he wasn't, and finally they appeared to be satisfied that he was nothing more than a numskull, and grudgingly gave orders that his belongings be returned to him and that he be released.

"I'm giving you a ride back to Amman in my jeep," Bonaparte told him, brusquely refusing to acknowledge Pierce's expression of gratitude, "and then I'm going to shove you on the first plane out of this country, understand?"

"No thanks," said Pierce.

Bonaparte scowled at him.

"I can't ride in cars," Pierce added, "nor in planes either."

Bonaparte ground his teeth together and made a gargling sound in his throat.

"I've gotten in cars once or twice when I had to, during emergencies," Pierce explained, "but this emergency's over now, so I'll just say thanks again and goodbye, and be on my way." He reached out to shake Bonaparte's hand, but Bonaparte wouldn't accept it, so Pierce gave him a military salute instead. Then he turned and walked off in haste, for the firing squad was preparing to murder the other prisoners, and he wanted to get away from the place as fast as he could.

"Where the hell do you think you're going?" he heard Bonaparte shout after him, but he merely waved and kept walking.

In a few minutes, a jeep pulled up beside him. Bonaparte was sitting in the back.

"Get in, Davis," Bonaparte ordered, indicating the seat beside the driver.

"No thanks," said Pierce, who kept walking.

"I said get in!"

"Listen, Mr. Bonaparte, I'm either a walker or I'm not, and if I am, then walking's what I'll stick to, and I've decided no more cars no matter what, so thanks again for saving my life, and good luck to you," Pierce replied. He saluted Bonaparte once more and kept going.

Bonaparte had the jeep stop. He jumped out of it and caught up with Pierce. "You damned fool, you don't even know where you're going!"

"I'm going east, Mr. Bonaparte. First there'll be Iraq and then Persia or Pakistan, I forget the exact order they come in," said Pierce, striding on rapidly across the sandy plain and wincing in anticipation of the sound of rifle shots.

"And you don't have any papers," Bonaparte said in exasperation, keeping pace with him. "You'll just get picked up again."

"Well, that's just one of the risks you take when you walk, as I guess you know."

"Davis, I don't know, because I stopped walking long ago, and for the last time, I'm telling you to get in that jeep."

"I swear I can't," said Pierce. "I'm bound to walk."

"Davis, don't tell me you've walked all this way."

"It's the truth."

"I don't believe you."

"You don't have to believe me."

Bonaparte, hurrying along at Pierce's side, kept glancing at him suspiciously. "Davis, I'm willing to believe you, for you're a big enough fool to do it, but don't you realize what they're doing to you? You're no better than a slave! Look at you—you've got no more meat left on you than a cockroach, and you've weathered up like a signpost—but you're still letting them exploit your body and destroy your soul with mind-killing drudgery for the sake of their profits."

"Nobody's exploiting me."

"They're paying you."

"They haven't paid me since I saw you outside of Pittsburgh."

Bonaparte seemed flabbergasted. "You mean you didn't get that contract back? You aren't getting paid to walk?"

"I'm paying my own way," said Pierce.

"Then you're walking for nothing!"

"I've got my own reasons, Mr. Bonaparte."

A volley of gunfire behind them indicated that the firing squad had done its work. Pierce lengthened his stride.

"Davis, I'm beginning to think I'd have done you a favor by letting them execute you back there," said Bonaparte, panting in the effort of matching Pierce's pace. "I've never before encountered a more futile human creature than you with your damned walking, which is of no benefit to anybody including yourself, and slow down a trifle, because I'm out of shape and smoking cigarettes again. Don't think I couldn't get back in shape, Davis," he added fiercely, "if I wanted to teach you another lesson in walking like I did before, which I wouldn't waste my time doing now, for I've got better things to do."

He made Pierce stop while he lighted a cigarette. Pierce, glancing back, saw that the jeep was waiting some distance behind them.

"I never intended to walk around the world, Davis," said Bonaparte, after he'd caught his breath. He sucked deeply on the cigarette, staring moodily down at Pierce. "My purpose was to dramatize the struggle against imperialism, and in Africa I found a better way than walking." He flung the cigarette away, but then lighted another one. "I joined the pan-African movement, Davis," he said, pacing back and forth. In his uniform, he seemed even taller than Pierce remembered him, and his manner was more abrupt and commanding than before. "They've sent me here to recruit volunteers for our war against the enslavers of men," he continued, "so you can understand that when I meet a fool who's wasting his energies pointlessly, it makes me angry." He measured Pierce with a calculating look. "There's misery and hunger and cruelty in this world, Davis, don't you realize that?" he said, speaking more composedly, but with an impatient edge to his voice. "God gave you a pair of legs, but he gave you a conscience as well, and two eyes to see the crimes and injustices committed by the few against the many. Any donkey can walk around the world, but it takes a man to stand up and fight against exploitation and outrage. It isn't too late for you, Davis," he went on. "A fellow with your pig-headed stamina can be of some use to us, and your color wouldn't keep you from joining, for many of our Moslem brothers are white, too. If walking's what you want to do, I can promise you plenty of it—but it'll be walking for a cause and a purpose, walking for the sake of your brothers in this world, walking that isn't just sheer idiotic meaningless movement. I mean walking with a direction to it," Bonaparte rapped out, his deep voice rising so forcefully that Pierce took one backward step. "You're walking one big empty circle now, and you'll end up no better than you started out!" He stood glowering down at Pierce. "You hear me, Davis? You're walking nowhere! Now it's time to start walking somewhere!"

Pierce made no reply. For several moments the two

men stood staring at each other as though listening for the echo of Bonaparte's words.

"Well, I can't quit," said Pierce finally. "You may be right, but I'm right, too, and even if I'm wrong, I can't quit."

Bonaparte dropped his cigarette and stamped on it. "Look out there, Davis," he snapped, pointing ahead to the dusty eastern sky. "You know what's waiting for you that way? The desert, Davis, and when the wind works up in the desert, a man caught alone there gets buried alive, and his lungs fill with sand and he suffocates, and a year or two later when they find him, he's dried out like a raisin." Bonaparte turned abruptly away and signaled to his driver, waiting far behind. The jeep started toward them. "You'll die out there, Davis," Bonaparte said. "If you don't die from the sand, you'll die from the sun, or you'll die in the mountains or maybe in the sea, but in any case it'll be a fool's death, Davis, a death for no reason, a death died out of obstinate foolishness and ignorance!"

"There is a reason," Pierce said. "I wouldn't have gotten this far without a reason."

"What reason?"

"Maybe not a single reason. Maybe lots of reasons. Each step is a reason."

"Each step is nothing but a step, Davis, and if you take a million steps, that's just a million times nothing at all."

"No, that's not right. One stone is a stone, but forty million stones are the Pyramids or the Great Wall of China, and forty million steps is what I figure I'll have taken before I'm through, so all those steps won't be wasted. They'll amount to something."

"They'll amount to a lot of damned nonsense,

Davis," said Bonaparte angrily. The jeep came skidding up beside them, shooting up plumes of dust.

"Listen, Mr. Bonaparte," said Pierce. "You were the one who really got me started walking. You told me about how I'd have to suffer—"

"I said no such thing, Davis."

"Well, anyway, you said I couldn't walk as long as I knew I could quit—and now I know I can't quit."

"You can damned well quit this minute."

"No, you're wrong," said Pierce. "And that's where the suffering comes in. When you set out to do something, like walking, you've got to sort of suffer your way inside of it—and if you can do that, if you can actually get inside, then you can't get out any more, and you don't want to get out, either, because it's become a part of you. That's what's happened to me. I've gotten inside of walking. I've suffered my way in there. That's where I am, and that's where I've got to stay."

Bonaparte climbed into the back of the jeep and sat there looking out soberly at Pierce.

"So walking and me, we're the same thing now," Pierce said, "and the world I'm walking on, that's part of me, too, because I've got the feeling that the world has been working up into me step by step, and it wants what I want. I want to walk, and it wants me to walk. That's what it's been pushing and guiding me along to do, and that's what I'm made for now."

The driver gunned the engine of the jeep suggestively, but Bonaparte gave him no signal to leave.

"And if that reason doesn't satisfy you," Pierce said, stepping back and grinning, "then you'll have to ask the world about it, don't ask me, and you'll have to ask it with your feet, walking."

"I don't know why I wasted my time with you,

Davis," Bonaparte said, but less harshly than before. "I've never heard such a lot of foolishness before in all my life, and here you are, walking around in a desert climate with your head uncovered, and with a sun like they've got here, those precious brains of yours will get scrambled in no time."

So saying, he took off his headdress and flung it to Pierce. Then he snapped his fingers at his driver, who swung the jeep around and went off at top speed. "Good luck, Davis," he shouted. Pierce waved, but Bonaparte didn't look back, so Pierce put on the headdress, and went walking on his way.

Mr. Mordenstahl's labors in behalf of the Pierce Davis Memorial were beginning to produce results. During his long career in business, he had scratched many backs and rolled quite a few logs, so he had favors to claim, and he claimed them in the form of pledges to contribute to the construction fund.

Moreover, he had achieved what he had wanted from the beginning—a site, and not just any site, but a site at the very spot in Spark where the world-walk had begun. For this he had had to win the support both of the mayor, Arnold Biedler (who owned the drugstore there), and of Judge Davis, who was politically important as well as being the spokesman for the family.

A certain amount of compromise had been necessary in each case. Mayor Biedler's favor was obtained only when Mr. Mordenstahl consented to make the Memorial utilitarian. That is, it was to consist of a two-level parking lot to relieve the traffic congestion that prevented shoppers from having easy access to centrally located stores, such as the mayor's own. For this work, which would involve the widening of Main Street through the removal of a row of magnificent elm trees that had stood for a century, the town would pay half, largely from federal funds earmarked for such purposes. The Memorial structure itself would be built on top of the parking edifice, and Mayor Biedler cared not what it was, provided it didn't draw pigeons.

Judge Davis did care. He had had a great personal affection for his nephew, but he felt that of all the Davises who had lived in Spark over the years, Pierce was the least worthy of such recognition, and he knew that the townspeople felt that way, too. The idea of having a stone effigy of Pierce looming permanently over a raised public parking lot, where it would undoubtedly be visible even at the courthouse, five blocks away, struck him as being excessive. He did not state his objection in so many words, but Mr. Mordenstahl had little difficulty in determining the source of his reluctance, which was overcome only after the proposed Memorial plan had been revised, and revised again. The final scheme called for the Memorial to be not a statue but a simple globe—and the inscription on it was to be so designed that persons on the street or in nearby buildings would be able, with the naked eye, to distinguish clearly one word and one word only, and that word would be "Davis."

Sometimes Mr. Mordenstahl was troubled by the concessions he'd been forced to make. Was it right, he wondered, for a monument to a walker to be erected on top of a parking lot for cars? And shouldn't he have fought harder on the question of the name? He consoled himself with the thought that Pierce had been a modest fellow, and that he had made his living fixing automobiles, so that having them underfoot, so to speak, wouldn't be inappropriate. "And anyway," reflected Mr. Mordenstahl, "nothing much gets done in a democratic society without compromise, which guarantees that the best interests of the community are represented, and thank God this isn't Communist Russia or Red China."

He wasn't collecting as much money as he'd hoped to. Tirelessly he visited longtime business acquaintances in city after city throughout the country, but they gave sparingly, and some of them predicted he'd never raise what he had to have, especially if he had to resort to public subscription.

"What the American people want is a real hero, C. L.," one of his magnate friends told him one day.

"But Pierce Davis *is* a hero. He died a hero's death."

"That doesn't count for beans, C. L., and you know it. That fellow Davis was supposed to walk around the world, you say, and he didn't make it."

"He tried."

"He *failed*, C. L."

"Yes, but—"

"The American people don't like failure, C. L. The very idea makes their flesh creep. There's something about failure that stinks, and we don't like it and we won't stand for it. I don't even like to hear the word mentioned."

"I didn't mention it."

"The American people want monuments to success, not failures. Look at that city out there, C. L. It wasn't built by failures."

Mr. Mordenstahl did take a look at the city spread before him. He saw the grimy ruins of the slums that were cut by superhighways where thousands of automobiles crept gasping, he saw the million rising vapors of industrial sweat that fouled the air and dimmed the sun, and he saw the river, black with sludge.

And he said nothing in reply, but quietly departed.

Later, alone, he pondered. His friend had been right, he supposed. And yet he had doubts. "There's nothing so terrible about a little deserving failure, is there?" Mr. Mordenstahl asked himself. "Take my own case. When I was successful, I was too busy and worried to enjoy life much, and in fact the only real happiness I've had in years has been the result of my failure. Success has its good points, no doubt, but a little of it goes a long way, and maybe failure has more to be said for it than people think, so it could be time to give failure a chance."

From this he went on to wonder whether success had not been celebrated enough—or indeed, too much. "What has all this success brought us, anyhow?" he said. "Maybe what we need in this country is some good honest failure!" Yes, he thought, perhaps the lesson of the world-walk was not that Pierce had tried and died, but simply that he had, on a noble but human scale, failed. If so, then shouldn't the Pierce Davis Memorial be a monument to failure?

Mr. Mordenstahl was still in possession of his senses, however, and suspecting that such ideas would not be too persuasive among the businessmen he planned to approach for funds, he resolved to keep them to himself.

Pierce found it too hot in the daytime to do much walking, for he had entered the true desert, so he began walking at night. He tried to reckon his course by the stars, which he'd been taught to do years before by Mr. Braden, the scoutmaster in Spark, but he'd forgotten the essentials, and although he believed that he was heading east toward Persia, via Iraq, he was actually going southeast into the Arabian Peninsula.

He encountered a further difficulty, in that he had departed from whatever roads there might have been in those parts. This meant that he came upon no towns or settlements of any kind, and for days at a time he wandered alone, his survival depending on chance meetings with Bedouin families, from whom he obtained food and water in exchange for such items he carried as they happened to fancy. In this way Pierce parted from some postcards he'd bought in Jerusalem, the St. Christopher's medal he'd gotten from the monks in Syria, the spare set of clothing he carried in the pack, and finally, the pack itself, which was worth a mere handful of figs, so he was left with virtually nothing further to trade, except for his headdress and canteen.

The lack of a road troubled him at first, but the more he thought about it, the more he found it a proper way to walk. He realized that roads hadn't been built for walkers. They'd been made for sledges and carts and chariots and carriages, and finally for motor vehicles, all of which had raised dust in the faces of walkers and shouldered them off to the side, or had run them down or forced them out of their natural state as walkers by making riders out of them. He wondered in fact if roads weren't the enemies of walking men, and he decided not to use them in the future, if he could help it.

He discovered further that he was losing the normal use of his senses. The desert had no odor to speak of, its mirages made a mockery of his vision, and its vast reaches were virtually soundless. His sense of taste was restricted to figs, and by now he was so accustomed to walking that he took little heed of the tactile sensations involved, so altogether he was somewhat disembodied. Still, he was worried by the fact that he soon would have nothing at all to eat or drink, and although he thought he might be able to manage just as well that way as before, he couldn't remember reading about anyone else who'd ever done it successfully, so one night when he saw a light flaming brilliantly in the distance, he assumed it was a Bedouin encampment, and plodded thankfully toward it.

By dawn he was close enough to the light to see that it was the flare of natural gas being burned off at an oil well; on the plain beyond were visible other wells, pipelines, a cluster of baked clay huts, some camels, motor vehicles, and a large building bordered by palm trees.

Pierce passed the group of huts, into which Arab families were crammed in destitution and poverty, and headed toward the main building of the oasis, which was a magnificent structure with balconies and colonades. In front were parked three air-conditioned American limousines, glistening with polish. Several men in white uniforms were working around the grounds as Pierce came into sight. One of them approached him, and after discovering that he was no ordinary desert castaway but a foreigner, conducted him to the rear of the building, gave him a meal and a change of clothing, and let him lie down to sleep in a corner of the kitchen.

In the late afternoon Pierce was awakened and led into the main section of the building. He had no idea where he was being taken, but as the corridors and rooms he passed through became progressively grander and more elaborately appointed, he supposed he would be presented to the chief personage, a sheik or a prince, perhaps, or possibly a sultan.

At the end of a carpeted hallway, he was greeted by a gorgeous Arab girl in a miniskirt, who ushered him into a large air-conditioned office, paneled in mahogany. On the floor was an enormous Persian rug, on the walls were splendid tapestries beaded with jewels, on the desk were three ivory telephones, and seated behind it was a lively little man with keen blue eyes who wore a tailored white suit, a silk cravat pinned by a ruby, and, as he rose to acknowledge the entrance of his guest, a welcoming smile that changed to an expression of wonder and disbelief.

"It's either Pierce Davis or an illusion by the same name," the little man exclaimed, rushing around the desk to clasp Pierce's hand, "and don't tell me you walked all the way from Turkey, fella, for the mere thought of it would floor me."

"Hi, Mr. Roach," said Pierce. "What are you doing here in Iraq?"

"Pierce, you missed a road sign somewhere, for this is Arabia," said Roach, "but have a chair, fella, unless it violates your principles to sit down."

Pierce sat down, and Roach directed his secretary to provide some refreshments.

"Pierce, you'll be amazed to learn that I've been thinking of you lately," Roach said briskly, "and I've got a tremendous proposition for you up my sleeve, but first let me know where you've been and how come you've slenderized yourself so much."

While the secretary passed a plate of sweetmeats and served brandy in crystal goblets, Pierce recounted the adventures he'd had since he'd seen Roach in Turkey.

The mention of George Bonaparte's name brought a look of sadness to Roach's face.

"Pierce, I sweat blood to get George established as a world-famous walker," he said with a sigh. "Nothing was too good for him, and I was glad to slave in his behalf, but then what did he do but throw it all away by getting himself jailed as a Red, which damned near destroyed me with shame and worry, Pierce, but I didn't stop working for him, because I'm not the kind to turn my back on a buddy in need, far from it. No, sir, once Roy Roach is on your side, he's there for life, no matter how rocky the trail may be," Roach went on, accepting a jeweled water-pipe which his secretary had prepared for him. "Well, I heard later they deported George to Tanzania, and now you tell me he's involved in this pan-African thing, which is a bad business, Pierce, as it's bound to stir people up against their rightful leaders, and thank God we don't have any such trouble in this sunny little kingdom here, where I am honored to serve as chief adviser to His Imperial Potency—that's the king, Pierce, whom you won't see today as he's worn out from his labors on projects to help his people, and besides he's taking a cure for the syph, which is known as the royal disease in this country, as the entire ruling family is laid low by it from time to time, including those who happen to be queers, but a finer bunch you'd never find, and as for my own humble contribution," said Roach, fingering his ruby cravat pin, "I'm in the diplomatic service, in a manner of speaking, for I'm representing a consortium of American oil companies, and my job is to keep His Magnificence happy so he won't sell his oil to foreign powers who might use it for aggressive purposes and besides we need it ourselves to defend Asia, which is in terrible shape, Pierce, as I learned from bitter experience when I was in India, where you wouldn't believe the corruption that goes on, and the greed of public officials demanding more than their specified share in certain arrangements," Roach added, his voice trembling as he recalled private outrages, "which makes it a relief to be in a place like this where the needs of the people have absolute priority—which reminds me of that proposition I have for you, Pierce, which is a wonderful job right here, as we need a man with your technical background to take charge of the Imperial Garage and be sure that the Cadillacs are kept in grade-A shape."

"I'd like to help you out, Mr. Roach," said Pierce, "but because of my walking, I've gotten a kind of prejudice on the subject of cars."

"Pierce, I am well acquainted with your feelings in that respect," said Roach, a bit impatiently, "and I would sooner stab myself to death than see you enter a car as a passenger, but this job merely requires that you lift the hood, fella, and stick your hand in there to tune the engine up."

"I know that, Mr. Roach, but I'd still rather not have anything to do with cars."

"Pierce, in the name of our friendship I'm asking you, as these Arabs here ruin two Cads a month with their carelessness."

"I'm sorry, Mr. Roach," said Pierce, "but I can't, and I'll tell you why. It's been my experience that a man with a purpose in life has got to stay true to it, regardless of the consequences."

"Pierce, after all the sacrifices I've made for you—"

"I appreciate that, Mr. Roach," Pierce broke in firmly, "but I've got my honor as a walker to think of, which means no cars for me in any form."

Roach gave him a long, reflective look. "Your decision, fella," he said, rather shortly. He peered into a folder he withdrew from his desk, and then he said: "Pierce, I admire your spirit, and I'm going to take a leaf from your own book, for when it gets down to ideals, I've got a few of them myself, and one of them is giving my old buddies a boost whenever I can, no matter how much trouble may be involved. So I'll tell you what, Pierce. It just so happens that a business acquaintance of mine is passing by tomorrow morning on his monthly rounds, and since he's going your way, I'll arrange for you to travel along with him at no expense to yourself, and he uses a caravan of camels, Pierce, so you can walk along with him, and in that way you won't get lost or stranded in the desert, how about it?"

"That would be swell, Mr. Roach," said Pierce. "I can't thank you enough."

"Save your thanks, Pierce, for I don't deserve them," Roach told him modestly, which was no less than the truth, for the next morning Pierce had manacles snapped on his wrists and was marched out to where the caravan was waiting. There he was chained behind one of the camels, and was stimulated to walk briskly along in the odorous wake of this beast by a whip-wielding guard. As there were quite a few other men similarly manacled and chained, and groaning from the lashes of whips, it took Pierce little time to realize that Roach's business acquaintance pursued the most ancient of commercial callings, and that Roach had sold him into slavery.

Mr. Mordenstahl had two rather unpleasant experiences in India that April.

First, the scheduled opening of a new chemical fertilizer plant was delayed because a group of ecological radicals had invaded the place and damaged some of the equipment before the police could expel them, and Mr. Mordenstahl was forced to twiddle his thumbs for two weeks while repairs were made.

During this period, he did some sightseeing, and it was at the sacred city of Benares, as he was observing the passage of pilgrims along the banks of the Ganges, that the second disturbing event took place.

From the procession of devotees a filthy, bearded worshiper emerged and made his way toward Mr. Mordenstahl. Such was the composed asceticism of his countenance and so revolting were the rags that clung to his wasted body, that Mr. Mordenstahl supposed him to be a fakir, and reached into his pocket for some alms.

But when the fakir greeted him by name, Mr. Mordenstahl realized with vexation that he was nothing more than an American hippie.

"Remember me, Mr. Mordenstahl?" the hippie asked with a gentle and guileless smile.

Mr. Mordenstahl reluctantly shook the proffered hand and inhaled the pungent odor of the human wreck that stood before him. "Of course I do," he said, but he didn't, although there was something familiar about the fellow. "I never forget a face," Mr. Mordenstahl added gamely, wondering if this could be the ne'er-do-well son of Mr. Wentz, the corporation counsel in Duluth.

"I'm Pierce Davis," the hippie said.

Mr. Mordenstahl dropped the hand and stepped back a pace.

"Guess you don't remember the name, Mr. Mordenstahl, but I'm the fellow from Iowa you hired once to walk around the world."

Mr. Mordenstahl turned away and headed off, wiping his hand on his trousers.

The hippie hurried after him. "Listen, Mr. Mordenstahl, I realize you told me to stop walking and all that back in Vermont, so I don't blame you for still being angry, but I've got a little problem here you might help me with."

Mr. Mordenstahl silently strode toward the avenue that paralleled the Ganges.

"I lost my passport a few countries back," the hippie

said, "and I'm trying to get a new one because I've had a bit of trouble getting past border guards. It would speed things up at the Consulate here if you could vouch for me."

Mr. Mordenstahl paused at the edge of the avenue, looking for a taxi. He saw none.

"It's kind of complicated because they evidently got me mixed up with somebody else back in the States with the same name who died, so maybe you wouldn't mind just telling the man in the passport office that I'm Pierce Davis from Spark, Iowa."

"No," said Mr. Mordenstahl.

"Excuse me, Mr. Mordenstahl?"

"Pierce Davis," said Mr. Mordenstahl, "is dead."

"No, I'm not, honest. It's that other Pierce Davis the Consulate got told about when they asked."

"I saw him die," said Mr. Mordenstahl. He started walking along the avenue, but the hippie remained by his side.

"Well, I'm sorry about that, Mr. Mordenstahl, for I can tell he was a good friend of yours, and it's a shame I've reminded you of him, having the same name, but—"

"I've never seen you before in my life," said Mr. Mordenstahl abruptly.

"Well, you interviewed me in Duluth a couple of years ago, and then you hired me—"

"I never hired you!" Mr. Mordenstahl's voice rose angrily. "I don't know who you are, and I don't want to know, so don't tell me!" He signaled commandingly at an approaching taxi, which, however, was occupied, and cruised past him.

"Maybe you remember when I fell down in a telephone booth in Wheeling, West Virginia, I think it was."

Mr. Mordenstahl turned to face the hippie. "Look

here," he said in a choked voice, "I have no idea why you're trying to pass yourself off as Pierce Davis, the world-walker, and I don't care a cow pie what your racket may be, it won't work with me."

"Gee, Mr. Mordenstahl!"

"Pierce Davis was ten years younger than you are," Mr. Mordenstahl burst out, reddening. "He didn't have lines all over his face, and he wasn't as skinny as a billy-goat, either. He was a clean-cut decent boy from a fine Republican family in one of our great agricultural states where chemical farming was practically invented and where they don't go around tearing down fertilizer plants!"

"Cross my heart, I'm me," said the hippie, as Mr. Mordenstahl went storming off. "I don't know how many Pierce Davises there are," he added, easily catching up with the older man, "but I'm one of them, and Iowa's where I come from, and walking's what I do."

"You have nothing whatsoever in common with Pierce Davis," Mr. Mordenstahl cried out. "You aren't fit even to mention his name, let alone try to steal it! Pierce Davis was a goddamned hero and virtually a son to me, so if I don't know you, you're not him, and you don't re-semble him any more than a pissant resembles an eagle, and let me inform you that no deadbeat drug-fiend bum is going to besmirch the reputation of that poor dead boy while I'm around!"

"Well, I guess I don't look the same as I used to," said the hippie, hurrying to keep pace with Mr. Morden-stahl, who was striding furiously along, fanning his per-spiring face with his hat, "but you haven't seen me lately—"

"I refuse to discuss the matter further!" Mr. Mor-denstahl shouted.

"I've aged up some and gotten thin," his companion persisted, "which you'd understand if you knew what I've gone through."

"I don't want to hear about it!"

"I mean, anybody who's been crucified and shot as a spy and sold into slavery, that's bound to leave a few marks, Mr. Mordenstahl. They put me to work in a salt mine, and believe me, that salt gets right into your skin. Then after I escaped from there, I had to weave a little raft out of reeds to cross the Persian Gulf—"

"I'm not listening!"

"—which sank halfway over, so I had to swim all night like I did in Greece, but there were sharks, and then in Pakistan a camel bit me, and I went a week with only weeds to eat—"

"I'm not interested in your psychedelic experiences!"

"Well, if you don't recognize me, Mr. Mordenstahl, that's all right, although I sort of hate not to be able to prove that I'm me—"

A taxi pulled over to the curb in response to Mr. Mordenstahl's signals.

"—because a man's name isn't important except as a convenience," Pierce said, as Mr. Mordenstahl got into the taxi and slammed the door, "but when you stop to think about it, walking around the world isn't a convenient thing to do, so if in the process of doing it you lose all the ordinary conveniences, maybe it's better that way."

The taxi started off.

"All you really need in this world is a pair of legs, Mr. Mordenstahl!" Pierce shouted, but he could tell that his former employer hadn't heard him, for as the taxi went rushing away, he saw through the rear window that Mr. Mordenstahl had clapped his hands to his ears.

197

* * *

The farther Pierce went in India, the more it seemed to him that Mr. Mordenstahl might have been right, after all. "What I used to be I'm not now," he thought, "so it's no wonder he got mad when I said I still was, and if I showed up back in Spark, they wouldn't know me either."

His clothes were rags. He'd worn through the boots he'd gotten in Jerusalem, and a shark in the Persian Gulf had borne off his headdress (evidently thinking that there was a nice tasty head inside it), so Pierce was exposed top and bottom and a good deal in between. He could still walk, though. He walked better than ever, in fact. Having nothing to carry, and being relieved of much of his flesh, he found himself as lightfooted as a shadow, and although he suffered from hunger and a dozen other discomforts, they didn't trouble him much when he was walking, so he spent more time walking than ever before.

Roads he used only when he had to. For the most part he crossed the countryside. This sent him into thickets (ticks and leeches jumped on him there, and then, disappointed, dropped off), and over vast stony fields where troops of monkeys would scamper along beside him, plucking impudently at his wrists and ankles. He passed through the preserves of rural maharajahs, whose private tigers measured him with yawns. At rustic temples, he saw the surrounding grounds dark with pilgrims. He swam rivers where corpses clustered like lilypads, and leaped ravines over the heads of hopeful hyenas. He found cavern cities carved from hills. For food he borrowed leaves from the trees and locusts from the fields, and sometimes he came upon encampments of mystics who shared with him peculiar vegetables and unusual stews.

And all the time he kept imagining that the very earth beneath his feet was urging him on. He could almost hear it strain itself to point a way for him to follow. It turned torrents down to a trickle so he could cross them, it helped him up steep places with a friendly shove of wind against his back, and it blew dust in the noses of wild animals who started to take too great an interest in him. Looking back, he seemed to see his footsteps glowing like a golden track, and he wondered if that meant that he was cutting a worldwide pathway for other men to follow—and then he decided that was a prideful and unworthy thought, for in its way it suggested that the world was like Macy's window, only bigger, and that the world-walk was only an exhibition after all. "Nobody knows what I'm doing," he told himself, "and nobody would care much if they did, so maybe it's better to keep it private, just between me and the world."

So reflecting, Pierce left India, entered Nepal, and began to cross the Himalayas.

By anyone else's standards, Pierce Davis would have been lost at this point, for he didn't know where he was, he had no specific idea of where he was going, nor could he have described, with any degree of accuracy, where he'd been.

But this meant nothing to him. He knew he wasn't lost, for he was still on the world, which was all that counted, and he needed a guide no more precise than the sun, which he followed in the mornings and kept behind him in the afternoons. If someone had shown him a map, he would have glanced at it only out of politeness, for he had come to regard maps in the same way he felt about roads, that they served other purposes than those he had in mind, and so they weren't for him.

His passage through the Himalayas wasn't easy, even for someone who'd survived as many calamities as he had, but being ignorant of the fact that some of the things he was doing could hardly be done, he did them without worrying over them, and apart from the loss of a frozen earlobe and a couple of toes, he suffered less than might be supposed, although he resolved that if he walked around the world again, he'd choose an easier route.

On his way up one gigantic range he overtook a party of international mountain-climbers who were loaded with packs and tents and other paraphernalia, and roped together like a daisy chain. At the sight of Pierce ascending the icy precipice with no more equipment than his fingernails, his rags reinforced by rude garments he'd woven from twigs and grasses, the climbers halted in their tracks, and those who were Catholics crossed themselves.

An Australian member of the group, encouraged by the mild manner of this apparition, asked Pierce first if he were the Abominable Snowman and second if he might be the ghost of the English climber George Mallory (lost decades earlier on Mount Everest), and when Pierce said he wasn't either of those celebrities, the Australian asked him what he was doing, to which Pierce replied modestly that he was just out for a walk.

"And what are you doing?" Pierce asked in turn.

"We're going to conquer the mountain," the Australian informed him.

"But you can't really conquer a mountain," Pierce objected.

"What I mean is that we're going to climb to the top

of it," the Australian explained, "and so we'll be able to say we've dominated it, you see, and then we'll climb down again and go off and conquer another one."

"Well, that's the wrong point of view," said Pierce, disapprovingly. "If you want to take a walk or go climb a mountain, that's all right, but if you set out to conquer something, it'll fight back, and you and it will both wind up losing. In the case of this mountain," he added severely, "if you conquer it, then the next thing you'll want to do is build roads on it and resort hotels and carve ski runs out of its sides, and then somebody'll come along like Mr. Mordenstahl did in Vermont and want to flatten it out. What I'm saying is that if you can't treat the world with a certain respect, you've got no business being on it."

He hoped that the climbers might invite him to supper, but as they had calculated their necessary supplies down to the last ounce, the thought never entered their heads, so he bid them goodbye and went scrambling on into the snowy mists above. When he had vanished, the mountaineers took counsel among themselves and readily concluded that he hadn't existed, it being well known that the combination of sun glare on the snow and a low oxygen content in the air produces frequent hallucinations among climbers at high altitudes.

In Tibet, Pierce fell in with a nomadic tribe which happened to be going in his direction. These people herded horses, but they didn't ride them; they walked instead, so Pierce felt comfortable among them, and then, too, he wasn't excluded from their conversation, for they didn't have any—or, more exactly, they communicated not in words but by the movement of their bodies, and as Pierce went farther along in their company, he perceived that this silent speech of theirs was based on walking. At first he supposed that theirs was necessarily a primitive language, well enough suited to the simple life they led but incapable of conveying complicated thoughts. The better he learned it, however, the more he realized that it was a subtle and sophisticated means of expression indeed, for there were countless delicate gradations in the ways in which they walked, and in how they held their heads while they did so, and whether they slumped or not, or kept one shoulder higher than the other, etc., so that Pierce, a novice in this language, hoped that in his ignorance he wouldn't say anything that would offend his companions.

The nomads stopped walking on rare occasions only, and sat or lay down more seldom still. For food they foraged as did their horses, eating berries, nuts, and grasses, and drinking milk from the mares. At night they slept either standing up or leaning against each other in pairs, which practice Pierce adopted, too, and in time found that he rested quite well that way.

Walking was not only their way of life, it was life itself. When a member of the tribe became too old or ill to walk any longer, he was considered to have died, even though there was still breath in him, and after the tribe had "chanted" (i.e., walked) a farewell service around him, he was left behind to expire unattended while the rest of them walked on. Likewise, the creation of life was too important to be excepted from the pattern of walking. That is, copulation was performed only in a standing position, or, when the partners were unusually adept or feeling frisky, it was actually carried on at a walk, and frequently in broad daylight, too, which occasioned no embarrassment to anyone (except to Pierce, until he got accustomed to it).

Pierce had never been handy with languages. He'd

had a bit of Spanish in college, plus a semester of Latin, to learn medical terms, but he hadn't been able to get the hang of it, and from his sojourns among the Germans, Turks, Arabs, and other peoples he'd encountered, he remembered only a smattering of words, and many of these he wasn't sure of. The walking language, however, he made rapid progress in, as it seemed to be more adapted to his personality and experience. It wasn't easy, for unlike ordinary languages, it had to be mastered by the entire body, not just by the brain and the vocal apparatus, so Pierce was pleased by the daily evidence of his increasing facility. At the same time he was deeply impressed by the fact that, since walking was the same thing as talking among these people, and since they were almost always on the move, their conversations went on ceaselessly all day, so that this outwardly silent company of nomads, proceeding across the Tibetan plateau, was actually as voluble as a troupe of actors perpetually on stage.

Because of this flow of public self-expression, the nomads were unmarked by the social and personality conflicts that arise from secrecy and misunderstanding. If one person was jealous of another, he was by the very nature of his life required to talk about it, not merely to a confidante, but to everyone in sight, which meant, in practical terms, the entire tribe. The purgative effect of such explications kept unruly passions easily in check.

"You can't keep anything to yourself around here," Pierce reflected, and as he had become fairly fluent in the walking language by this time, he automatically expressed this opinion physically to those around him, and they in turn began spiritedly to discuss the matter (for the nomads loved a good argument, and would willingly walk through a dust storm rather than break off an interesting debate). Pierce informed them that elsewhere in the world people communicated with one another by uttering noises from their mouths, which the nomads could hardly believe, and when he spoke a few words, to show them how it was done, they found it so ludicrous that they hopped and skipped about in paroxysms of walking laughter.

Pierce sometimes worried that he was cutting a poor figure in this walking culture. After all, he was a foreigner, and he knew that no matter how well he learned the language, he'd always walk with an accent. His companions took great pains to ease his mind, assuring him over and over again that he walked as expertly as anyone could who hadn't been born to it (and it was true that nomad babies walked at an extraordinarily early age), and that although he occasionally stumbled over some complicated phrase, or was tripped up by subjunctive clauses, he vented his thoughts quite clearly for the most part (despite a tendency to ramble).

As a further evidence of their friendly regard for him, they urged him to take a wife. Pierce explained that he was married already, but this objection made no sense to the nomads (whose standards, it must be admitted, were not those prevailing in Iowa), so at length he decided it might be a discourtesy for him to decline the honor. Besides, he was much attracted by the young lady who was proposed for him. Her face was rather long, it was true, but her brown eyes were lustrous and inviting, and she had a sultry way of arching herself and widening her nostrils that made Pierce positively sweat, and after she had actually rubbed up against him and blown in his ear, he resolved that the wedding should be postponed no longer.

According to tribal custom, newlyweds were granted the privilege of walking apart from the rest of the tribe for a week, for reasons of privacy. Pierce and his bride spent the allotted period in ardent conversation (it must be remembered that for the nomads speech and action were identical). Sometimes they strolled along, sometimes they trotted briskly or went galloping in abandon, or leapt and plunged through the fragrant wildflowers as they sought to express the entire passionate vocabulary in which the walking language was remarkably rich. Pierce's nomad consort was so fully conversant with the wide range of amorous avowals available that he supposed she'd benefited from several previous honeymoons, but he wasn't any more troubled by this than she was, which was not at all. Just as he'd learned a new language that he'd seemed to have been preparing for with his walking feet all along, so he realized that he was naturally and easily adopting moral attitudes which, shocking as they may seem, were at least suitable for the casual life that the nomads enjoyed, and, having shed his inhibitions, he found that he had shed his clothes as well, but as his energetic mate was in a like state of nature, and as she appeared more beautiful to him that way, with her fine black hair blowing in the wind and her glossy skin gleaming in the sunlight, he only wished it all had happened sooner.

Still, the nuptial week came to an end, and the loving pair rejoined the tribe, and not long after that the nomads reached the apogee of their seasonal circuit and prepared to turn back. Pierce was tempted to remain with them, as they begged him to do, and spent a troubled day pacing out the pros and cons of the matter, while the nomads shuffled out muted comments to indicate their sympathy with his difficulties. Finally, however, Pierce concluded that he had to continue the world-walk, which decision the nomads accepted with regret, insisting that he return to them one day, which he promised to do if he could. They took a ceremonial leave by walking backward. Pierce did the same, and thus he watched their farewell remarks for a long time across the widening stretch of plain that separated them, until they dwindled in the distance, and their walking voices were lost to his sight.

From his earliest days as a walker Pierce had been bothered by the recurrent sensation that someone was following him. This had so nagged him at first that he'd hidden behind trees at the side of highways in Illinois and Indiana, to spy out this supposed pursuer, who, however, had never appeared, and he finally concluded that he was the victim of a psychological phenomenon produced by the loneliness and uncertainties of walking, so he resolved to worry no more about it.

Still, the feeling returned, in Europe as well as in America, and in Asia more than ever. Sometimes he sensed it as the echo of his footsteps, sometimes as a rush of air, or the beating of wings, or the humming of rain in a forest, and then again it seemed to be the absence of all sound, a blank space behind him that walked when he walked, but he could never catch sight of it, nor could he decide whether it was amiably disposed toward him or not.

He spoke to it once in a while. "You're a persistent creature, whatever else you are," he'd say over his shoulder, "and you've come a long way from Iowa, all right, but if you're hanging back out of modesty, don't do it, as it's high time we got personally acquainted." He never got any response to these overtures, however, and for long periods he wasn't aware of the presence behind him, and he supposed it had gone off on other business, or had gotten tired, and quite frequently he forgot about it altogether.

As he walked across the vast and sparsely inhabited reaches of Sinkiang, he realized that his invisible companion seemed closer than ever, and bolder, too, for when he glanced back over his shoulder, he occasionally glimpsed something that wavered for an instant at the edge of his perceptions, and then dissolved. He tried to strike up a conversation with it, using the walking language of the nomads, and although he had the impression that it replied to him in the same way, the responses were too faint for him to hear (or, to be more exact, to see). "That's all right," Pierce would assure his ghostly partner. "It's not your fault I can't quite understand you, but we're making progress, so don't get discouraged, and I'm sure we'll have a nice chat one of these days."

During his long trek in northwestern China, Pierce became aware of other interesting phenomena as well. He found that he could go for days without food or water, and that when he did feel hungry, he could satisfy his appetite with a few handfuls of soil, which didn't seem so strange to him when he reflected that plants and trees sustained themselves well enough on such a diet, and they were as much alive as he was, weren't they? Besides, he knew that the earth contained all sorts of nourishing elements, and the more he thought about it, the more he wondered why other people hadn't learned to live off the land directly, thus dispensing with all the bother of planting seeds and waiting for crops to appear. On the other hand, he supposed that, as they generally lived in one place, they had plenty of time for such refinements, whereas he, being constantly on the move, had to take life as he found it, raw.

Another unusual thing he noticed at this time was that insects and animals didn't trouble him. He walked through curtains of mosquitoes without being bitten, and waded serpent-clogged marshes unharmed. In the forests, wolves loped by without giving him so much as a sniff. Bears and jackals ignored him, and wildcats didn't even blink when he passed them by. He encountered few humans in those parts—a few miners or geological surveyors, an occasional agricultural settlement, and shepherds with their flocks—and these persons, too, paid him no more attention than if he'd been the shadow of a cloud. For his part Pierce went on his way without saluting them, as he didn't know their language and required nothing from them, nor did he feel the need for more companionship than he got from his unseen follower.

In the middle of the Gobi Desert, Pierce sighted a lean, wind-weathered boulder which, he perceived as he came closer, was actually a gray and desiccated old man standing in a contemplative attitude, unmindful of the lizards that sped up and down his sides or the tiny spider which had spun its web in his left ear. Pierce decided that this must be one of the Eastern hermits he'd heard about, and not wanting to lose the opportunity of exchanging views with such a personage, he greeted him with a ceremonious walking phrase. This produced no reaction from the hermit, but Pierce was reluctant to try any words of actual speech, for it had been many weeks since he'd last said anything aloud, and then the sound of his voice had alarmed him. Moreover, he had no reason to suppose that the hermit would understand English, or, for that matter, any other spoken language. "That old fellow very likely has been standing here like a rock for quite some time," Pierce thought, "so if he's able to communicate at all, which isn't certain, then he probably does it like the rocks do, if they do, and so I'll have to learn his language (provided he has one) if I want to talk to him."

So Pierce planted himself a pace away from the hermit, folded his arms in the same way the hermit folded his, and concentrated on learning what he supposed would be the language of non-movement which the rocks and sands might use when they had anything to say to one another. It wasn't easy, as the old man's lizards transferred their attentions to Pierce, tickling him considerably, and then several storms came howling across the desert, freighted with stinging sand, and Pierce's legs, accustomed to walking, kept twitching in complaint against the restraints of standing. Yet with the passage of several days or weeks or months (Pierce couldn't tell how long it was), he began to pick up the rudiments of the hermit's language and gradually acquired a passable fluency in it.

After an exchange of amenities (which took time, as the hermit was far from garrulous, and sometimes considered a remark for half a day before uttering it), Pierce introduced himself as a world-walker, and was surprised when the hermit replied that he'd once been a world-walker, too.

"You really walked around the world?" asked Pierce.

"Several times," said the hermit. "I forget how many."

"Well, that's news to me," said Pierce. "I didn't think there were any other world-walkers."

"There've been quite a few of them," the hermit informed him, "and some are still walking."

"No kidding," Pierce exclaimed. "Well, it's a shame I haven't met any of them, but I guess our paths haven't crossed."

"You wouldn't recognize them."

"I wouldn't?"

"No, because they keep to themselves, and they don't tell anybody what they're doing, and they stay out of the way."

"I can understand that," said Pierce, "because that's how I've been doing it lately, but tell me, what do these other world-walkers do after they've finished their walk around the world?"

"They do it again. If a thing's worth doing once, it's worth doing twice."

"That makes sense to me," said Pierce, "and I've often thought that this first walk of mine was just a trial heat, or a leg-stretcher, you might say, but all good things come to an end, it seems, and in your case, you've obviously stopped walking, and how come?"

"Standing is better," said the hermit.

"I can't argue with you," Pierce said, "since standing is something I know little about, but it strikes me that each man has a pair of legs to use, and walking's the natural thing to do with them, while if standing had been the original idea, then instead of legs we'd have gotten a pedestal or some such thing."

"You'll stand, too, sooner or later."

"That may be," said Pierce, "but I doubt it."

Two full days went by before the hermit produced his next statement. In the meantime there was an eclipse of the moon, and a damp wind hurried in from the north, which made moss form on Pierce's knees.

"Walking is mortal," said the hermit.

"I guess that's right," said Pierce politely.

"Standing is immortal."

"It is?"

"Standing is being without mortality," the hermit explained the following week, "and thus it is endless."

"That's one way to look at it," said Pierce, "and I'll

have to admit that it's a subject I haven't given much thought to, but here you've picked a pretty lonely place to plant your feet, and wouldn't it be more interesting elsewhere?"

"This wasn't always a desert," the hermit rejoined. "Once it was a lake, and once it was a land of flowers and forests, and once there were walled cities with towers, and once or twice the glaciers descended, and all these things will come again."

"That's worth waiting for, all right," said Pierce, "provided you've got the patience, but if you walked, you could search these things out, you see, and besides, life without movement must become a little boring sometimes."

"The earth moves."

"That's what the scientists say," Pierce replied, "but I've never noticed it myself."

"The stars move. So do the sun and the moon. The sides of the mountains crumble, bit by bit, and the sands are constantly shifting in the winds. Biological life goes on," added the hermit. "There are insect empires all around that rise, decay, and fall, and microorganic systems are forever struggling and developing."

"Well, I can tell you're an expert on standing," said Pierce, "and you sure make the desert sound like a lively spot, and after I've gotten walking out of my system— which at this moment I honestly don't think I ever will— maybe I'll give standing a try, just for a change, but before I forget, I've got a question to ask. When you were walking, if you can remember back that far, did you ever have the feeling that somebody was following you?"

"Yes."

"And did you try to find out who or what it was, but couldn't, no matter how hard you tried?"

"Yes."

"And did you have the sensation that the farther you walked, the closer it came up behind you?"

"Yes."

"Until you could practically see the edges of it almost?"

"Yes."

"So tell me," said Pierce. "What is it?"

"The Other Walker."

"What walker?"

"We call it the Other Walker," said the hermit, and in a flash of lightning (for it was night again, and storming) Pierce could see each seam and ridge of his granitic old countenance, "but it's death."

"What's that?"

"Death."

"Oh," said Pierce.

"When you see the Other Walker, you see death, and that's the last sight you see," the hermit said. "Standing is better," he added.

"I hadn't thought about death."

"If you want to stand, there's plenty of room right here," said the hermit.

"I mean, I never thought of death as walking."

"You could stay where you are," said the hermit. "I wouldn't mind."

"I always figured death might drop out of the sky like a bomb, or grab you in bed when you're sick," said Pierce, "but to walk behind you on tiptoe for thousands and thousands of miles, I wouldn't have imagined it."

"I know lots of stories," said the hermit, "to help pass the time."

"Well, if life walks, then death can walk, too, I guess," said Pierce. "There's no law against it. Still, I'm inclined to give life the edge in the matter, although I've got to admit that death has never given me any trouble, so I've got no complaints, but it seems to me that life's the one that's out in front."

"When you know the language better," said the hermit, "you can listen to the gossip of the sands, and the wind brings fresh news every day."

"If death's a walker, then we've got something in common, so it can't be so bad."

"It's been a long time since I had a friend," said the hermit wistfully. "He was a walker, too, but he didn't last. He eroded," the old man explained, "before his time. But I can tell you're made of sterner stuff."

"I'd like to oblige you," Pierce told him, "but I've got to be on my way, for I've still got some distance to go."

"It's a pity you won't stay," said the hermit.

"Next time around I'll drop by for sure," Pierce promised, with some difficulty disengaging his feet from the sand, and flexing his arms, which he'd kept folded all that time. He reached out to give the hermit a farewell handshake, but couldn't find a hand to clasp, for the old fellow was all of a rocky piece, each portion of him being more or less like every other, so Pierce contented himself with patting what would have been a bony shoulder, if the hermit had made greater concessions toward maintaining a human form. Then he set out walking.

"Standing is better," he heard the hermit's voice echoing rather plaintively up behind him from the direction of the boulder.

"Sorry to disagree," Pierce replied without looking back, as he didn't want to chance seeing the Other Walker quite so soon, "but man's a walking creature, in my opinion, and as long as I'm a man, walking's what I'll do. A dolphin can think, and a beaver can build, and the

213

ants can make cities, and in fact there's hardly a thing a man can do that something else can't do, too, except walking," he said, and it seemed to him that the winds lifted his words and hurled them booming across the desert and over the mountains that ringed it all around, and at the same time, too, he heard secret voices whispering agreement in his ears, as though all the men who'd ever walked had been waiting there as spirits to encourage him. "Walking's what makes man different," Pierce cried out. "Walking, it's what a man's supposed to do! It's what a man has got to do! If he lives, he walks! Man walks!"

Part
FOUR

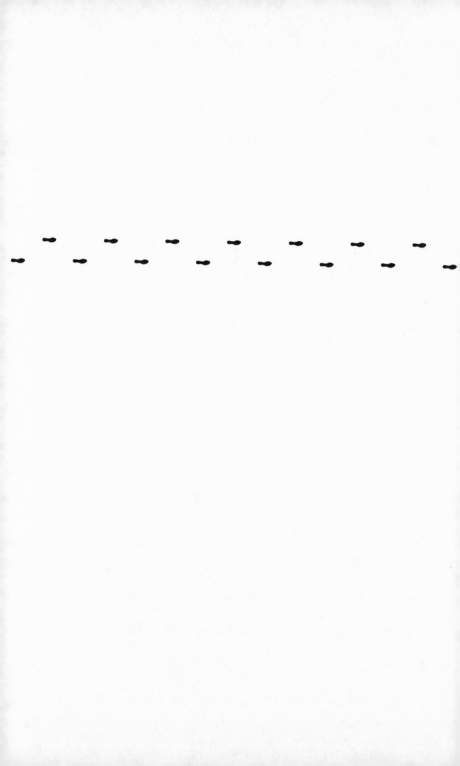

By this time, it should be plain enough that in the course of his walk around the world Pierce Davis changed greatly from what he'd been when he started out. This change wasn't so much in character (for Pierce was always a simple fellow, and became if anything even simpler), nor was it only in appearance (although if Mr. Mordenstahl had wanted to recognize Pierce in India, he would have been hard put to do so); rather, Pierce's capacity to absorb new experiences had expanded so considerably that these experiences became a part of him, and he became a part of them, to a degree unknown to those who've never done anything so conscientiously as he did his walking.

It was, in fact, almost as if a new Pierce Davis had walked up out of the old one, outdistancing him and leaving him far behind—so far behind, indeed, that one might say that Pierce as he'd once been had gotten lost or used up along the way, and that in his original form he now existed only in the memories of others. In any event, a note or two may be in order concerning those who knew the old Pierce best, and who (every so often) remember him.

Natalie has achieved her ambition and more. She has become not only head nurse at the Wright County hospital, but also an assistant director of the hospital itself, and twice has served on Iowa delegations to regional nurses' conventions. She keeps a framed photograph of Pierce in a bureau drawer at home. When anyone asks about her late husband, she explains that he was in the automobile business and died during an exploring expedition in Asia. Little Stephanie, who resembles her so closely in appearance and temperament, inherited nothing from Pierce except a propensity for inopportune laughter, which Natalie is certain she'll outgrow long before she enters medical school.

After the death of his brother (which will be touched on later), Judge Davis retired to a permanent fishing vacation (in Canada, as there are no more fish left in Iowa's rivers). Not needing to keep his mind keen for legal matters, he has taken freely to the bottle, so his memories of Pierce and of all other things, too, are somewhat fuzzy. He thinks of his nephew once or twice a month, usually when hiking parties come tramping through the underbrush to disturb his streamside vigils, and then he grumbles that walkers ought to keep to the roads that were built for their use.

George Bonaparte is a major general in the Pan-African Army (and, at the present writing, the military governor of the Transvaal, with headquarters in Johannesburg). Assuming that Pierce died in the desert, General Bonaparte decided that it would be appropriate to honor the walker's memory by naming after him the lightweight but hardy boots issued to his troops. Thus it has come about that—as in the case of the Wellingtons, called after the great Duke—Pierce's name has passed into the common language. Throughout those African countries where such footgear is needed (and in parts of Europe and Asia as well, for the style has found favor and is spreading), a man looking around the house for his boots will ask his wife where she put his Piercedavises.

Roy Roach made a lightning trip to Paraguay two years ago, and has remained there since, declining all invitations to travel elsewhere. He is currently public relations director of the International Civil Justice League (an association of Paraguayan citizens of foreign origin, which opposes what it considers the iniquitous worldwide spread of extradition legislation). His present secretary, Miss Hildegarde Vogelweide, answers all his routine mail for him and writes that Roach never heard of anybody called Pierce Davis.

After the dedication of the Pierce Davis Memorial, Charles L. Mordenstahl resigned from the Duluth agricultural company and purchased the old family farm of his boyhood, six miles west of Butternut, Minnesota. There he has embarked on a program of organic agriculture that is a complete and eccentric denial of his professional past. He won't use so much as a pinch of chemical fertilizer, nor will he tolerate any pesticides whatever, and in fact when a neighboring farmer hired a plane to do crop-dusting, Mr. Mordenstahl knocked it out of the skies with a shotgun blast. (Although the pilot escaped injury, Mr. Mordenstahl was sued for damages. He conducted his own defense with characteristic vigor, declaring that he'd been protecting nature against armed aggression. He attempted to introduce, as a defense exhibit, a stack of dried cow pies, but the judge wouldn't allow it, and, as might be expected, Mr. Mordenstahl lost the case.) To this day the hale and white-headed figure of the onetime seed king may be seen patrolling his weedy but remarkably flourishing fields, and if he is asked about Pierce Davis, while he still insists that Pierce died in the earthquake in Turkey, the mere mention of the name causes Mr. Mordenstahl to raise his head hopefully and glance west, as though expecting at any moment to see the world-walker striding toward him.

The farther Pierce went, the more of a walker he became, and as he went very far indeed, he achieved the unconscious goal of every man who pursues something with singleminded intensity. He became what he did; that is, he wasn't so much a walker as walking itself.

He got so absorbed in what he was doing, moreover, that the customary rules which limit the possibilities of less dedicated men seemed to be suspended for him at times. How else could he have scaled the Himalayas as he did, or learned the language of the rocks? If Pierce was aware of these mysterious and even miraculous elements in his walking, he didn't say so, for by now he was reluctant to discuss his walking with other people. He didn't think they'd have been interested, for he supposed that people by and large don't care about anything that isn't spectacular. Walking is too ordinary. Anybody can walk. Even walking in space, which the astronauts did, got dull after a few steps.

So Pierce kept on walking alone and in silence, walking almost secretly, in fact, as though he had finally passed into the shadowy ranks of the shy and modest world-walkers mentioned by the Gobi hermit. His further public appearances became rarer, and virtually accidental (and in some cases of doubtful validity). Still, a few episodes may be worth recording, even if they cannot be assigned with complete confidence to the further stages of Pierce's walk around the world.

In the winter following Pierce's encounter with Mr. Mordenstahl in Benares, Soviet border guards arrested a man who'd swum the Amur River from China and arrived in Siberia covered with mud. He had no papers, nor would he speak, but instead kept prancing about like a turkey cock until the authorities got tired of such antics and locked him away. As the visitor was racially a Caucasian, the guards thought he might be an American escapee from a Chinese prison camp, but they had no opportunity to verify this theory, for the next morning his cell was empty, he having departed they knew not how nor whither.

Late in that same winter, a family of Eskimos living south of Shishmaref, Alaska, reported having seen a human male walking across the frozen Bering Strait—which exploit, being most unlikely because of the sub-zero temperatures, they later conceded probably hadn't happened, and decided that what they'd actually seen had been a skinny polar bear.

There were subsequent stories—a gold prospector in the Yukon told of seeing human footprints manifest themselves mysteriously in the snow right past his camp, and a mining project near the Peace River, in British Columbia, was forced to suspend operations for a week when drillers insisted that the rocks were begging them to stop—but the relation of these dubious reports to Pierce Davis is speculative at best, and one is obliged to do no more than mention them and pass on to Pierce's letter to Natalie.

When this letter was written is unknown, as it was not dated, and the envelope which contained it was so smudged and filthy by the time it arrived that no postmarks could be discerned (indeed, no stamps were on it, and Natalie had to pay fifty-seven cents in postage due). Presumably Pierce wrote it in Asia, when he was impoverished, which would explain both the lack of stamps and the unusual writing materials employed; that is, he wrote not on paper but on leaves, some of which crumbled his thoughts to dust, and, for the want of commercial ink, he manufactured his own from substances best left to the imagination (suffice it to say that the Clarion postman delivered the letter with a pair of tongs). Nor did Pierce's handwriting add to the attractiveness of his message, for it was so jerky that one suspects he scribbled it while actually walking, and beyond this the very stretch and stride of his sentences appear to have been dictated by the nature of the land beneath his feet, for at times his expression labors, as though climbing, and then again it speedily descends, or veers aside as if to avoid a rock or tree, but in general the letter proceeds at a regular, not to say monotonous pace, with little more use for periods than a walker has for rests.

Excerpts from the surviving leaves of Pierce's letter follow:

". . . maybe you wonder why I ever went walking and why I kept it up so long and why I'm still doing it, which I used to wonder about a lot, too, and it was a long time before I knew, because it's the simple things in life that are the hardest to understand, and walking, that's about the simplest thing anybody can do.

"I started walking when I was about a year old, like everybody else does, and then after while I forgot about it, the way everybody else does, too, and the only difference was that I took it up again later on, but by then I couldn't remember what it really was, so it took me quite a while to rediscover walking and what it meant.

"Which is strange, because anybody can look at the face of a little child that's just learned how to walk, and the answer's there—and it's joy, that's what it is, and why people should let that slip away from them and lose it just because they grow up, I can't understand.

"What I mean by joy is that a child who's learned to walk realizes that he's complete right there and then. He's on his feet at last, and he understands that he's a human creature with two legs to walk on, and these two walking legs of his make him the same as everybody who's lived in the world, so all of a sudden he knows what he is and where he is, and he's happier at that moment than he'll ever be again.

"And then he grows up and he stops walking, and he loses that happiness he had, because he forgets what he really is, and he starts imagining that he's lots of other things that he isn't. There was a state trooper I met in Iowa who thought he was partly a gun and partly a patrol car and partly a pair of sunglasses, and if there was a piece of man left in him, he'd forgotten it, but anyway he told me that the highways were built for cars, not for people, and that was the truth, although I didn't realize what that meant at the time. It was the same way with cities, which were made for the buildings and the elevators and the streets that are in them, so finally I stopped using the roads and didn't go near the cities.

"But before the roads and cities existed, the world was there—and the world was made to be walked on. Walking, you won't hurt it and it won't hurt you. And if I've sort of overdone walking, maybe it's because I've been trying to make up by myself for all the walking that isn't being done. Sometimes I think I'm the last walking man, so I've got to keep walking until somebody else starts, and if nobody else decides to do it, I can't quit.

"I used to think walking was lonely, but it isn't any lonelier than other things you do by yourself, like breathing or thinking or sleeping, and it sure isn't lonelier than not walking, and after a while, when you've gotten the knack of it, you see all sorts of things on the earth that you couldn't see otherwise, and if you think these things aren't worth seeing, then you'd better take another look at the face of the child who's taking his first steps, for he sees it all, he sees it the way it has to be seen, he sees himself in the world the way he ought to be—walking."

The dedication of the Pierce Davis Memorial was to have been held on March 17, 197_, that is, on the third anniversary of the beginning of the world-walk. Because of various problems in financing and construction, however, the ceremony had to be postponed several times over a period of weeks, and finally, at the suggestion of Mayor Biedler, it was decided to combine it with the July Fourth Independence Day celebration.

By that time the Main Street parking lot had been completed and was actually in use. Its cement paving was already stained here and there with oil, and one steel ramp guard had been buckled by an erring motorist, while in the foundations beneath, a community of rats had moved in among the litter of candy wrappers, apple cores, cigar butts, and sandwich ends which the workmen had deposited there.

At the very top, mounted on a steel pedestal, was the Memorial itself—a globe of reinforced concrete (although, because of financial exigencies, not reinforced quite as much as originally planned). Being a representation of the earth itself, it was not precisely round but rather elliptical—a bit too much so, in the opinion of Mr. Mordenstahl, who had visited the project several times during its construction. Another little defect, in his view, had resulted from the treatment of the finished concrete with a new substance designed to repel pigeons. This, after several rains, had imparted a splotchy yellowish tinge to the surface, and in fact Mr. Mordenstahl feared that the Memorial resembled nothing more than a gigantic lemon. However, at the moment it was shrouded in canvas for unveiling purposes, and Mr. Mordenstahl was able to convince himself that his speech of dedication would gild these imperfections with golden words, as he celebrated, to the citizens of Spark, the deeds of their fellow townsman.

July 4 dawned hot and clear. The ceremony was scheduled to begin at eleven, and by ten-thirty Mr. Mordenstahl was in his place on the wooden reviewing stand which had been set up at the parking lot. His speech was in his pocket, where he kept fingering it. He also kept pestering the workman who had been assigned to advise him on how to haul aside the canvas at the time of unveiling, wanting to be sure that everything would work properly when he yanked on the cords.

Soon the other dignitaries arrived to take their places. These included Judge Davis and Pierce's father, Dr. Davis, who had to use a cane but otherwise bore no marks of his stroke, except for the fact that the muscles on the right side of his face still sagged, which made him look perpetually tipsy. Also on hand were the mayor, members of the Spark city council, the commander of the local American Legion unit, various ministers, the sheriff, the chief of police, etc. With one single exception, everyone was in some kind of uniform. Dr. Davis and several others were in their Legion attire, some wore military reserve uniforms, the ministers were costumed as chaplains, and Mayor Biedler, lacking anything better (he'd been 4-F in World War II), appeared in a scout-master's garb, which, being faded and dim with age, caused him somewhat to resemble Field Marshal Montgomery in the desert wars, a likeness the druggist heightened by carrying a riding crop under one arm and frowning militantly into the sun.

The lone civilian was Mr. Mordenstahl. He'd been invited to wear a uniform if he had one (and he did have an old sailor suit stored away somewhere), but he had decided not to, on the grounds that Pierce had gone walking in ordinary clothing, and so his spirit ought to be represented in the same way. Still, Mr. Mordenstahl felt rather conspicuous in his light-gray suit, and he wondered whether he shouldn't at least have pinned his Good Conduct Medal on his breast pocket, for even the women there—the police matron, Mrs. Gulliver, and Miss Foley, a retired WAC captain—were in uniform (Natalie, who presumably would have worn a dress, hadn't been able to come down from Clarion because of a last-minute administrative emergency at the hospital, or at least that was the reason she gave when she telephoned Mr. Mordenstahl at his hotel the night before).

As Mr. Mordenstahl sat among the assembled guests of honor on the reviewing stand, he had the opportunity to reflect on the appropriateness of the decision to hold the dedication of the Memorial on American Independence Day. "Pierce was, after all, an American boy," he thought, "and his mission was to carry the finest essence of the American spirit around the world—or halfway around it, anyway—and what more fitting tribute could be paid to his memory than by these traditional patriotic exercises in the heartland of America, where, in a few minutes, his fellow citizens will march as he marched, while Old Glory flutters in the wind?"

As it happened Mr. Mordenstahl had not seen a Fourth of July parade for some years. He assumed that this event had altered no more than the Constitution itself, and as his perceptions were somewhat soggy with nostalgic expectation, he did not immediately realize that there had, in fact, been a bit of a change.

The first units to pass by the reviewing stand were several open convertibles containing the surviving veterans of past wars (including old Mr. Dunstan, well into his nineties, who had charged up San Juan Hill with Teddy Roosevelt). These enfeebled gaffers obviously couldn't have been expected to march, Mr. Mordenstahl knew, and he could well understand why, in view of the heat of the day, the town authorities had provided buses for the schoolchildren (who leaned out of the windows waving little flags), and also an open truck to transport the high-school band.

Still, Mr. Mordenstahl was a little surprised to note that the following contingents of uniformed men, representing the various services, likewise appeared in trucks or open cars—and indeed, he observed that of all the participants in the parade, not a single one proceeded on foot, so that, instead of the respectful silence of the crowd being punctuated by the inspiring tramp of marching feet, there was only the rumble of engines and the rubbery singing of tires.

When he ventured to comment on this to his neighbor, a state senator in the uniform of a reserve Marine captain, he was informed that wheeled transport was more modern and efficient, and faster besides, and it would enable everyone to change clothes and get home in time for the baseball double-headers on TV.

The parade was no swifter than the patriotic speeches that followed it. These, too, rolled expeditiously out of the mouths of the speakers as though the phrases themselves, smoothed and rounded by long usage, were wheels designed to hurry whole pages of text away as quickly as possible. Mr. Mordenstahl, his pedestrian attention dodging this oratorical traffic, noticed that the crowd of citizens, such as it was (and it wasn't much, for most people had stayed home or gone driving into the country), was observing the festivities while sitting in parked cars or leaning out of the windows of the buildings along Main Street. Try as he might, Mr. Mordenstahl couldn't see a single person who might properly be described as standing, except for a ragged tramp, so emaciated as to be almost wraithlike, who had wandered up from somewhere and was observing the proceedings from beneath the awning of the drugstore, with a placid and agreeable smile.

Mr. Mordenstahl paid no heed to this disreputable figure, as he was preoccupied by the rapid pace of the celebration. His own speech, so carefully prepared and rehearsed, now seemed to him heavy and lumbering and old-fashioned, and much too long as well, so he plucked it out of his pocket, snatched his pen, and began cutting it, for his long experience as a public speaker had taught him that an address which doesn't respond to the mood of the listeners might as well not be given at all. His time was short. Mayor Biedler was at that very moment rising (with some difficulty, as the scoutmaster's uniform was tight) to introduce him, so Mr. Mordenstahl had to abandon any hope of rational editing. He simply ripped a handful of pages from the middle and stuffed them into his pocket, and, as the introduction was a brief one, he had no sooner completed this operation than he was required to rise, his tattered speech in his hand, and advance to the microphone with his customary public expression of genial assurance.

He couldn't begin speaking right away, however, for several World War II tanks which had taken part in the parade were clattering by on their return trip to the Armory. They made a tremendous racket. Mr. Mordenstahl beamed graciously, waiting for the tanks to pass. This gracious beam remained on his face for no short span of time, for he discovered that the disappearance of the tanks did not result in a corresponding diminution in noise, as the engines of several automobiles parked here and there along Main Street burst into life. People were starting to leave. From in back of him, too, came the rip and roar of ignited motors, for parking had been permitted on the new lot in the space not occupied by the reviewing stand. One driver, eager to descend the ramp without delay, honked his horn a few feet behind Mr. Mordenstahl, making him wince and duck instinctively, and to fear, in a moment of alarm, that he might be run down by a car even as he sought to dedicate a monument to walking.

Mr. Mordenstahl determined to wait no longer, and he at once launched into his text—or so he tried to do, but unfortunately he thrust himself too close to the microphone and spoke too loudly, which produced an earsplitting scream of feedback in the public-address system, and he was forced to wait some more until this noxious phenomenon had spent its considerable force.

"We are here to celebrate the achievement—" Mr. Mordenstahl began more cautiously, but he got no further, for the demon of feedback still lurked in the wires, threatening once again to utter its horrible metallic cries, and then, too, some boys were setting off firecrackers in an empty garbage can around the corner on South Street, which made the very pavement ring, while all the time the automobiles of departing citizens were snarling and grumbling along.

"We are here to celebrate—" Mr. Mordenstahl whispered. He hesitated, confused. He couldn't find his place. His text, disarranged by his crude efforts to shorten it, now presented page 7 to his eyes instead of page 1. Had he by mistake excised the opening of the speech and not the middle? He pulled the rejected sheets from his pocket and fumbled among them. One was, surprisingly, totally blank—but no, that was his spare handkerchief.

"We are here," declared Mr. Mordenstahl, in mounting desperation. Some pages slipped from his fingers. Bending to retrieve them, he bumped his head against the microphone, producing a dolorous echo. "We are here," he repeated, struggling up, red-faced and sweating, but now his voice was totally lost, for the vibration of the automobiles had loosened the amplifier connections, and the loudspeakers were mute.

"We are here," Mr. Mordenstahl insisted, to himself. Glancing around, he saw that the citizens of Spark had now completed their evacuation of the area. A block away were visible the rears of the last few cars, their brakelights occasionally flickering. Many of the dignitaries on the reviewing stand had slipped away, too. "We are here," Mr. Mordenstahl informed the useless microphone. To his surprise, he heard a feeble ripple of applause. Those who had remained assumed that his speech was over, as they heard no further sounds. Mayor Biedler and the state senator got up to congratulate the speaker, initiating a general rising.

"It's not over yet," Mr. Mordenstahl complained. Casting away the shreds of his undelivered speech, he seized the cords that held the Memorial shrouds in place. "I hereby dedicate this enduring monument to the memory of Pierce Davis, the world-walker," he cried out in an enormous voice—but these words, too, were vanquished as soon as they emerged, for as Mr. Mordenstahl tugged on the cords, and as the canvas fell cleanly away to reveal the yellowish concrete globe above, twelve jet fighters flashed by in the sky en route to an air show in Missouri, and the resulting sonic booms effectively disposed of Mr. Mordenstahl's last, valiant efforts to make himself heard in the town of Spark, Iowa.

Even if he had been heard, his words wouldn't have made much impression, for at that same moment, there occurred, most inopportunely, two little disturbances which distracted the attention of the few remaining persons. The police, having become aware of the presence of the ragged tramp noticed earlier by Mr. Mordenstahl, had pounced upon this unwelcome guest, and were hustling him away, ordering him to quit the town immediately—and then, more important, there took place in the lower portion of the reviewing stand what turned out to be the final and fatal collapse of Pierce's father, Dr. Davis. Several town notables at once gathered up the stricken physician and carried him over to the sheriff's car, in which he was rushed to the hospital. Judge Davis was driven there, too, by sympathetic friends, and in fact the entire place was soon emptied of all human and mechanical occupants, except for Mr. Mordenstahl, who remained alone on the reviewing stand beneath the Memorial, still holding a shroud cord in one hand.

"I've been an idiot," he thought, and slowly he began to descend from the stand. Main Street, though deserted, still smelled of gasoline fumes and slightly trembled to the hum of unseen distant traffic. His own footsteps on the pavement were the only ones he heard—or were there others, not far away? Mr. Mordenstahl glanced about, but he saw not a soul, and so decided that what he'd heard had been the echo of his own dejected steps.

"I've been an idiot," he told himself again. "You can't build a monument to a hero. If a man's a hero, he builds his own." And just before he turned the corner, he paused for one last look at the Memorial. "You're as useless as I am," he called out to it sadly, "so you might as well fall down right now."

The Pierce Davis Memorial did not fall, but neither did it long remain to grace the meager skyline of the town.

The following day a gust of wind blew off the first letter of the Davis name, causing people to suppose that the parking lot globe was actually an advertisement erected by the Avis car rental agency, and then an inspection by the town engineer revealed that the sonic booms had weakened the structure itself, cracking it in a couple of places, so that in the second week of August the Memorial was demolished and junked as a hazard to motorists parking their cars under it.

It should be noted that Dr. Davis's collapse occasioned a bit of comment, for several persons seated near him at the time reported that he had risen to his feet just when Mr. Mordenstahl had jerked on the cords, and that he'd been observed to extend his left arm, pointing, and heard to utter the word "Pierce" before he fell, and it was asserted further that he had pointed not up at the Memorial but rather straight ahead of him, out into Main

Street at a spot on which his staring eyes appeared to be fixed—and yet, the street having by then emptied, there had been nothing to be seen there (apart from the insignificant tramp, being hurried off by the indignant police). So it was universally acknowledged that the old doctor had been struck at the fateful moment by his imagination only, and by the time the funeral was over, no one thought any more about it.

Nor was any particular credit given to the retired schoolteacher, Mrs. Muncie, who quite matter-of-factly remarked that Pierce Davis himself had walked past her house that very Independence Day, heading east. "He said he'd walked around the world once and was going to do it again," the old lady said, "and when I told him he was still a fool to do such a thing, he just gave me a smile and went on his way like he did before."

Thus Pierce's walk around the world ended as it had begun. Or, rather, it didn't end. It would have been just a beginning—a leg-stretcher, as Pierce told the Gobi hermit—for he'd found his destiny in the dust his walking feet had raised, and a man's destiny doesn't quit after the first time around, or the second time, either. It goes on. It may go on forever, in fact, since they say that the spirit outlives the flesh, and if that's true, then it doesn't matter how far Pierce went or how long he lasted, for somewhere in the world he walked around the spirit of Pierce Davis is bound to be walking, walking still.

5